WINDY CITY SINNERS

7/29/16

To John — With all
best wishes. Hope you
enjoy my Chicago
tale.

Cheers!

Melanie Villines

WINDY CITY SINNERS

A MAGIC REALISM CRIME NOVEL

MELANIE VILLINES

SUGAR SKULL PRESS
LOS ANGELES, CALIFORNIA

ISBN 13: 978-0692504437

ISBN 10: 0692504435

EMAIL: sugarskullpress@gmail.com

COVER PHOTO: Chicago skyline by Maciej Maksymowicz, used by permission.

An earlier version of the first chapter, "Queen of the May," appeared as "Windy City Sinners" in *Chicago Quarterly Review* Vol. 17/2014.

Sugar Skull Press publishes contemporary crime novels as well as classic and gothic mysteries.

For available titles, please visit our website: sugarskullpress.com.

Please direct inquiries to sugarskullpress@gmail.com or contact us at:

Sugar Skull Press
P.O. Box 292357
Los Angeles, CA 90029

For my mother

Chicago is not the most corrupt American city.
It is the most theatrically corrupt.
STUDS TERKEL

CHAPTERS

PLACE: Far Northwest Side, Chicago, Illinois

NOTABLE FEATURES: Cemeteries, forest preserves, Little Poland, Little Italy #2—and rumored to have the highest per capita gun ownership in the city, thanks to the high density of police officers and members of the Chicago Outfit in the area.

TIME: Turn of the 21st century

1

QUEEN OF THE MAY

WHEN THE ENTRY BELL RINGS AT H&V DRY
CLEANERS, Virginia Martyniak peers over the rim of her
bifocals and sees a man in a black woolen ski mask.

It's the middle of May—and even with a cold spring, it isn't
chilly enough for a ski mask. There's only one explanation.

Good God, Virginia thinks, not here!

It's been all over the news how a man in a ski mask has been
holding up dry cleaners in Wrigleyville—but that's on the other end
of town. Lord in Heaven, here he is, Virginia thinks—right in my
own store.

Virginia can't move, can't speak—feeling as brainless and
immobile as her dressmaking dummy. She watches as the man
bolts the door, flips the sign to "closed," and lowers the
shades—blocking out the morning light.

She doesn't even budge when he pulls out a revolver and
points it at her chest. Virginia knows that her bulky beige dress
and fluffy gold hair make her an easy target in the darkened
room.

Good Lord, Virginia thinks, this is the Far Northwest Side
of Chicago—things like this don't happen. All the cops live
around here!

"I wont yer cash, Mama," the man says in a South Side drawl.

In the dim light, Virginia glances away from the gunman to
the framed icon of the Blessed Virgin that stands on the
counter. She says a silent prayer: *Holy Mother, keep me safe.*

Virginia sees the robber's eyes dart towards the sacred
image—they seem to flash with recognition. But what would a
black man know about the Queen of Poland—the Black

Madonna of Czestochowa—even if they are both black? Most black people, Virginia believes, are not Catholic—and few, if any, she thinks, are from Poland.

"Move it, Sista," the man snarls, waving the gun.

Virginia tries to comply, but her arthritic right foot has fallen asleep. Dear Jesus, please help me move, she prays. If I don't give the man the money, he'll think I'm resisting. I'm not resisting, I just can't move!

Virginia isn't ready to die. She's sure she has some kind of sin on her soul. She hasn't been to Confession in a good long while. Father Spinelli gives such harsh penances—even for trifling sins. But, Virginia wonders, what is sin? Sometimes, there are extenuating circumstances—like now. If I had a gun and killed this man, would I be guilty of murder?

Please, O God, please help me get through this! I vow to lead a blameless, spotless life from henceforth now and forever amen. But even as she makes the promise, Virginia knows it's impossible. She's a human being and will sin—in thought, word, or deed—despite her best intentions.

Virginia walks as fast as she can—but the cash register seems as if it's on the other end of the earth. She gropes her hands along the counter, pulling herself toward the register—as if moving through a magnetic field toward a resisting pole.

"Hurra it up, Woman," the man says.

When she reaches the register, Virginia feels triumphant—as if she's just scaled the top of the globe. She slams her hand on the old machine's lever, and the drawer shoots open with a ding.

How unlucky that this happened on a Monday, she thinks. I just put two hundred dollars in the register! Lord, I can't afford to lose this money. I work hard for it. And now this do-nothing just breezes in and wants to take it from me. Dear God, how can you allow things like this to happen? Is there no justice in this world?

But Virginia decides to take this up with God later—for now, she'll turn over the money and try to keep from getting shot.

She rips the bills out of their slots and bundles them into a pile, which she slides onto the counter. The man folds the bills in half—his hands graceful, despite the leather gloves—then crams the wad into the pocket of his black leather jacket.

When the robber turns to leave, Virginia is glad he's going, happy she's getting rid of him, thrilled that he hasn't harmed her.

But then she sees the man's eyes turn toward Gertrude, her dear Gertrude. The plastic goose sits on a small table behind the counter—along with a brimming box of outfits. Right before the robber stormed in, Virginia had dressed the life-sized lawn ornament in a white wedding gown and veil.

"The bird, too," the man says.

When he demands the goose, Virginia's maternal instincts take over. "You can't have her!" she screams.

Virginia scoops up the goose, stumbles through the shadows to the back of the store, and fumbles with the door. But the man rushes after her and wrenches the goose from her arms.

"No, no, no!" Virginia howls.

She kicks the man in the shin and tries to knee him in the groin, but he manages to push her away—knocking Virginia against the back door.

Then he skips to the front of the store, snatches up the box of costumes, stuffs the goose inside, and unbolts the door.

Virginia tries to race after him—but her aching foot is like an anchor holding her back. She is almost sixty years old and shouldn't be working at all, except she has to—they can't afford hired help.

As he makes his exit, the man turns and says, "You sure got nice hair, Blondie."

Her hair! It has set Virginia apart her entire life. Virginia was born with a cap of soft yellow curls that have only grown more rich and lovely with age. At fifty-nine years old, Virginia still does not have a gray hair on her head.

People come up to her in the street and try to touch her hair—acting awestruck, as if her golden locks are something from a fairy tale or a holy picture.

Then there are the men—always making passes and making nuisances of themselves. Virginia is a married woman—photos of the happy couple hang on the walls, and a thick gold wedding band proclaims "no trespassing"—but nothing discourages these unwanted advances.

Virginia considers herself a plain person. She's tall, big-boned, almost twenty pounds overweight, and never wears a speck of makeup. Still, the men don't seem to care that she has a homely face and an awkward body. It's only her hair that they see—each one a fool for a blonde head!

After the robbery, Virginia sinks to the floor, puts her face in her hands, and weeps. The robber's remark has brought back a lifetime of pain she's suffered because of her beautiful hair. And he ran off with her beloved Gertrude! And all of Gertie's lovely clothes!

"My baby!" she cries. "My poor baby!"

❦

As Marek Jablonski weaves through the Chicago side streets, with their rows of neat little houses and tidy lawns, he starts to feel normal. The crime now seems like a movie he'd seen—an American movie with a robber and a gun at a dry cleaning store.

The worst part was coming face to face with the Queen of Poland—as if his country's beloved Black Madonna had appeared to rebuke him.

Marek checks his rearview mirror to make sure no one is following him. Then he looks at his face in the mirror. He'd pulled into an alley a short time before, and used cold cream to remove the black greasepaint from his eyelids and the area around his eyes.

Marek grabs a tissue from the dashboard and wipes away a dot of black paint. He takes a deep breath. The last trace of his most recent crime is gone.

Now, he'll drive around for a while—until it's time to pick up his grandmother at the cemetery.

It's May, and the dead city has come to life. Flowers exclaim spring like a rainbow of punctuation marks. The birds sing, the squirrels romp, the sky is a Madonna-robe blue.

Yesterday was Mother's Day. Marek is glad it's over. He misses his mother. He'd phoned her in Poland, crying the whole time. He wants to go home, but has to wait. He needs to return as a success—a man with money, a man who can start his own business.

As Marek weaves through the "P" streets that mark the edge of Chicago—Pacific, Page, Panama, Paris, Pioneer, Pittsburgh, Plainfield, and, finally, Pontiac—he notes the Blessed Virgin statues in people's front yards. Even from a distance, Marek sees the scorn in each Virgin's eyes. He tries to avert her gaze—but he has to look, he has to accept the Holy Mother's disdain.

The Virgin statues are of different types—some are white plastic, filled with sand; some are white plaster. Others are painted with a blue cape, with green snakes at the Madonna's feet—but they all wear the same sad expression. They all seem to say: "Marek, you have broken my heart."

Yesterday at church, on Mother's Day, Marek had witnessed the May crowning of the Blessed Virgin—the Holy Mother of All. The little children had sung in high sweet voices: *"Oh Mary we crown thee with blossoms today, Queen of the Angels, Queen of the May."* Then everyone had knelt and responded as the priest recited the "Litany of the Blessed Virgin Mary." After each invocation of the Virgin's name, the gathering had responded: "Pray for us."

Marek needs the Virgin Mother to pray for him now—so he will get away with his latest robbery. But he knows the Madonna will not hear his pleas.

✂

Virginia feels as if her spirit has left her body, and is off somewhere observing her shaking shell.

Gertrude is gone! And Virginia loves Gertrude more than anything in the world. Yes, she loves her husband—but that's different. Her love for Herb is a given, like a mountain. Her love for Gertrude is like a tree—something that grows and changes and keeps Virginia enthralled.

Virginia pounds her fists on the floor and moans, "Gertrude! Gertrude! My baby."

Her whole life, Virginia, more than anything, has wanted a child. She'd prayed, gone to doctors—even made a pilgrimage to Lourdes.

Her attempts had been futile, her longing like an eternal flame. Nothing had worked, nothing had helped—until Gertrude had entered Virginia's life.

✂

Marek pulls onto the main drag, Belmont Avenue, and drives past the gas station where he works. He sees a tanker truck pouring gasoline into the ground. Yes, Marek thinks, you walk on the surface, but there is so much under your feet: the gasoline, the sewers, the pipes, the cables and wires, the water—perhaps, as in the case of the Virgin, even snakes.

Ahead, the traffic slows as a worker in a neon vest and hardhat directs cars past a work zone. As Marek sits in his car, he sees what looks like a bright orange egg pop out of a round

16

hole in the street. Then a man in an orange hardhat emerges from the manhole.

Marek knows why the men are working underground—they're checking the gas lines to avert another disaster. A submarine sandwich shop had exploded a few nights before. The place was closed at the time, and no one had been hurt. But for days, people in the neighborhood had discovered bits of bread and meat in trees, and plastered to the sides of their homes.

Yes, thinks Marek, there is so much beneath your feet. You walk around oblivious to the danger—but it's there, just waiting for an opportunity to explode.

At last, the traffic starts moving—and Marek veers onto a side street. The houses glow in the May sunshine—as if their bricks were polished during the night by elves from the nearby forest.

His grandmother had purchased her small brick house because it's near the "safe" city limits and close to the forest preserves—almost like living in the country. She can walk just one block and see a clear view of the sunset through the pines.

The location also gives Busha easy access to the cemeteries that mark the edge of town. Like the neighborhood itself, the cemeteries are filled with Italians. The bereaved relatives visit the graves often—leaving potted plants, bouquets of silk flowers, balloons, holy pictures, statues of saints, and other small gifts. His scavenger of a Grandmother finds this irresistible.

Marek turns onto Cumberland Avenue and pulls into Queen of Peace Cemetery. In the distance, he sees Busha scuttling from grave to grave. She plucks up her small treasures and stuffs them into shopping bags.

Marek parks near a statue of the Blessed Virgin that's at least five feet high. Someone has woven a crown of silk flowers and placed it on the Virgin's head. The Madonna also wears a cape made from an old plaid bathrobe. It's May, the month of Mary, and people want to show their dedication.

Marek feels like lighting a cigarette—as he always wants to do when idle, while waiting. But he'd given up smoking for Lent. And even though the Lenten season has been over for a month he has not resumed his habit. It makes him feel righteous to deny himself something he enjoys so much.

Busha raises her open hand to show five fingers—meaning she will be there in five minutes. Sometimes Marek wishes he could go through life not talking, just exchanging simple signs with other people. The more you talk the more you dig a hole, he thinks, just like the graves in this cemetery.

✂

As she writhes and weeps on the floor of H&V Dry Cleaners, never for a moment does Virginia say to herself, "It was only a plastic goose."

No! Gertrude is Virginia's baby—and a baby is a baby, no matter what form it takes. The feelings are the same—a fierce love, a primal protectiveness. When the baby is robbed, kidnapped, absconded, the mother is bereft, inconsolable, desolate.

Not that Virginia hadn't started out wanting a real baby, a child of her own she could love and dote on—a child that would spring from her womb and give her life true meaning.

But God had never answered these prayers—no matter how many promises Virginia had made, no matter how many things she'd offered to give up.

At times, she'd even considered taking up smoking or drinking—so she could renounce them and get points with God. But this was silly, foolish—how can something be a sacrifice when you don't want to do it in the first place?

The only thing Virginia had gained from her desire for a child was a heap of sin—most of all she had indulged in envy, one of the seven deadly sins.

For as long as she can remember, Virginia has felt a burning jealousy when anyone—a relative, a friend, even a customer—

had announced a pregnancy. Her envy was so strong that Virginia feared she might harm the other person's unborn child. She didn't want to hurt anyone—least of all a helpless baby. Virginia just wanted a child of her own. Why did God give her these longings if she couldn't have what she wanted?

For many years, Virginia had prayed for a miracle. Even after menopause, in her early fifties, she'd still prayed. Didn't Sarah in the Bible bear Isaac when she was an old woman?

But when Herb gave her the plastic goose a few Christmases ago, Virginia got so caught up in caring for Gertrude that she accepted her fate. She would go to her grave as a barren woman.

And now Gertrude is gone! Virginia feels as if her heart has been crushed to gravel. She will never be able to give that much love to another goose—or any other type of lawn ornament or stuffed animal or doll or even dog or cat. No, she had given it all to Gertrude.

And where is Gertrude now? What is happening to her? Virginia tries to push back thoughts of anyone harming or ill-using the goose. But a series of horrible visions run across her mind. Oh, my poor Gertrude! My baby! Virgin Mary Mother of God, please keep her safe!

2
LADY MADONNA

WHILE HE WAITS IN THE CEMETERY FOR HIS GRANDMOTHER, Marek Jablonski occupies his mind by testing his memory and mathematical skills. He recalls his robberies, remembers how much he'd stolen at each location, then totals up the figure.

He has about two thousand dollars—hidden behind a panel in his bedroom closet. But he needs at least ten times that much before he can go back to Poland.

Marek decides he's wasting his time with petty robberies—they're safer than robbing banks, but the returns are so piss poor. No, Marek tells himself, I need to make one big haul—and then be done with it and go back home.

Marek looks around—at least five minutes have gone by, but Busha is still pilfering the plots. As he bides his time, Marek watches a family of geese graze on the graves—a mother and her babies, four of them.

Marek thinks it odd that there's so much life in the cemetery—lush trees, vibrant flowers, fat geese, squirrels, rabbits, birds of all colors. He even spots a young buck, its budding antlers golden in the May sunshine.

Marek sees a flash of red, and follows it with his eyes. A robin swoops onto a telephone wire that drapes across Belmont Avenue. Marek gets out of his car and looks up toward the bird, now singing from the wire.

Then, all Marek can see is wires. They're strung from pole to pole, hanging everywhere. He looks at the rectangles of blue sky through the black cords. Small puffy clouds seem to hang there like laundry on a clothesline.

Marek imagines he can leap in the air and land on the wires. He'll walk the length of the city—all the way to Lake Michigan—high above the streets, suspended between heaven and earth. He'll be like God, watching everyone below, seeing all.

It's the way he'd felt back home—walking the high wire in the flea-bag circus his family dragged from town to town.

He'd been the star, the one people came to see. A bigger, better circus had offered him a job. His older brothers turned jealous, then turned on him—hinting that they'd drop Marek when hanging from their hands, with no net below.

The family circus was an embarrassment, a disaster—and Marek wanted to escape. But he was trapped—if he left, he was a traitor; but if he stayed, he was a prisoner.

He had taken the only way out—Busha's longstanding offer of a one-way ticket to Chicago and a better life in America.

For the thousandth time, Marek curses himself for coming to this country. He berates himself for believing Busha's lies. As soon as he got off the plane, Marek realized why Busha had lured him from Poland. She's getting old and needs a private slave to keep her house in top condition.

It would have been much better, Marek thinks, if I had remained in the ridiculous circus. There, at least, I was the star attraction.

Virginia tries to stifle her sobs, so she can call for help. She crawls behind the counter, reaches up and clicks on a lamp. Then she yanks on the phone cord, and the telephone clatters to the floor—its bells clanging.

The sound makes Virginia think of her childhood tricycle—the one with the little bell on the handlebars. For a while, she just stares into space, remembering the high-pitched ding-ding of that bell. Then she snaps back, picks up the telephone receiver, and cradles it to her chest.

She hears the dial tone blaring like a piece of hospital equipment. Virginia remembers holding her mother's hand in the hospital when she died. Virginia blanks out again, thinking about how her mother had suffered at the end, how thin and frail she was, how helpless.

Virginia shakes her head, trying to recall what to do. She squinches her eyes shut. Then a thought shoots into her mind. She opens her eyes and looks on the counter. It's still there! Sitting on a small easel is her most prized possession—her precious icon of the Queen of Poland, the Black Madonna of Czestochowa. Thank God the robber didn't steal it!

❊

Marek feels in his pocket for the money he'd robbed from the dry cleaners—a few hundred dollars, he guesses—what he'd earn in a week at the stinking cesspool of a gas station.

He's also snagged the porch ornament, which is in his trunk, along with the bird's outfits, his black leather jacket, his ski mask, and his gun. The revolver had been as easy to obtain as the toilet paper that bulges from Chicago's supermarket shelves.

Marek hopes Busha will give him credit for at least a week's room and board for the bird and the clothes. He shouldn't have to pay Busha at all—not with all the slave work she has him doing all the time.

Marek doesn't worry that the blonde from the dry cleaners will recognize the bird on Busha's porch. How can someone prove ownership of a plastic bird when there are so many in the neighborhood? As for the clothes, he'll say his mother had sent them from Poland.

Mama! How Marek misses her and all his friends and relatives back home—even his scheming brothers. A sinking feeling starts in Marek's heart, then spreads like hot lead through his body. The homesickness makes him feel heavy and nauseated, as if he's building up gravity and will soon fall through the earth—leaving a large black hole, a bottomless stinking grave.

Marek longs for home, for his own country—where he can realize his long-held dream of opening his own nightclub. He'll start a new career—performing as a hip-hop artist called MarVin. Marek has spent much time learning the rhythms and the moves from videos he watches on TV.

But, in the meantime, Marek is stuck in America—in a dead-end job, living with his lying Busha. He needs more money than he can earn in any work available to him in this country. He has no choice but to steal, he tells himself.

Marek takes a deep breath and slaps himself on the cheek—trying to shake off the longing for home and anger at Busha. He wants to leave the cemetery—now! But Busha is like a bull, an ox that cannot be rushed. He has to wait until she is ready to go.

Marek gazes at the cemetery's giant Virgin Mary statue. He makes the sign of the cross and says the "Hail Mary." Right away, he feels much better—as if he's just taken a deep drag on a cigarette.

✄

The replica of the holy icon—the Black Madonna—had belonged to Virginia's mother. It was the only thing she'd brought with her—other than the old clothes on her young body—when emigrating from Poland.

Virginia thinks of her dying mother—of how Mama had worked her life away in the clock factory and it had killed her. Those glow-in-the-dark clock faces that she'd spent her life painting! In the end, they had killed her with bone cancer.

"Please, O Holy Queen of Poland, help me remember that phone number! I need to call the police!"

Marek sees hBusha coming closer, her shopping bags abloom with silk flowers. Marek's heart jumps, thinking Busha is ready to leave—but she dawdles at each and every grave.

The old woman looks as pleased as a well-fed bear. It's just as she had told him—the Monday after Mother's Day is the annual jackpot. The Italians had outdone themselves showing respect for their dead matriarchs.

Marek knows Busha is as elated as if she'd won a Vegas jackpot. But, for him, the day holds only drudgery. He'll drive Busha home with her booty, listen to her nag about the remodeling chores, then go to work at the miserable stinkhole gas station.

How he hates it! Having to wear a shirt with his name in an oval patch on his pocket. People calling him "Mark" all the time. "Mark, give me a package of Marlboros. Mark, give me an instant lottery ticket. Mark, give me a roll of Life Savers. Mark, give me a candy bar. Mark, give me five dollars on tank three." How he hates the demands, the familiarity—not to mention getting called by someone else's name.

Marek laughs at the irony. Yes, he thinks I am "marked"—a fool in a light blue shirt with my name on the pocket, a sap sitting like a caged pigeon in a brick booth with bulletproof glass.

He laughs again, feeling a bitter taste in his throat. In his little booth at the gas station, he is like an anti-priest in an anti-Confessional. People come to his small cubicle to feed their vices—for cigarettes, and lottery tickets, and candy, and gas to take them God-knew-where. Yes, they come to indulge their sin—not to have their sins forgiven.

Marek can no longer stand the indignity of the job. He'll turn in his notice—just as soon as he comes up with an idea, one big plan that will get him all the money he needs to go back to Poland.

The numbers 911 float into Virginia's head. Her hand shaking over the dial pad, Virginia manages to peck out the digits. When she speaks, the operator doesn't understand what she's saying. Virginia takes a deep breath and after a slow, painful struggle gives the woman the information.

When she hangs up, Virginia pulls a black rosary out of her skirt pocket and begins to pray.

�֍

Five minutes turn into ten, and ten minutes turn into fifteen, but Busha is still not finished. How Marek hates to wait! So many painful thoughts spring to his mind when he's idle.

His worst recent memory now surfaces. He recalls how his hopes of a good-paying job in America had cracked apart. Every time the terrible memory comes back to him, Marek feels as if his soul is filled with the stench of rotten eggs.

The husband of Busha's lady friend Bronislava had promised to get him work as a truck driver making fifteen dollars an hour. The man planned to get Marek a license by bribing someone at the Secretary of State's office. Marek's English and knowledge of the complicated driving rules were too poor for him to pass the test any other way.

But then a big scandal had broken out after a truck driver had rear-ended a van—killing seven children. When it came out that the driver had paid a bribe for his license, the news media swarmed all over the story—uncovering many others who had lined the pockets of State officials. The "License to Kill" story has been headline news for months, and an army of political hacks is on the way to prison.

So, just like that, Marek's fifteen-dollar-an-hour truck-driving job evaporated—and, with it, Marek's last hope of making decent money.

After the job fell through, Marek found himself a good-paying position—holding up dry cleaners around the city. These are easy targets—middle-aged or older women alone in the store, with at least a few hundred dollars in the drawer.

Until today, he'd only hit placess in a distant neighborhood, near Wrigley Field. But Marek can't go back there—all the dry cleaners in the area are on "special alert." So, why not rob a place near where he lives? It's as far from Cubs' Park as you can get—all the way on the northwest edge of the city.

He has no other options besides stealing, Marek tells himself over and over. He's nineteen, he has little formal education, and his English is worse than poor. No, he doesn't have too many employment prospects. He's just another immigrant sucker slogging away in the salt mines of minimum wage America.

Yes, he'd been poor in Poland—but it was his own country, where he could speak the language, where he had friends, family, respect.

Back home, the family could not even afford to feed the roller-skating bear that had performed with them for years. They had been forced to sell poor Pasha to a pet food company. This was the final blow—the final heartbreak that had sent Marek to the telephone to call Busha for the ticket to Chicago.

But, right now, hating his life and hating his humiliating job and not knowing whether he will be arrested for his crimes and despairing that he will ever make something of himself, Marek feels that perhaps the bear had ended up with the better deal after all.

3

MOTHER GOOSE

WHEN POLICE OFFICER JERRY VALENTINO ARRIVES,
it takes a while for him to get Virginia to calm down. She sobs
from deep within, shaking and muttering to herself.

The officer tells Virginia he needs a description of the man.
Through gasps and tears, Virginia says it was a black man in a
black ski mask, with a black leather jacket, black jeans, and a
black T-shirt. She describes the man as about six feet tall and
weighing about two hundred pounds. He had black eyes.

"How do you know he's black if he was wearing a ski
mask?" Officer Valentino asks.

"He sounded like those rap singers on TV," Virginia tells
him.

Jerry Valentino scans the store. It's hard to believe he's
back on patrol, wearing a uniform, handling cases like this. Just
a few weeks ago he was working undercover—where he'd
worn his own clothes and made his own sweet schedule. But all
of a sudden, he was put on "soft duty"—non-emergency patrol
calls. No explanations.

Jerry figures he's under suspicion for aiding and abetting a
fellow officer who'd been arrested for running a drug ring. So
far, he hasn't been accused. But Jerry figures the FBI will pay a
visit any day now. Meanwhile, he's back in uniform.

"Was he wearing gloves?" Jerry asks, transfixed by
Virginia's blonde hair.

"Yes," she sobs. "Black leather gloves."

"So you didn't see his skin?" Jerry says, smiling at Virginia.
There's something about the woman—even if she is old
enough to be his mother.

"No," Virginia answers, blotting her eyes and nose with a wad of tissues.

"How much did he get?" Jerry asks, suppressing the urge to stroke Virginia's hair. His wife had walked out on him six months before, and it's been a long time since he'd touched a woman.

Virginia knows what the man is thinking. Will I never get any peace, she wonders.

In her younger years, she'd tried to dye her hair black, but her scalp had broken out in oozing sores. She has no choice—she has to bear the curse of blondness: the leering men, the unwanted attention, the crude advances.

"He got about two hundred dollars," Virginia says in hiccupy voice, trying to suppress her sobs. "And my goose and her clothes!"

"Goose?"

Virginia opens a photo album and flips to page after page of Gertrude in various outfits.

"He got Gertrude!" Virginia wails before she faints—wobbling to the floor like a reflection in a fun house mirror.

When Jerry Valentino tries to lift Virginia, he feels pains rip up his back and he, too, falls to the ground.

After work, Marek goes home to the small brick house he shares with his grandmother. When he sets the plastic goose on the plastic-covered sofa, the bird seems out of place in her stylish bridal ensemble.

Marek feels the goose's black eyes bore right through him—an accusing look that seems to say: "What am I doing here?" Marek averts the goose's gaze and heads for the kitchen. He's always hungry.

After stuffing himself with the stuffed cabbage Busha had left in the oven, Marek rolls into the living room and turns on the television—the station that plays videos by hip-hop stars.

Since his arrival from Poland three months before, Marek has been unable to improve his accent—except when imitating the blacks in the videos. The ability comes in handy when he's robbing a dry cleaning store in a ski mask. Marek has jet black eyes—so didn't have to invest in colored contact lenses.

Marek doesn't want a black person arrested for his crimes. Besides, he doubts this will happen. After all, how can the victim identify a masked thief? While Marek feels sorry about imitating the voice of a black man, what other choice does he have? If he uses his own voice—with his thick Polish accent—the police will find him, he's sure of it.

But, for now, he won't think about his crimes or his homesickness or his unhappiness. He'll just relish his delicious solitude.

Busha is gone every weekday from four in the afternoon until two in the morning. She works as a cleaning lady at an office building near O'Hare Airport—about fifteen minutes away.

During his free evenings, Marek practices with the hip-hop artists—even though he's supposed to be stripping the woodwork and doing other endless chores around the house.

Tonight, as he dances and sings along with an artist called Dr. 2B^2—and pictures himself in Poland, as MarVin, the rap star—Marek's attention is drawn to the goose on the sofa.

Blood rushes to Marek's face—all of a sudden, he feels guilty about taking the bird, as if he'd stolen a baby from its mother. Shame speeds into his mind and heart—a mixture of guilt and fear that makes Marek's testicles contract and gives him slicing pains across his groin.

Marek sits down and tries to reason with himself. Yes, the blonde had really liked the bird. But she's rich, she owns a business—a sign in the window says: "Herb and Virginia Martyniak, proprietors." Later, Marek had looked up the word in his Polish/English dictionary. Yes, Virginia Martyniak could afford another bird—a whole flock of them.

When Grazyna Jablonski comes home after midnight, the first thing she notices is that her grandson has not removed one speck of old paint from the woodwork in the dining room.

Earlier in the day, when he'd dropped her at home after the trip to the cemetery, Marek had promised to make big progress that evening on the woodwork. He is a worthless swine, she thinks—just like his good-for-nothing dead grandfather!

Grazyna regrets sending for her grandson, sorry she'd offered to help—when he, sniveling about the doomed bear and bad blood in the family, had phoned asking for a plane ticket and a place to stay. Doesn't the ingrate understand that everything has a price?

She should have left him drowning in the bad blood! She sees a whole red ocean of czarnina—her country's famous duck's blood soup—with Marek's head going under for the third time. She's an old woman and still she works every day. How can this oaf sit around watching television at her expense!

Grazyna needs to get her house into tiptop shape. She purchased the boxy brick home fifteen years before, and the value has shot up. Many consider this little neighborhood—eight blocks wide and six blocks deep—the City's prime rib.

The area is on the edge of town, where all the city workers want to live. Besides that, it's close to the forest preserves—and almost like living in the country, with wildlife, even deer, all around. Yes, it's a wonderful place to live—cozy, with sturdy homes, safe streets, and a nearby Catholic church.

Whenever a house comes on the market, somebody races to buy it. Most of these are homes of the prevailing Italians, who are dying off—and buried nearby, oh, those lovely flowers! When the Italians vacate their premises, and this world, Polish buyers swarm around the properties—offering high sums of long socked-away cash to buy the trim and tidy houses.

The latest assessment on Grazyna's home is for three hundred thousand dollars—and she'd only spent forty thousand for the place and had paid it off long ago. She can take that big chunk of money and buy a nice apartment building, make a large down payment—and then live off the rents and be the queen of her own castle for the rest of her life.

To make sure she gets a high price for her house and finds just the perfect apartment building—in a nice neighborhood, at a great bargain—Grazyna has made a pact with Saint Stanislaus of Krakow. She has promised to visit the priest at Saint Francis of Assisi Church, and plead with him to install a statue of the Polish saint. This is Grazyna's insurance policy—when a saint is on your side, nothing can stand in your way.

She'll sell the house as soon as all the remodeling work is finished—Grazyna knows this will increase its value maybe another fifty thousand dollars. She needs to get the repair work done by the end of the year, so she can put the house on the market the following spring.

Her grandson will have to keep up his end of the agreement. Yes, Grazyna admits, she didn't tell the boy he'd have to do this work until after his arrival. But did he expect her generosity to come without a price?

✄

As he sleeps on the living room floor—despite the blaring television—Marek dreams of a way out of his troubles.

He knows a girl, a Polish girl, Anna, from the disco. She works at a bank. She's in trouble—because she'd embezzled thirty thousand dollars to feed her shopping addiction. Now she's about to get caught. She needs to put back the money right away. What if they set up a robbery? Marek can pose as a robber and Anna will give him the money—about fifty thousand dollars. Then he'll keep twenty thousand and give her back the money she needs to repay the bank. This can work, his dreaming self tells him.

If he'd remained asleep, Marek's dream may have drifted away—but Busha wakes him with kick in his kneecap at just the right moment.

✂

Grazyna clicks off the program where the black people are singing. Marek snaps awake from his spot on the floor, remembering his dream with relief and gratitude. Yes, the plan can work.

Grazyna speaks to Marek in Polish, though he's tried again and again to get her to speak English so he can practice.

"I would not have brought you here—at great expense!—from Poland, you lazy slug, if I thought you would not help your poor Busha with even a few small jobs."

An argument looms like an open trap in front of him, but Marek decides the sidestep it. The woodwork stripping is no small job, but why quibble about it now? He has just figured out how to end his problems—and is sure that Anna from the bank will be only too glad to go along with the plan.

"Busha, I have brought you a gift," Marek says, pointing to the goose on the sofa.

Marek intends to bring up the business about getting credit for room and board in a few days.

"Only crazy Americans have plastic animals on their porches and in their yards!"

"But she is so sweet in her wedding dress," Marek says.

"I will only have saints or the Virgin in my yard!" Grazyna says.

She has grown quite fond of the plastic statue of the Virgin Mary that sits in her front yard. She prays to it often.

"Tomorrow, you will finish the woodwork—or you will find yourself a new place to live!"

Marek rifles through the outfits, holding them up for his Grandmother to admire. But, to Grazyna, her grandson is as transparent as Saran Wrap.

"Try to get someone else to give you money for the stupid goose," Grazyna says.

Then she goes to bed. All that trouble, Marek thinks, and for nothing.

But the next morning when he shuffles half-asleep into the kitchen, Marek spots the goose sitting on a chair. Grazyna has dressed the bird in a little sailor suit.

Marek knows better than to say anything. But he has a feeling that things will work out, after all.

4
SINS OF OMISSION

DURING THE INCIDENT AT THE DRY CLEANERS, Officer Jerry Valentino had wrenched his back—big time. He'd spent a week in the hospital undergoing tests and getting physical therapy, and another few weeks at home in bed.

Now, here he is, on sick leave, doped up on Vicodin, vegged-out on his deck chair, staring at the forest preserves, and worrying about how to get rid of the cocaine hidden under the floorboards in his attic.

Jerry is scared beyond shitless that Frank Czmanski is about to rat him out as an accomplice. But Jerry didn't do anything except let Frank hide the drugs in his attic. Now Jerry has to move the drugs someplace else. He can't dump them—if and when Frank gets out of prison, the stupid shit will be back looking for his stash.

Jerry knows he should have refused when Frank asked for the favor. But Jerry had allowed his longtime partnership with Frank in the force—and his code of police brotherhood—to cloud his judgment and make him do the dumbest fricking thing he had ever done in his dumb fricking life.

Jerry is so jumpy and in so much physical pain he can't think at all—let alone come up with a good hiding place for over a million dollars worth of coke.

As his body sweats and his mind strains, Jerry glances up and sees three cats jump over his back gate. Jerry hates cats. And the neighborhood has been overrun with them ever since the idiot across the street started feeding the strays— the same moron who has that big black mailman living with him.

When the cats jump into his yard, something snaps in Jerry. Cats are bad luck—if he lets them invade his space, the FBI will be next.

With one hand against his sore back, Jerry limps into his kitchen and pulls the revolver from his holster. He hops outside, brandishing the gun.

"No trespassing!" Jerry yells.

The cats saunter up the sidewalk with a languid ballsiness that infuriates Jerry even more.

Jerry pulls the trigger. He misses the cats, but the noise sends them scurrying over the fence.

Jerry gapes at his gun. Holy Christ, he thinks, what the hell am I doing? I could get in deep, fricking shit for something like this. He glances around, wondering if anybody saw him. Then he staggers into his house. He decides he'd better spend the day in bed.

✄

For a week after the robbery, Virginia wears the same pink and white checked nightgown and stares out the kitchen window at the spot in the backyard where she used to sit with Gertrude.

Herb Martyniak doesn't know whether his wife is deep in thought, or doesn't have a thought in her head. She seems blank and distant, but there's an undercurrent to her vagueness —like the filaments that rattle in a dead light bulb.

Herb tries to get Virginia to eat or go outside, but she remains listless and nearly lifeless. Herb's eyes fill with tears every time he looks at his wife. She seems like a sad statue: *Grieving woman in gingham nightgown at kitchen table.*

Herb visits the garden supply store and buys another plastic goose. But Virginia won't even look at it. He puts the goose in the yard, so Virginia can see it from her spot at the window. Herb figures that his wife will feel sorry for the naked goose—

and pick up her sewing things and start to make some outfits. But Virginia acts as if the goose is invisible.

This isn't the first time over the years that Virginia has suffered these spells. Every few years, she'd get remote and silent—either staying in bed for days or not moving from a chair. Herb knows it's because Virginia wants a child. By the time Virginia gave up hope, they were too old to adopt.

They'd thought of becoming foster parents, but Herb knew it would kill Virginia if the child went back to its parents or to another home. When Virginia gets attached to something or someone, she won't let go.

If they'd had money, they could have hired a surrogate to bear their child. In a way, that's what God had done when Mary had borne Jesus. She is the surrogate mother who had carried and given birth to God's child.

Herb knows there's only one answer—find Gertrude. But the police aren't about to spend manpower on a case like that.

He wishes Virginia had a relative or a friend to comfort her. But Virginia has no parents, no siblings, and no real friends—just passing acquaintances that float in and out of the dry cleaners. What friends she'd had over the years, she'd dropped or alienated out of jealousy as soon as one had become pregnant—or even a grandmother.

As a last resort, Herb calls the rectory. He doesn't have much confidence in Father Spinelli—the priest has an oily insincerity that Herb finds repellent. But Herb is desperate.

Father Spinelli has no quarrel with his vows of poverty and chastity. But he is incensed at the parish's constant demands on his time—with no letup, now that Spinelli is the de facto head of Saint Francis of Assisi Church.

A few months ago, the former pastor had been whisked away for an indefinite stay at a retreat house—while the

Archdiocese investigates morals charges against him. In the meantime, Spinelli has to bear the load—with the humiliating title of "acting pastor." The least the Bishop could do is give him the job—after all, Spinelli is doing the work. But, over the years, the priest has failed to ingratiate himself with his superiors—never volunteering for task forces or extra duties.

Spinelli knows it'll take half of forever before the Archdiocese finds a replacement—the priest shortage gets worse each year. When the time arrives, Spinelli is sure the new pastor will come from Africa, or India, or the Philippines—the only places where the Church has a rich mine of willing prospects. To these men, the priesthood is preferable to starvation and squalor.

Spinelli doesn't care for Church politics—and doesn't care about getting ahead. All he wants is time for his personal mission.

The priest is never more content than when he has a few spare hours for his musical compositions. If he only had the time, the priest feels, he could write some first-rate pieces. His recurrent, fervent prayer is to become the greatest priest/composer in history—outstripping even the formidable Father Antonio Vivaldi.

But Spinelli is always called away to some emergency or another. He has to listen to old ladies' health problems in grimace-inducing detail. He has to coach basketball, emcee bingo two nights a week, plus say Mass every day—four times on Sundays. He has to visit the sick in the hospital, give the last rites, perform weddings, baptisms, and funerals—plus hear Confession.

But right now, Spinelli has a whole delicious hour for himself. He's just getting into a satisfying stretch of music when his housekeeper calls him to the phone. He tells her to take a message. But Sophie says the man keeps calling and calling.

"Is man with wife having goose robbing at dry cleaner," the plump Polish housekeeper tells the priest.

Father Spinelli throws down his pencil. He still hears notes humming in his head, but knows they are lost forever.

✂

Jerry Valentino is locked away in his air-conditioned bedroom in a torment of twisted sheets and even more twisted thoughts. Over and over, he sees the FBI break down his front door, cuff him, and haul him off to prison.

He has to find a place to hide the drugs. But he can't pry up the floorboards in his attic—his back is too screwed up. What he needs is a helper, somebody he can trust without question. But Jerry trusts no one anymore.

The doorbell rings. It makes a happy ding-dong sound that Jerry has always liked. But the doorbell sounds different this time—as if the ending tone is a chord from a Requiem Mass.

Jerry stumbles to the front door—the pains in his back getting more intense with each step. He peeks through three little windows set up high in the door and sees the ink-black face of the local mailman—the boyfriend of the imbecile across the street that feeds the cats.

Jerry looks at the man's face—divided into three distinct sections by the windows. *One God in Three Divine Persons* pops into his mind—something from a catechism lesson long forgotten.

✂

As Jerry stares at him through the window, Emmett Dobbs takes off his mailman's hat so the cop can see his big, bald, scary-looking head. He sets his face into a stony mask.

He'd seen the cop fire a gun at Dennis's cats. Emmett's mind is full of threats and revenge—nothing physical—he just wants to scare the piss out of the animal-hating freak.

38

If anything happens to the cats—especially the big orange one—Dennis will be hell to live with. Emmett doesn't need that kind of stress right now. He's about to take off and do nothing but work on his paintings and his sculptures. He needs things calm at home.

Emmett isn't about to let this lowlife cop destroy his domestic harmony—or the only thing that gives him any real satisfaction. He lives for the two weeks out of fifty-two when he can paint—nothing is going to mess it up for him.

For the past year—ever since he'd moved in with Dennis—Emmett has been the only black person in an all-white neighborhood. At first, he'd felt the usual fears. Over the years, things hadn't changed that much when it came to race relations in the City of Chicago.

But Emmett has an advantage—he is six and a half feet tall and dark black. He has a huge shaved head. People are afraid of him. They avert their eyes when they see him coming, or just nod, then dart into their houses like mice fleeing a tom cat.

Right now, Emmett isn't afraid about confronting the short Italian cop. Emmett knows he can make a lot of trouble for the midget if he tells about him firing off his goddamned gun. The motherfreaking cops don't want no bad press.

Slaving his life away in the post office all these years has given Emmett one advantage. He knows how to file grievances, understands how the wheels of government work, realizes you don't have to take no shit—even if you are a black man working for a white boss.

❀

Jerry can see the veins in the man's eight-ball head throb as he pounds on the door with his big-ass black fist.

"Leave the mail outside," Jerry yells through the closed door.

"I ain't got no mail for you. I got a personal message."

"What's that?" Jerry says.

"I know what you did this morning, Cisco Kid!" Emmett says.

Cisco Kid? What's the dickhead talking about, Jerry wonders. Is it a racial slur—does he think I'm Mexican? With his swarthy Sicilian coloring, Jerry is often taken for a Latino or even an American Indian—and he hates it.

Wait, maybe he's talking about my gun, Jerry thinks. He feels his stomach flop over a few times.

"Get out of here," Jerry says, without much spark.

"Hey, gunslinger, I gotta talk to you," Emmett tells him, baring his teeth into a terrifying, cheerless smile. It's the same look that causes dogs to turn tail on his postal route.

Jerry knows there's no way the asshole is going to leave. Should I call the police, he wonders. But what if the force arrives and this goof tells a wild story about what had happened with the gun this morning.

Jerry unlocks the door and cracks it open. The man sneers down at him. There is almost a foot difference in their heights and a hundred-pound difference in their weights.

"What do you want?" Jerry whispers, his eyes darting up and down the block.

"You don't want me talkin about it out here," Emmett says, the scary grin still on his face.

Jerry glances around, then opens the door.

Emmett steps into the hallway and looks around at the living room. Just as he'd suspected—gold Italian-Provincial furniture, lamps with hanging glass do-dads, fake flowers in high vases, and a cheap-looking painting of what he assumes is Mount Etna in an ornate gold frame over the sofa. On the television, there's a framed picture of Saint Anthony of Padua—Dennis has one just like it at home.

"Let's go in the back," Jerry says, dragging his feet toward the family room.

The décor here is more to Emmett's liking—fireplace, polished wood floors, simple, modern furniture. Jerry eases himself inch by slow inch into a chair at a dinette table, and indicates the seat across from him with a nod of his head.

Emmett sits down, the flimsy chair creaking under his weight. They stare at each other across the table.

"You shot at some cats this morning," Emmett says, spreading his massive hands, palms down, on the table.

Jerry doesn't say anything. He knows better than to incriminate himself.

"Shooting a gun like that could get you in some deep shit, Mr. Po-lice Officer," Emmett says, flicking away a toast crumb.

"What do you want?" Jerry asks.

"Leave Dennis's cats alone."

Jerry lets this information sink in. The guy's name is Dennis. The man isn't just the "gay idiot" anymore. He's Dennis. He's a person, a human being, with a life and hopes and dreams and fears and pain and problems and cats. This all washes over Jerry until he feels as if he's drowning. He can't stop himself—he breaks into loud, blubbering sobs.

Emmett had never expected this. Man, he thinks, I'm good. It sure didn't take much to bring this sucker to his knees.

5
KYRIE ELEISON

WHEN FATHER SPINELLI ARRIVES IN A HUFF OF BLACK ROBES, he steps across the threshold as if embarking on a tour of the lower depths. As Herb leads the priest to the kitchen, he can feel Spinelli's hot glare against his back. The priest is acting as if he's doing Herb a favor. But this is your job, Herb thinks. Don't act like I'm a gravy stain on your satin vestments!

The priest glances at Virginia in her spot by the window, then nods for Herb to leave the room. Relieved, Herb decides to go on a quick run over to the dry cleaners. He has to check on how things are going with the kid he'd hired to run the place in Virginia's absence. Plus, he has all those pickups and deliveries to make. Thank God, Herb thinks, that the priest had shown up.

After Herb leaves, Father Spinelli pulls up a padded kitchen chair and sits next to Virginia. He hopes things will come to a quick and satisfying conclusion. He has to get back to work.

"What is bothering you, my child?" the priest asks, even though Virginia is almost a decade his senior. The priest's words are comforting, but his tone is strident. Virginia picks up on his tone, which echoes inside her head.

Virginia closes her eyes, and feels as if she's floating. She hears noises—like a gnashing of teeth. She sees a black whirlpool, then she's looking into a deep pit. She hears weeping and wailing. Then she sees clothes in a gigantic washing machine—she sees shirts and jeans and underwear and socks and other items tossing and turning through a large window on the side of the machine. She sees words—names of sins: greed, sloth, wrath, and hundreds more—tumbling inside the machine. Then she sees dirty water run out of a hose under the washer. The sinful words go down a drain into the ground. The washing machine opens, and the clothes float out—as white as goose down. The black whirlpool fills with bright light. The weeping and wailing and gnashing of teeth are gone—replaced by pleasant sighs.

The priest checks his watch. Virginia has been silent for at least two minutes. He can't sit here all day!

Virginia opens her eyes and stares at the priest. She sees the word "pride" on his forehead.

"You're suffering from the sin of pride," she says in a flat, matter-of-fact voice.

"What makes you say that?"

"I can see it in your face," she says, then turns to stare out the window.

God, no, the priest thinks. Not this! He figures Virginia has suffered a mental breakdown—and he'll have to stay with her for hours. All his personal time will get eaten away by the woman—and how the priest hungers to get back to his musical work!

Spinelli knows the nature of Virginia's problem—he's heard her confession many times. She's a hysterical, post-menopausal woman that has never borne a child. Many times over the years, she's confessed to envy against her friends and had railed against God. Now, once and for all, the woman has lost her mind.

It seems to Spinelli that Virginia is hearing things. She inclines her head as if listening to a voice. She nods, then turns to the priest.

"Another priest is standing behind you. He has red hair," Virginia says.

At first, Emmett is glad he'd caused Jerry to break into tears—hell and hallelujah, the asshole cop feels guilty about shooting at Dennis's cats! But after a few minutes of listening to Jerry sob and sniffle away, Emmett just wants him to shut the hell up.

Emmett glances around the room for a box of tissues, and spots one on the shelf above the fireplace. He doesn't want to help, but can't stand to look at the cop's snotty face anymore.

When Emmett sets the box in front of Jerry, the cop stares at it for a moment—then grabs a fistful of tissues and blows his nose and wipes his face.

"Thanks," he says, the effort of speaking sending him into even deeper sobs and moans.

Emmett doen't know what else to do or say.

"So, we're all set then?" he says, just to say something.

Jerry stands up, slides open the glass doors, steps onto his deck, and spots a gang of cats lolling on his lounge chair. The cats open their eyes and say "meow" in unison.

From his spot at the dinette table, Emmett sees three of Dennis's cats trot into Jerry's house.

Jerry hobbles inside, following the cats.

"Get the hell out of here!" he screams.

Emmett jumps up and rushes after the animals. The nervy felines have already made their way into the Italian-style living room.

"Kitty, kitty, kitty," Emmett says in a sorrowful voice that sounds to Jerry like something from the Latin Mass.

Kyrie eleison, Jerry remembers. *Christe eleison*. As he shuffles after the cats, Jerry recalls what the words mean: *Lord have mercy. Christ have mercy.*

Yes, he says to himself, Lord have mercy! He hears a crash of crystal in the living room—the tall vase with the silk lilies that his wife had been so proud of!

Jerry's back seizes up and he can't move. He's paralyzed in the hallway between the family room and the living room.

He hears Emmett, again calling out: "Kitty, kitty, kitty." Only it sounds like *"Kyrie eleison, Kyrie eleison."* Lord have mercy.

Yes, Lord have mercy, Jerry cries as he crumbles to the floor. He hears more crashes, then a tearing, ripping sound, then tinkling glass, and the booms of Emmett's feet as he tries to capture the animals.

Have mercy on me, Lord, Jerry prays. *I am just a man, I am weak, small, finite, fragile, only human, and there is only so much I can take. Have mercy on me, O Lord, your sinful servant who goes through life getting shot at, terrorized, maligned, mistreated, full of guilt and shame and pain and loneliness. Have mercy! My wife leaves me because I won't talk, but there is so much to say and I don't know how to say it, I am only a man, one man, I am flawed, lacking, my kids are gone, cats invade my home, I have a pain worse than death that besets me at every twist and turn of my back, before this the kidney stone almost killed me with more pain, before that the cyst on my leg, worrying about cancer and dying, and wasting away, and having been on this earth and accomplishing nothing! Lord, have mercy on me, a sinner! Forgive me for aiding and abetting a drug king! Forgive me for betraying my duty as a police officer. Have mercy on me, Oh Lord. Send me a helper, Oh Lord. Have mercy!*

Jerry thinks he's whispering this confessional plea in his mind, but he's screeched it out loud—and Emmett, despite the din the cats are making, hears every word. The mailman has to sit down and take a breath. He eases himself onto the sofa and covers his face with his hands.

The cats, sensing the prevailing mood, flop down on the black leather recliner and curl up for naps.

Father Spinelli turns and looks behind his chair. Of course, he sees nothing. But a priest with red hair? Can the woman mean *il prete rosso*, "The Red Priest"—Antonio Vivaldi?

"He says you will never become greater than he," Virginia states, happy to report this unwelcome fact to her nemesis.

"Who is saying this?" Spinelli asks.

Virginia looks behind the priest, and inclines her head as if listening.

"Father Antonio Vivaldi," she tells him.

Right away, Spinelli sums up the situation. The woman's recent shock and distress have released some kind of latent psychic powers. The priest figures the woman has picked up the information about Vivaldi from his subconscious. He decides to ignore what she's just said.

"Virginia," Spinelli says, "I'm here because your husband is very worried about you. He wants me to help."

Virginia glares at the priest. She loathes Father Spinelli—and knows that scorn for a priest must be one of the worst possible sins. Still, these feelings are beyond her control.

Father Spinelli has been cold and unfeeling to her over the years—offering no sympathy when she'd gone to him for counsel about her desire for a child. During her Confessions, when she'd admitted her envy against pregnant women and her anger at God, the priest had lectured her in a shrill voice—and had given her several rosaries each time as penance.

No more! She will never put herself in that position again—she will never ask Spinelli for advice or compassion. She will never go to him for Confession—or the Sacrament of Reconciliation, as the Church now calls it.

"I don't need your help," she tells him.

"Virginia, you haven't moved from the window for days."

To spite him, Virginia gets up and walks into the dining room. She sits at the piano and starts to play. Spinelli stands in the doorway and listens. The woman plays with artistry and skill—and the music is sublime, something he's never heard before.

When Virginia finishes, she closes the cover on the piano keys, and sits with her hands folded in her lap.

For a few moments, the priest can't speak. Then he clears his throat and says, "That was lovely, Virginia. What is the piece called?"

Virginia listens for a few moments, her head tilted to the side.

"It's called 'Seven Oceans' by Antonio Vivaldi," she says.

"I've never heard of that work," Spinelli says.

"Of course not," Virginia replies. "He just wrote it."

✂

Emmett listens, but doesn't hear anything from Jerry's end of the house. He tiptoes into the hallway—and sees Jerry on the floor, not moving, his fingertips touching his face.

Emmett bends down and listens for the sound of Jerry's breathing, then taps his shoulder.

"Ahh!" Jerry wails in pain, his hand shooting to his lower back. "Help me find my pills!"

Emmett jumps up and glances around, trying to spot a prescription bottle. As Jerry moans in agony on the floor, Emmett searches the place—and after almost giving up locates the pills under the cushion of the gold sofa.

He rushes into the kitchen and runs water into a glass. Then he walks over to Jerry, offering him the pills and the water.

"Help me sit up," Jerry says, realizing he'd used the word "help" in his last two pleas. Yes, he needs help—in so many different ways.

Emmett puts his hands under Jerry's arms and yanks him up. It hurts, but Jerry is too worn out to utter a sound.

Jerry throws the Vicodin into his mouth and gulps the water. He sighs. Then he starts to laugh with as much abandon as he'd cried.

"Man, those pills work fast," Emmett says.

Jerry laughs harder, holding his stomach and falling over onto one shoulder. Again, Emmett boosts him up.

When his laughter subsides, Jerry asks: "Where are the cats?"

"On your chair taking a nap," Emmett says.

Jerry starts to laugh again. He can't stop.

Man, this motherfreaker is one emotional basket case, Emmett thinks. He feels exhausted from the whole encounter.

"I hate cats," Jerry says between belly laughs.

"I figured," Emmett responds.

"But they seem to like me," Jerry says, tears of laughter streaming down his sunburned cheeks.

Emmett can't stop thinking about the "confession" that Jerry shouted out a short time before. Emmett knows better, but decides to bring it up.

"You stole drugs?" he asks.

Jerry stops laughing, like a soundtrack cut off. He stares into Emmett's face. A thought occurs to him: *Maybe this is the black guy that robbed the dry cleaners.*

6

MOTHER MAY I?

GRAZYNA JABLONSKI WIPES HER BROW WITH THE BACK OF HER HAND, then rests her elbows on the old push mower. How she loves her little patch of earth on the Far Northwest Side of Chicago! She does all the yard work herself—fearing that Marek might mangle her cherished hedges, stomp on her perfect lawn, and not bear the proper reverence for her flowers.

As she admires her garden, Grazyna tries to remember when the yard had last sported real flowers. It seems like a long, long time ago. For many years—during the spring and summer and fall—she had pampered and tended the hearty blooms.

Grazyna didn't mind the extra work—but there was no way to keep up with it. Whenever she'd spot a weed or dead flower, it felt like a blight on her soul—something best eliminated altogether.

With silk flowers, Grazyna's yard—front and back—can bloom year-round. Grazyna replaces the flowers every few days—so they always look bright and fresh. With four cemeteries near her home, she has a nonstop supply of new stems.

Grazyna doesn't see this as robbery. Silk flowers are expensive, after all. And what good are they to the dead? The flowers look much better in her yard. The departed souls have told her as much. She confers with them, asking for their consent before she takes the flowers. Grazyna considers herself fortunate—life is so much simpler when you receive permission for an act that most people would deem a sin.

After Jerry Valentino threatens to turn in Emmett for holding up the dry cleaners, he makes an offer. If Emmett helps hide the cocaine, Jerry won't report him as the robber.

Emmett is innocent, but knows nobody will believe it. He's the only black person in the neighborhood. Besides, as his dumb luck would have it, the robbery happened on his first day off in weeks—and he'd slept the entire day. Dennis had spent the morning at the animal hospital—a couple of his cats had urinary tract infections—so Emmett has no alibi. He has no choice except to help the crooked cop.

✄

Again, Grazyna starts to push the mower—the sweet bouquet of fresh grass intoxicating her. She loves mowing the lawn—such a pleasant, mindless, monotonous task! It's so relaxing, so freeing—her body floating along, her thoughts drifting from present to past to future with no effort.

From time to time, she admires her wondrous flowers—and congratulates herself on her artful arrangements. How could it be wrong to take the flowers, when they bring her so much joy—and the dead people in the cemetery can never give them any real appreciation?

Long ago, Grazyna had understood that certain sins—lying, stealing, cheating—are only wrong when viewed from a particular perspective.

Is it wrong to answer with a lie when the other person has no right to ask you the question? Is it wrong to take something that does not belong to you when the other person has much and you have nothing? Is it wrong to remove a diamond ring from the toe of "Large Ludmilla"—a woman too huge to wear the ring on her finger—as the circus's fat lady snored away, when you need to sell the diamond on the black market to buy two tickets to America, for yourself and your fire-eating husband who has a brother in Chicago that will sponsor you if

50

you can pay your own way there? Is it wrong to leave your two sons behind with your relatives in the circus, when you have the chance of a better life and can send money home and then bring them to join you someday? Is it your fault that you never saw the boys again, except in pictures, because the Communists would not let them leave? Is it your fault that when they could get out, they did not want to go? Is it your fault that you never went back to visit them, afraid that you would be captured and tortured by the authorities for a crime you did not commit? Did you not always send money home, even after the lazy good-for-nothing infernal fire-eater died from drink and left you a poor widow who had to pay off his gambling debts, this the same stinking-excuse-of-a-man who had kicked your poor dear German Shepherd Princess and made her lose her pups, the poor babies falling from their mother's womb like thick red tears, Princess howling at the loss, mourning, heartbroken, never the same again, not eating, wasting away to nothing, nothing, just bones and sad haunted eyes. Is it your fault?

When Grazyna wakes up from these thoughts, she has already mowed and raked her backyard. Grazyna crosss herself and says a "Hail Mary" for her dear departed Princess, who is buried below—in this tiny cemetery for one.

Jerry instructs Emmett to remove floorboards from the attic, take out the cocaine, and with great care funnel it into a plastic Virgin Mary statue.

The statue has been sitting in Jerry's basement for over six months. His mother had given it to him after Annette walked out with the kids—saying the Virgin Mary would help reunite his family—but Jerry had never gotten around to filling the statue with sand.

Jerry wonders what his mother would think if she saw him holding the Virgin upside down, while another man fills her with cocaine. Jerry's hands shake and sweat while he grasps the white plastic statue—sometimes sliding down the Virgin until they are clasped around her head. Jerry prefers this—he can't bear to look in the Madonna's face.

Since Emmett isn't a Catholic, he has no qualms about using the Mary statue in this way. He just wants to get the whole pain-in-the-ass business done with.

Emmett wonders what Dennis would think if he saw him now. Dennis is a devout Catholic—he goes to Mass every Sunday and has a lot of statues and holy pictures around the house. Dennis's favorites are Saint Anthony, Saint Sebastian, and Saint Francis of Assisi—the patron saint of animals.

"Where you goin'ta put the statue?" Emmett asks Jerry.

"In front of the house across the street."

"By the Jablonskis?" Emmett says. "The old Polish lady?"

"Yeah, her."

"They already got one over there," Emmett says.

"It's gonna be a switch."

Emmett shakes his head.

"What's the matter?" Jerry asks.

"You can't leave cocaine out in the hot sun," Emmett says.

"What're you talking about?"

"I seen it on a news show. It says how that's why these coke smugglers from Colombia are always so in a hurry to get the stuff to its destination. Cocaine is a perishable item. Unlike heroin or marijuana, which holds up for a long time."

"Well, I'll just have to take my chances."

After what seems like hours, they're finished. Jerry feels relieved when he places the Virgin in an upright position on the basement floor.

"Come back at four a.m.," Jerry tells Emmett.

"Shit, why?"

"We gotta make the switch when nobody's looking."

"Why not midnight, then? The sidewalks roll up around here at ten," Emmett says.

"The old lady doesn't get home from work until two—and her grandson stays up late. All the lights in the house are usually out by three. We gotta make sure the both of them are asleep before you do it."

Right away, Emmett tries to think of what kind of excuse to give Dennis. Emmett decides to keep it simple—he'll just say he's getting up a little early because it's a heavy bulk mail day.

After Emmett leaves, Jerry eases himself up the basement stairs—his back screaming with every step. He lowers himself onto the sofa—and thinks over the plan. There's no reason it won't work. Emmett will take the coke-filled Virgin and switch it with the one in the old lady's front yard across the street. This way, Jerry can keep the drugs hidden in plain view—and leave them there for the indefinite future.

Jerry is glad he's about to get the drugs out of his house. But he's still nervous—his body feels like a bundle of twitches. He jumps at every sound—even the hum of the refrigerator seems to go right through him.

From the corner of his eye, he sees a flash of orange. Earlier, Emmett had booted out all the cats—or so he claimed. Now, a long, lanky orange cat is sitting next to Jerry on the sofa.

The cat looks in Jerry's eyes, never blinking. Jerry feels as if he's in a trance. He watches as the cat's front paws slide onto his leg. The cat inches into his lap—then rests its head on Jerry's chest.

The cat purrs, and seems to send waves of relaxation through Jerry's tense body. Jerry closes his eyes. The purring is so soothing. Jerry puts his hand on the cat's head—and floats into a deep, delicious, drug-free sleep.

❧

Grazyna rolls the mower to her front yard. She sees the mailman coming up the block. She hopes he has a letter from her sons in Poland, but the boys—now men in their forties—almost never write anymore. It seems that the older they get, the more they blame Grazyna for abandoning them as children. Still, each day Grazyna prays they will write—and each day she asks the mailman the same question.

"Mailman, please, you having letter for me?"

Emmett always hopes he'll miss Mrs. Jablonski during his route. He's afraid that one day he'll reach his limit and just bust her in the chops. The same question every damn day. When's she gonna get the message?

"Here's your mail, Mrs. Jablonski," Emmett says, "you find out for yourself."

As he walks away, Emmett thinks: I am the messenger; I am the bearer of news both bad and good. Emmett knows that in days-gone-by, people used to kill the messenger if they didn't like the message.

Yes, he thinks, mine is a dangerous occupation. The dogs are the least of it. People waiting for government checks, people mad because you brought them too many bills, people disappointed because they didn't win the Publisher's Clearinghouse Sweepstakes—always having to deliver everything rain or shine. The mailman is the most important person in most people's lives, but one of the least respected.

Oh how I wish I could just do my artwork, and never have to deliver another piece of mail!

"Mailman, please, you having letter for me?"

※

After the mailman leaves—giving her no letters from Poland—Grazyna makes the sign of the cross and begins to recite the "Hail Mary" in front of her plastic statue of the

Blessed Virgin. This is her repayment to the dead people whose graves she'd gleaned for flowers.

The two-foot plastic statue stands right below Grazyna's living room window, surrounded by a circle of silk flowers. Yes, it is true that Grazyna had taken the Virgin from another yard. But the older Italian couple had two statues—and who needs twin Virgins? Besides, she'd prayed to the Holy Mother, who had given Grazyna permission to take the statue.

"Amen," Grazyna says, finishing her dutiful prayer. Then she makes the sign of the cross once again, and begins to mow the lawn.

This time, her thoughts rest on the recent past. A few weeks before, she'd taken the Virgin statue on her way home from work—at two in the morning, when the Italians were asleep. She had opened the plug in the bottom of the plastic statue and allowed the sand to run out. When empty, the statue was light and easy to carry.

When she got home that night, Grazyna filled the Virgin with coarse tan sand—which she'd removed from a construction site, after asking permission from Saint Joseph, the patron saint of the building trades.

Grazyna had taken the sand, over a period of days, during her forays into the cemeteries. Builders are putting up new condos near one of the graveyards. Grazyna wonders why anybody would want to live next door to a burial ground. But not everyone is able to confer with spirits the way she can.

When he finishes his postal route, Emmett goes home and tries to work on his current canvas. Emmett loves to paint—the picture taking shape, the colors, the smell of the acrylics, the feeling of his brushes. But this time, every dab of paint is uninspired. Emmett throws down his brush.

Thank God, Dennis is at work—he'd know something was up, for sure. He can always take one look at Emmett and just know.

Emmett goes downstairs and paces around the house—Dennis's cats following him from room to room. He feels like shooting the mewling, moaning, miserable felines himself.

The mailman is sure as shit sorry he'd ever gone over to complain about the cop firing at Dennis's cats. But Emmett knows he has only himself to blame for getting involved in a mess like this.

Emmett flops into the recliner and flips on the television—anything to distract his mind from what's going to happen later when he has to sneak the coke-filled statue into the Jablonskis's front yard

The television screen blooms to life—filled with the smiling face of the queen of television talk shows. Of all people! Every time he sees that woman, Emmett thinks of his mother—and he doesn't feel like thinking about his mother right now. But it's too late. The floodgates are open—and his Mama comes rushing in.

Emmett hears his mother telling him: "Emmett, don't you go doin nothin rash and foolish."

Again, she advises him: "Don't go callin no attention to yourself. Try to stick in the background. Don't let nobody know what you're really thinkin."

For most of his life, Emmett heeded his mother's advice. But living in the white neighborhood—with people who seem afraid of him—has emboldened Emmett. It's as if all his pent-up rage at last has an outlet. If somebody gives him shit or pisses him off, they sure as hell goin'ta hear about it.

But nobody in the neighborhood has ever given Emmett any cause to erupt in an angry fit—until today, when the cop fired his gun at the cats. Emmett hates the goddamned yowling, pissing cats himself—but that doesn't mean somebody else can get away with trying to kill the freakin felines.

Yes, today, Emmett had indulged his sense of outrage. He had acted in a rash and foolish way. And now he's paying the price. You just never know, Emmett thinks, where a particular action will lead. It's like dominos—one event, one action sets off all kinds of other actions and events.

Emmett feels like kicking himself in the ass. He's helping a criminal hide cocaine! This is the kind of thing that sends people to prison for life.

During all his years, Emmett has always been the good boy, the dutiful son, the kid that stayed in the house after school and never got into any trouble. He'd found a nice, safe, stable job at the post office. He paid his bills on time, didn't speed on the highway, and always sent a thank you note when somebody gave him a gift.

Still, he thought, here I am aiding and abetting a dirty cop—the last thing I thought would happen when I woke up this morning.

But no matter how far you try to stay away from trouble, Emmett thinks, somehow it just finds you.

✄

When she gets home from work, Grazyna stands before her statue of the Blessed Virgin and says the "Hail Mary." Then she walks up her front steps, picks up the plastic goose—dressed in a sea-foam green organdy dress and straw hat—and trudges into the house. It's two in the morning—and, after a long, tiring day, Grazyna will at long last get a little rest.

✄

At four a.m., Emmett removes the plastic statue of the Virgin Mary from Grazyna's front yard. He replaces it with another that looks just like it. The only difference is what's inside—a million dollars in cocaine—and a tiny "X" in black magic marker on the bottom.

Emmett tells himself he'll just do as Jerry asks. If the whole freakin plan blows up, Emmett will say he didn't know what was inside the statue. He was just doing a favor for a neighbor with a bad back.

7

THE WAGES OF SIN

NOW THAT VIRGINIA IS UP AND WALKING AROUND,
Herb is careful not to disturb her. She's still acting strange—
preoccupied and distant—but at least she's talking, eating, and
sleeping. Herb figures he'll just go along with anything she
says for a while.

When Virginia mentions she intends to change the name of
the dry cleaners and buy new signs, Herb knows it's a crazy
idea. They can't afford new signs. They struggle just to make
the rent each month. Virginia advises Herb to cash in their
IRAs. The signs will be a good investment, she tells him.

"Oh," she says, "and I'm going to need an electric piano,
too."

After the signs are in place, Virginia returns to work. Over a
month has passed since the robbery. The store reopens under its
new name on the first day of summer.

The business is now called "Redemption Dry Cleaners." In
smaller letters, under the name, it says: "Wash your sins away."

During Father Spinelli's recent visit, when Virginia had
experienced her vision—the giant pit in the earth with the huge
washing machine that removed sins—she thought it was just a
dark symptom of her sorrow over losing Gertrude. But the
visions wouldn't stop. Day and night, she'd see the black pit,
hear the weeping and wailing, and watch as the sins flowed out
of the hose beneath the washing machine. She realized that
God was calling her to a mission. She had to heed the call.

But Virginia decides to give herself an exit clause. If she does this for God, then God will have to do something for her. Within a year, she'll have to conceive a child.

Virginia has no desire for sex right now—the thought makes her feel ill. She can't even stand to be in her own skin—let alone allow Herb to touch her. Each nerve in her body feels like a painful flame.

If God is to answer her prayer for a child—either by curing her nerves or through divine intervention—she'll continue to do His work at Redemption Dry Cleaners.

✄

Giovanni Gammeri is a tiny man who's had a huge crush on Virginia for years. He works as a limousine driver and has to wear a uniform shirt. He owns just three. It gives him a good excuse to visit Virginia every other day.

When Giovanni looks up at the looming new sign—"Redemption Dry Cleaners"—his olive skin pales. He feels his heart grow tight—sure that the robbery has caused Virginia to sell the business.

When he enters the store, he's thrilled to see his beloved behind the counter.

In his forty years of life, no woman has affected Giovanni the way Virginia does—her every movement and gesture shoot straight to his soul.

"Virginia! Amóre!" he beams.

"Good morning, Giovanni," says Virginia, businesslike as usual.

"Is so good to see you again!" Giovanni seems to sing, as if his life is an opera. "I am so worry about you! You are okay?"

"Fine," Virginia says.

Giovanni takes a deep breath, as if trying to inhale Virginia's essence. To him, she has always seemed like Anita Ekberg in the movie *La Dolce Vita*.

"Mia camicia," Giovanni says, offering Virginia his shirt.

"We have some new rates, Giovanni," Virginia replies, handing him a large receipt.

"Just do like usual, Virginia," Giovanni says, staring at her hair.

"Things have changed," Virginia tells him.

"Please to me explain, Virginia." How he loves the sound of her name!

Virginia goes over the receipt with Giovanni—explaining that at the top, there's a space to write the item of clothing. Across the receipt, in five columns, are lists of sins—with different rates for the various sins.

"Non capisco, Virginia," Giovanni says.

"I can look at your shirt and name the sins you committed while wearing it," she says.

Giovanni has no idea what Virginia is talking about. But it doesn't matter. He loves her with his heart and with his soul.

He nods and says: "Per favore, Virginia."

Virginia gives the man a long look through narrowed eyelids. Then she examines the shirt for spots, stains, and soil. She checks off boxes on the receipt. Then she adds up the fees.

"It will cost you $35.99," Virginia says.

"But the shirt, it is not cost so much!"

"Maybe you should buy a new one."

"How if maybe you just take only one or two sin away this time. What cost is then?"

Virginia crosses out a few items on the receipt, then totals the figures.

"If we remove lasciviousness and cupidity during this wash cycle, the total will be $5.99."

"Yes, Virginia," he says. "Gràzie."

"You really should have lust removed from this shirt. But that by itself is a fifteen dollar sin," she tells him.

"So maybe next time, Virginia," he says.

Virginia points to a kneeler—one she'd instructed Herb to purchase from a religious supply store. Giovanni bows his head, folds his hands, and falls to his knees on the padded red bar.

Virginia sits at the keyboard and plays for about thirty seconds. It's one of the compositions Antonio Vivaldi has channeled through her. The music, Virginia believes, is like a stain remover that loosens the sins on the clothes before they enter the dry cleaning solution.

Giovanni closes his eyes, soaking up Virginia's delightful music. He loves her more than ever.

She ends the brief musical passage and stands up. Giovanni follows her example. Then he just stands gazing at her.

"Thursday afternoon," Virginia tells him.

"Yes, Virginia," Giovanni says, as he bows and backs out the door—flushed with bliss.

✄

For a week, two cleaning ladies at the office building have been talking about the new church—Redemption Dry Cleaners. They tell Grazyna the holy place is right in her neighborhood.

"Why do I need a new church?" she asks in Polish.

"At this church, they take away your sins and clean your clothes at the same time," Dorota tells her.

"Yes, and what do they charge?" Grazyna says, the left side of her lip curling up in a sneer.

"Different things, depending on the sin and the item to be cleaned," Bronislava explains.

"I don't believe in wasting money!" Grazyna says, nostrils flaring.

Dorota and Bronislava hear this all the time—it is Grazyna's litany. Grazyna is the most frugal woman they've ever known. She won't even buy toilet paper—each night, she stuffs a roll in her purse before leaving for home.

"Still, it is wonderful, this place," Dorota says. "I feel better than I have in years."

"I go to Saint Francis of Assisi," Grazyna says. "It's an Italian neighborhood, so the church is named for an Italian saint. Still, I am talking to the priest to have the church put up a statue of Saint Stanislaus of Krakow, in honor of the Polish people who are moving into the area."

"Well," says Dorota, "you go to church. You must give donation, pay for lighting candles, it costs you something."

Grazyna doesn't respond to Dorota—the simple woman just would not understand.

Grazyna has talked to God, asking if He wants her money. She tells God she doesn't think so, seeing how the Church is so rich and has so many buildings and money and property and possessions. God has told her she is correct. He doesn't need her money. He has plenty.

Herb believes that Virginia has lost her mind. But he loves her so much, he can't bear the thought of putting her away anywhere. Yes, the mental asylum is nearby and he can visit her each day. But Herb won't think of it.

Anyway, what harm can her screwball ideas do? She's acting like herself, except for this sin business.

The dry cleaners doesn't clean anything on the premises. It hasn't in years. Herb and Virginia bundle up everything and send it to a big commercial operation in the suburbs. Still, no one inquires where the clothes are cleaned or how the sins are removed. People accept the service as another mysterious sacrament.

Herb's tolerance for Virginia's innovations do not go unrewarded. In just a week as "Redemption Dry Cleaners," they make as much money as they'd cleared the entire previous year.

Location, location, location, Herb thinks. What a boon that we're living in such a hotbed of sin. And who knew?

8
THE WIND CRIES MARY

SOMETIMES, Father Spinelli remains in the confessional for hours without anyone entering the cubicle. God knows, he has better ways to spend his time. But he has to stay in the hot box—whether any sinners enter or not.

Then Spinelli learns why penitents are so scarce. They're having their sins removed at Redemption Dry Cleaners.

Spinelli can't believe it. The absolute gall of the woman—trying to compete head-on with the Catholic Church!

The priest feels his bile rise as he remembers his last encounter with Virginia. The woman claims she's channeling Vivaldi's music. The mere idea makes Spinelli feel as if his stomach will erupt in a volcano of acid. How can he—or anyone—function when a rival comes back from the dead to compete?

Spinelli pops a Tums into his mouth, then slides shut the window of the Confessional—if anybody deigns to stop by, they can go to hell! Business is closed for the day!

He rushes out of the hushed church, into the hellfire July afternoon. Spinelli will pay a visit to Redemption Dry Cleaners—and deliver a personal sermonette to Virginia.

For the first time in weeks, Jerry gets dressed in more than jogging shorts—a painful procedure that takes him over an hour. Jerry is feeling edgy—he needs to get a close look at the coke-filled Virgin to make sure everything is okay.

He doesn't want to stroll for no reason—it'll look suspicious—nobody does that in this neighborhood. If somebody is just out walking—without a dog, without a stack of envelopes, without a shopping bag—it makes other people nervous, thinking the person is an outsider or a vagrant casing for a robbery.

Jerry leaves his house through the front door—waving a pile of envelopes like a flag that says: *I've got a good reason to be on the street.* He grabs the handrail and hobbles down the steps. Then he drags his heels to the corner, crosses the street, and stuffs his envelopes in the mailbox. He shuffles back down the block—this time on the opposite side of the street.

As he inches along, Jerry feels he's looking at his street for the first time in years. All these little brick houses, he thinks, holding in all these little lives—mine included. All these little patches of lawn—watered and mowed and raked then watered and mowed and raked again.

Some people have awnings on their houses—awnings with initials on them. There's a "P," an "L," and an "R." What are these people's names? Why are they so proud of their initials? If they sell their homes, will it have to be to someone whose last name starts with the same letter?

Jerry looks toward the front windows—white curtains, green drapes, bare windows, a sofa shoved up to the window, a little dog yapping, a vase with fake tulips, pink ceramic kittens, a rainbow decal, a dusty plant, a "Warning, we call police!" sign.

When he reaches the Jablonski house, Jerry stops and pats his pockets—as if he's dropped his keys. As he goes through this charade, Jerry checks out the Virgin Mary. She looks okay—in the right place, not cocked to one side, nothing spilling out the bottom.

But then Jerry notices something else—on the Jablonskis' front porch sits a plastic goose in a drum majorette outfit.

After the robbery at the dry cleaners, Jerry had looked through the goose photographs with the distraught crime victim. The drum majorette outfit had stuck in his mind because it looked like the one his ex-wife had worn when she'd twirled her baton with the high school marching band. The short skirt and high hat—and Annette's confident strut—had made Jerry fall in love with her thirty years before.

Whoever robbed the dry cleaners must live in this house, Jerry thinks. Virginia Martyniak said the robber was a black man—but the Polish cleaning lady and her grandson live in this house.

Jerry knows, just knows, that the grandson had something to do with the robbery—and no doubt the rest of the robberies at dry cleaners attributed to a black man in a black ski mask.

If the kid is involved in criminal activities, Jerry will have to move the Virgin. It's just too risky to leave the statue where it is—God forbid, the kid is not only robbing dry cleaners, he's also buying or selling drugs. Whatever the case, sooner or later the force will show up—maybe with dogs that will sniff out the Virgin.

But before Jerry jumps to conclusions—and enlists Emmett to relocate the Virgin somewhere else—he decides to keep his eye on the Polish brat for a few days.

�぀

Father Spinelli stands in a line that snakes down the strip mall, waiting for his turn to enter Redemption Dry Cleaners. It's early July—the month that gives Chicagoans their annual foretaste of hell. Spinelli is suffocating in his black woolen clothes, feeling as if he's about to keel over from heat stroke.

He's already been waiting an hour. The line creeps ahead, inch by slow inch. Many people are repeat customers, whose remarks only fuel Spinelli's rage against Virginia.

"I feel like new man," says an old Italian with a cane. "When first I come here, I am in wheelchair. But my anger and other sin wash away more with each cycle. Soon, I no more need this," he says, waving his cane.

"Tak," agrees a bent-over-with-age Polish man. "Before I wearing thick glasses. Now I seeing like young man. Sin spots cleaning from my soul."

The priest listens to other conversations. They all boast of miracles.

The woman is purporting to get rid of sin, the priest thinks. And now she's making people believe she's working miracles. Plus she's cleaning these people's clothes. How is the Church supposed to compete? We can't offer a practical service such as this. If this keeps up, she may franchise this operation and put us out of business.

The priest is fed up with his job, but he sure as hell isn't going to let Virginia take it away from him. If he leaves the priesthood—which, yes, he's considering—it will be his choice, not the doing of this unbalanced, post-menopausal pest of a woman!

�֎

Jerry sits in his van down the block from Marek Jablonski's house. He's been there an hour.

When Marek drives his rusty Nova out of the garage, Jerry waits until he turns the corner before following him. Several times, Jerry pulls over to allow Marek to get a half a block or so ahead. He notices that the Nova's license plates are smeared with mud and unreadable.

When Marek pulls into the supermarket parking lot, Jerry lags a few cars behind, before turning into the lot. He watches where Marek parks, then stops a few rows away. When Marek leaves his car, Jerry is stunned to see him dressed in an Uncle Sam outfit—complete with white beard and top hat.

Jerry looks around. Many people are dressed as Uncle Sam. A large banner on the supermarket reads: "July Jubilee! Uncle Sam Look-Alike Contest!" Jerry remembers that it's Friday, July third.

Jerry decides not to stick around. The kid can't be up to no-good during a costume contest at a supermarket.

Father Spinelli feels angry, envious, resentful, and many other sinful things as he stands in line. While he waits his turn, he hears strains of the Vivaldi compositions the woman plays after each transaction. Each note is like a Roman dagger in the priest's chest. Gall burns his throat. He stuffs a Tums in his mouth as if it's a communion wafer.

When his turn arrives, the priest steps up to the counter and faces Virginia. The woman is aglow—as if she's found her true calling in life. Spinelli snarls at her, but Virginia doesn't see it—she's looking at the priest's empty hands.

"What do you want cleaned, Father?" she asks.

"I do not require your service!" he says, pounding on the counter. "I've come here to tell you to cease and desist this sham!"

Virginia is sure the priest needs a long rest at a retreat house. After all, a small operation such as hers can't represent a threat to a huge conglomerate like the Catholic Church.

Spinelli hurls his half-roll of Tums at a huge framed portrait of a goose that hangs behind the counter in a sort of altar.

The crowd gasps.

"He's jealous!" a middle-aged woman says.

"Have your jealousy removed!" chimes in another woman.

People in line grab the priest and try to rip off his clothes so Virginia can clean them. But the priest utters a quick prayer—*Saint Michael the Archangel, defend us in battle!*—and manages to pry himself free.

He staggers out of the stifling store, then rushes back to the refuge of Saint Francis of Assisi Church.

The irony of his costume is clear to Marek. He's dressed as Uncle Sam—the American version of God the Father, the country's patriarch, the paternal know-it-all in a blue coat, red and white striped pants, long white beard, and top hat.

Perhaps the high hat disguises a pinhead, Marek thinks—like the poor souls that traveled with the circus in Poland.

Marek strides into the store, checking his costume against the others—his is by far the best! Years making his own trapeze outfits had sharpened his tailoring skills.

He sees Anna alone at the bank counter. It's two o'clock—the lull after the lunch-hour patrons and before the after-work check-cashing crowd. The other tellers have taken a break.

Marek is alone in line as he walks up to the counter and hands a note to Anna—a young blonde who looks like a fashion model, and aspires to the profession.

Anna plays her part well. She gazes down at the note, constructed from newspaper letters. It says: "Giving me $50,000 cash money. I having gun. Don't pulling alarm or I shooting!" It hadn't been easy to find the exclamation point for the note. The day before, Marek had combed the newspaper—there are few such punctuation marks in the *Chicago Tribune*. But the *Tribune*-owned Cubs had won after a long losing streak. The headline on the sports section had, of course, read: Cubs Win!

As she stares at the note, Anna tries her best to smooth her brow and wear her best vapid bank-teller smile. She will try, try, try not to give herself away.

Anna's face shimmers with restrained shock and surprise. The bank always says "safety first"—don't jeopardize anyone's life in a robbery. So, of course, she can't scream or alert anyone in the supermarket. Still, she has to show some emotion for the surveillance cameras.

Marek doesn't worry that the cameras will capture his image. He's well disguised in his striped outfit, white beard, white eyebrows, and tall hat. He's even wearing sunglasses.

Anna goes to the back room and stuffs money into a zipper bag—one that's supposed to explode with paint. She'll later explain why she didn't use an exploding bag—she'd ordered some, but they hadn't arrived.

When Anna returns to the counter, several more Uncle Sams are standing behind Marek. By their foot-shifting, toe-tapping waiting-in-line behavior, they don't seem to suspect a robbery is in progress. Anna hands Marek the large plastic pouch, and he stuffs it into a shopping bag. He then turns in his striped trousers and marches out of the store.

Anna pretends to faint—her excuse for not tripping the alarm after the robber took off. The other Uncle Sams call the store manager to report the passed-out teller.

In the meantime, Marek drives off—not too fast, not too slow. As he moves along, he rips off his beard and eyebrows, his hat and jacket and pants. While he does so, he feels as if he's peeling away his servitude in America. Yes, soon he'll be back home! He now has the money to open his nightclub!

He stuffs the costume into a green plastic garbage bag. Then he drives past the cemetery, to the Dumpster behind the condo construction site, and crams the plastic bag inside.

After he gets home, he hides the money behind the panel of his bedroom closet. The next day, he'll return thirty thousand dollars to Anna—and she'll put it back in the bank on Monday.

Marek feels no guilt. He thinks: If the bank is stupid enough to allow this to happen, it's the bank's fault. They should have better security. This will teach them a lesson.

9

CONCEIVED WITHOUT SIN

VIRGINIA OFTEN REMINDS GOD ABOUT THEIR BARGAIN—her continued service at Redemption Dry Cleaners in exchange for His help in conceiving a child.

It's Independence Day, and Virginia has the day off—a Saturday. It's been eons since she's had a free Saturday. She decides to spend the day in prayer and meditation.

Virginia has the house to herself—her in-laws are hosting a picnic in the forest preserves, and Herb has gone off to play softball, horseshoes, volleyball, and eat lots of rich food. He'd asked her to come along, but understood that she's just too tired for an outing in the hot sun.

Dear Lord, she prays, make me fertile, help me conceive.

Virginia tries hard to keep her mind on her entreaties. But the noise outside! It's still morning, but the bottle rockets and firecrackers and cherry bombs are already booming and blasting. Dear Lord, please help me concentrate!

She holds her beloved icon of the Queen of Poland, the Black Madonna of Czestochowa, to her chest and prays: "O Holy Mary, Mother of God, Blessed Mary ever Virgin, shine your eyes upon me, bring me a child." Then Virginia recites the "Hail Mary," and meditates on the image of the Black Madonna and her Divine Black Child.

Years before, when Virginia had made her pilgrimage to Lourdes, she'd met stalwarts who traveled to all the Marian shrines around the world. These are the Mary groupies—and they'd regaled Virginia with stories about the wonders of their cult. The best places, they'd told her, are the ones with statues or paintings of Black Madonnas—hundreds of locations around the world.

A member of the faithful had given Virginia a brochure that listed all the sites—from Austria to Zambia—and included what Virginia felt was an obscure write-up about the phenomenon. Two sentences haunted her: "On our dark journey of life, the Black Madonna is our guiding light. She is our own true nature, hidden in the cavern of our soul."

Virginia had read these words many times, but still wasn't sure what they meant. What is our "true nature"? Is it different from human nature? Are people just sinners by nature—or is there something higher, something better, deep down inside?

Virginia doesn't know the answers. She doesn't even understand the questions. But it doesn't matter. The Black Madonna speaks to her without words.

✂

When Jerry gets up on Saturday, July Fourth, he goes through his morning routine: coffee, radio, newspaper, cereal. But now he has a new feature in his habits. He opens the sliding doors to his deck and the big orange cat trots into the room, then rubs against Jerry's bare legs. Jerry pours dry cat foot in a bowl and sets down a fresh dish of water.

While the cat eats, Jerry munches his cereal and drinks his coffee and reads the newspaper. He always follows the same reading pattern: sports page, comics—then he scans the Metro section to see if there's news on the Czmanski case. Jerry can read between the lines—and figure out if the FBI is looking for accomplices.

The paper is full of important sports news—a two-game winning streak for the Cubs!—and there are some funny comics that Jerry reads twice. By the time he gets to the Metro section, almost an hour has sped by.

When Jerry sees the headline, "UNCLE SAM ROBS $50,000 FROM NORTHWEST SIDE BANK BRANCH," he stands up and scans the article. Then he throws on his clothes—even though his back is still a painful screwed-up mess.

Jerry knows who robbed the bank. And, just like that, a plan shoots into Jerry's mind. He'll confront Marek Jablonski, take the money, then return it to the police department—saying he'd found it in a trash bin at the cemetery when visiting his father's grave.

Jerry remembers that it's his dead father's birthday—the son-of-a-bitch, may he rot in hell! To make the story believable, Jerry will have to visit the cemetery—right after he checks in on Marek Jablonski.

If Jerry finds a huge sum of money and turns it in, the force will realize he's an honest cop, the brass will stop thinking he's mixed up in criminal activities, and he can get the effin FBI off his back.

Virginia tries and tries to pray. But the July-Fourth booms and squeals and blasts have gotten louder and more nerve-wracking throughout the day—making it hard for her to think, let alone pray. By sunset there's no space between the sounds—the fireworks erupt nonstop.

After Herb arrives home at ten, he falls into a coma-like sleep. But after a Fourth of July filled with explosions, Virginia is edgy and weepy.

Antonio Vivaldi shows up with a new composition for Virginia to transcribe. Virginia tries to comply, but her hands shake—the constant kabooms outside make her feel as if there's an earthquake in her body.

"That's a half note—not a quarter note!" Vivaldi barks as Virginia fills in a black circle on the chart paper.

After a few minutes, he throws down her pencil and asks the dead priest to leave.

"Just make the correction, and let's move on," Vivaldi coaxes.

"Come back tomorrow," Virginia tells him, pointing to the back door.

Even though he's a priest, Vivaldi knows the ways of women—and understands that Virginia will not back down. He figures it best to leave without making a scene. Besides, he loves fireworks—and things are building up to the big midnight bang.

After Vivaldi's exit, Virginia sits in her darkened dining room—the sounds of the fireworks sending shooting pains through her head and stomach. She clutches her icon of the Black Madonna and recites her daily litany.

Holy Mary,
Holy Mother of God,
Holy Virgin of virgins,
Mother of Christ,
Mother of Divine grace,
Mother of the Church,
Mother most pure,
Mother most chaste,
Mother inviolate,
Mother undefiled,
Mother most amiable,
Mother most admirable,
Mother of good counsel,
Mother of our Creator,
Mother of our Savior,
Virgin most prudent,
Virgin most venerable,
Virgin most renowned,
Virgin most powerful,
Virgin most merciful,

Virgin most faithful,
Mirror of justice,
Seat of wisdom,
Cause of our joy,
Spiritual vessel,
Vessel of honor,
Singular vessel of devotion,
Mystical rose,
Tower of David,
Tower of ivory,
House of gold,
Ark of the Covenant,
Gate of heaven,
Morning star,
Health of the sick,
Refuge of sinners,
Comforter of the afflicted,
Help of Christians,
Queen of angels,
Queen of patriarchs,
Queen of prophets,
Queen of apostles,
Queen of martyrs,
Queen of confessors,
Queen of virgins,
Queen of all saints,
Queen conceived without original sin,
Queen assumed into heaven,
Queen of the most holy Rosary,
Queen of peace.

As soon as Virginia finishes the litany, she starts it all over again. She doesn't know how many times she repeats the Holy Mother's holy names.

All at once, Virginia feels as if her body is pulling in heat and light—as if she has on black clothes at the beach. It's midnight and the fireworks erupt in a wild big-bang explosion of sounds and light that shake the house and light up the dark room.

Virginia stares at the icon of the Black Madonna. In the flashing lights, the Holy Mother seems to smile, and her eyes appear to move.

�֍

Jerry Valentino shows up at the Jablonski house in the early afternoon. Before he pushes the bell, he hears pulsing music through the door—a counterpoint to the endless fireworks that boom all over the neighborhood.

Jerry made sure that Marek is home alone. He'd seen the kid's Grandma hop into a car with her lady friends. She was carrying a big plastic bowl of something—Jerry figured she went a Polish picnic and would be gone for a while.

When Marek answers the door, he's dressed in hip-hop clothes, sunglasses, and a stocking cap.

"Marek Jablonski?" Jerry asks, though he knows the answer.

"Who asking?" Marek says.

Jerry flashes his badge. Marek has the instinct to run out the back door—but knows that is just a temporary solution. He figures it will be better not to panic.

"What you are wanting?" Marek asks.

"I gotta talk to you," Jerry says, pushing Marek aside and entering the house.

Marek follows him, leaving the door open. Jerry kicks the door closed, then clicks off the television, walks to the sofa, and sits down.

Jerry throws the newspaper article about the bank holdup on the coffee table.

Marek stands in the middle of the room. He holds his lips together, as if incriminating words can fly from his mouth.

"You better hand over the money. Pronto!" Jerry says.

Marek's throat is dry. His tongue is stuck to the roof of his mouth.

"I said now, goofball," Jerry tells him.

Marek moves his jaw from side to side to get his mouth moving. He says: "I knowing nothing."

"I followed you yesterday," Jerry says. "I spotted the goose on the porch and figured you for the holdup man at the dry cleaners. I decided to keep an eye on you. I saw you in your Uncle Sam costume. I watched you go in to the supermarket."

"I not beliewing you," Marek says, embarrassed that he'd pronounced the "v" sound as it's said in Polish.

"You better beliewing it," Jerry says, mocking Marek. "You've been impersonating a black man and holding up dry cleaners for the past couple of months. And yesterday you robbed a bank."

"You are mixing up me and some other thing," Marek says. But he knows his flushed face and fluttery voice betray him.

"You shoulda thought twice before taking that goose—that drum majorette outfit is a dead giveaway."

Jerry realizes that, so far, his dialog has sounded like something from an old gangster movie. It's a deliberate choice—he knows that Polskis just lap up those crummy "Chicago cops and robbers" flicks.

Marek can't believe his bad luck. Why was he so stupid to take the goose? Such a small thing and it had tipped off the police! And, even worse luck, he still has the money behind the panel in his closet. He has a date to meet Anna in just a few hours.

Jerry pulls out his gun and yanks off Marek's sunglasses.

"I want that money!"

"You are to arresting me?"

Of course, this is the last thing Jerry intends to do. He doesn't want the cops nosing around the house—and maybe uncovering the coke in the front-yard Virgin.

"Tell you what, hip-hop," Jerry says. "You give me the money and I'll say I found it in a Dumpster. I'll turn it in and get all kinds of high praise for my outstanding police work."

"No," Marek says, "you will keeping money!"

"Read the newspaper tomorrow. There's gonna be a big story all about it."

"I having no money," Marek says. He tells himself: There were many Uncle Sams at the supermarket—how can the cop pin it on me, unless he finds the money?

Jerry waves Marek around the house, pointing the gun at him. He has no qualms about shooting the kid—and knows he can get away with it. He'll concoct some kind of story about going over to check on a disturbance and the kid trying to attack him and them struggling over the gun.

When they reach Marek's bedroom, Jerry cuffs the bank robber's hands behind him. Next, Jerry goes to the closet, removes a wall panel, and, wham, there's the money. He knows how criminals think.

Jerry finds a Jewel shopping bag in the closet and shoves the money inside.

Marek's eyes dart around the room, trying to figure out what to do, how he'll explain this to Anna. She'll never believe him. But then again if the cop turns in the money, she'll understand he's telling the truth. Still, she'll be in trouble. She won't be able to repay the thirty thousand dollars she stole from the bank.

And why is the cop not arresting him? It's so confusing! Marek will never understand this country!

Marek's lips quiver and tears stream down his face. What will he do now? He'll never get back home. Worse, he'd quit his job at the gas station this morning! He has no work at all—except the backbreaking jobs around Busha's house that he has to do for free.

Jerry aims his gun at Marek and backs out of the room.

"Don't go anyplace," he snickers. "Don't call anyone, don't do anything, don't talk to anybody. Get in bed and stay there. If Grandma comes home, say you're sick and can't get out of bed. After I turn in the money, I'll come back and unlock your cuffs."

✄

Jerry is so happy that he almost forgets about the pains in his back. The fifty thousand dollars is in the trunk of his car. Soon, he'll go to the police station and turn in the cash. But first, he has to do something he's never done before. He has to visit his father's grave.

The cop wishes he could come up with a better place to find the money, but nothing makes sense. He's on sick leave and isn't supposed to be out of bed. How can he explain finding the money, say, in a supermarket Dumpster—and what if the trash had just been emptied? The cops will check on things like that. He can't say he'd found it in his own garbage can—too big a coincidence.

As he pulls into Queen of Peace Cemetery, Jerry hopes he won't run into his mother or brothers at the grave. But as far as he knows, they never visit the old man on his birthday—just on Father's Day, and that was a few weeks ago.

Jerry is amazed he remembers the gravesite—the bastard was buried seven years before, and Jerry had never paid one visit since. If the cops ask, he'll say he'd dropped by to commemorate his father's seventy-fifth birthday. Yes, the miserable asshole would have been seventy-five today!

Jerry gets out of his van and shuffles through the grass to his father's grave. A thick slab of granite, three feet high, marks the spot. On it is an image of the Sacred Heart and written below: Rocco Valentino, Husband and Father, 1925-1993. Jerry laughs when he reads the word "father." What a fricking joke!

Jerry makes the sign of the cross—in case anybody is watching. It's always best when concocting an alibi to make it as believable as possible. That's why Jerry continues to pray, just to make the whole thing look real.

He says an "Our Father," then makes another sign of the cross. When he turns to leave, he notices a green gum wrapper near the headstone. Without thinking, he bends down to pick it up and his back seizes up. He's kneeling at his father's grave and can't get up.

Jerry doesn't want to kneel at his father's grave—even if the gesture will make his alibi more believable. He puts his hands on the gravestone and tries to push himself up. The gravestone topples over, with Jerry on top of it. He's lying on his father's grave, with his head on the gravestone like a pillow.

"Help! Help!" Jerry yells.

But nobody is at the cemetery. Everybody is at picnics and barbecues, in the forest preserves, at the beach, at the zoo, in the parks, at swimming pools, and at backyard parties. Only Jerry is celebrating Independence Day at the cemetery.

He tries to roll over, thinking he can crawl to his van and try to pull himself up by the door handles. But he's as stiff as a cadaver.

In the stifling heat, with no cover at all, exposed, out in the open, Jerry is afraid of sunstroke. He'll kick off on his own father's grave!

"Help! Help!" he cries.

But nobody comes. Jerry feels as if he's growing heavier and heavier. He closes his eyes. He hears birds and planes and the wind rustling through trees. He hears fireworks going off in the forest preserves. Then all the sounds blend into one big hum, a low rumbling, like a distant thunderstorm. The sounds fade and he's in a deep, silent place. Jerry figures he is dead or dying.

"How come it take so long you come by me?" Jerry hears his father's voice say.

"Am I dead?" Jerry says.

"No, I'm the dead one," Rocco Valentino's voice says. "You're just a living asshole."

Jerry doesn't want to admit it, but it's good to hear the son-of-a-bitch's voice.

"Now get outta here," Rocco says. "But don't wait no seven years to come back."

All of a sudden, Jerry can move. He springs to his knees, pulls up the headstone, pushes it in place, and then hobbles toward his van.

A good fake alibi takes a lot of real fricking work, Jerry thinks as he gets in his van and heads for the Dumpster where he'll pretend to find the stolen cash.

�֎

When she wakes up on Sunday morning, Virginia Martyniak has a big smile on her face—as if she'd had a night filled with marvelous dreams. But Virginia doesn't remember any dreams—she just feels a peaceful blankness.

Herb is still snoring beside her. Virginia decides to let him sleep for a while—the poor man is exhausted from all the sun and sports the day before. Besides, Virginia wants to be alone for a while—she wants to think her own thoughts and say a few prayers, without engaging in any morning chitchat with her husband.

Virginia only hopes she won't find Vivaldi lurking in the kitchen. If he is, she'll tell him she has to get ready for Mass—which is true. Virginia doesn't want to go to Saint Francis and listen to Father Spinelli's sanctimonious sermon. But she's still a member of the Church—and until she joins another parish, she has to go.

But best think of that later. Right now, Virginia feels wonderful. Even the prospect of an hour in Spinelli's harsh presence doesn't break her buoyant mood. She wonders why she feels so happy—but does there have to be a reason? Happiness, like love, often comes unbidden—and must be enjoyed while it lasts.

⁂

Sunday, July fifth, is one of the best days of Jerry Valentino's life. The front page of both Chicago papers blaze with stories about the outstanding police officer—himself—who'd found the bank's missing money and turned it in.

People phone him all day. His fellow officers call, his mother calls, his brothers call, his old schoolmates call. But his ex-wife doesn't call. And, behind it all, that's what Jerry had wanted most of all.

He wants to show her and show her good—see, Annette, I am an honest, upstanding police officer. No matter what you think, no matter what you suspect about my being mixed up with Frank Czmanski and his drug ring. See, Annette, you left me for nothing, for no reason. You are wrong about me, Annette. I am a good man, an honorable person, a decent human being. See, I found a lot of money and I gave it back. See, Annette, see, see, see!

⁂

Marek has no job prospects—but, thank God, Anna still has her position at the bank.

Somehow the bank people believe her story—that the man had taken eighty thousand dollars. When recounting what had happened, Anna wept, saying she didn't know why only fifty thousand had been recovered. She cried, and she looked sweet and innocent. And then she was safe—the robbery had covered up the thirty thousand in embezzled funds. She makes a personal vow to steal no more—at least not at this bank.

The bank is glad to recover the money—figuring the robber had in getaway haste thrown away some of the cash. All the time, newspapers include stories about stupid robbers who leave drivers' licenses, resumes, and library cards at crime scenes. Why not an even stupider robber who throws away part of his haul?

Marek hopes the police department will suspect Jerry Valentino as the thief—and believe that he'd kept the missing money—but he soon realizes the thought will never occur to the officials.

The police department is satisfied about the way the whole thing has worked out. A man in blue had recovered and returned most of the cash—it's a bonanza of good publicity.

This is a frickin' nailbiter—I laughed too and cry slapstick

10
SAINTS PRESERVE US

SUMMER COMES TO A CLOSE AND SEPTEMBER COOLS OFF THE CITY, but Father Spinelli grows more inflamed with each passing day. His musical work is uninspired and church attendance is down—all because of Virginia Martyniak! He can no longer fulfill his duties with any enthusiasm. Even his passion for his music has cooled down—only his hot rage makes him aware he's alive.

The doorbell rings. Spinelli covers his ears with his hands. He can't face whoever it is and whatever the person wants.

His housekeeper steps into the room. Sophie thinks the priest looks in bad shape. She figures he's been drinking.

"Officer Walentino come for wisit, Father," says Sophie, a recent arrival from Warsaw and still having trouble pronouncing "v's."

"Tell him I'm occupied," Spinelli groans.

"He waiting for showing to you something," Sophie says.

"What, in God's name?"

"Surprise for you," she says, frowning.

Sophie doesn't know if it's proper to say "in God's name"—but she figures a priest, if anyone, can get away with it.

Spinelli pushes himself from his chair, wondering if he'll have to wait for the afterlife—like Vivaldi—before he has time for his musical work.

When Spinelli steps out into the bright September afternoon, he sees Jerry Valentino standing next to a red van with its rear doors open. In the back, rows of two-foot white plastic statues of the Virgin Mary glare in the sunshine. Jerry's white teeth also glare at the priest. He is smiling, pleased with himself.

After hiding the cocaine in the Virgin Mary statue, Jerry had suffered a series of guilty nightmares. He wonders if Vicodin is causing the dark visions, but knows God might be trying to send him a message.

To make up for his misdeed, Jerry decided to buy a vanload of Virgin Mary statues and donate them to his fellow parishioners at Saint Francis of Assisi Church.

"What's all this, Jerry?" the priest asks, suppressing a yawn. He really doesn't care.

"Catholic Police Fund took up a collection. We bought these for the neighborhood," Jerry says.

"That's nice," the priest responds, but he really doesn't give a damn.

"So, if you could, you know, announce it in church on Sunday," Jerry tells him.

"Announce what?"

"That we're going to select houses at random to receive the statues. If somebody sees one in their yard, they should just leave it there," Jerry says.

"Fine," the priest snaps.

"I thought you'd be more excited," Jerry snaps back.

It's too much. A sob hiccups from the priest's mouth. He tries to hold back his tears, but in seconds his face is streaming.

"I'm overwhelmed," the priest moans.

The priest, of course, means he's overwhelmed with his duties, with his life, with every miserable part of his existence— exacerbated by the woman at the dry cleaners, who's removing sins, she claims, making tons of money, and channeling Vivaldi's music.

But Jerry interprets "I'm overwhelmed" as the priest saying he's awestruck by the wondrous gift.

Jerry smiles. Yes, this is the reaction he'd been expecting. The priest is moved to the point of tears.

Jerry leans against the van, happy and satisfied—the rows of Virgin Marys behind him like silent witnesses.

✄

When Grazyna hears the announcement that the Catholic Police Fund will place statues of the Virgin Mary in yards that don't have one, she decides to talk to the priest.

Father Spinelli feels only half there as he stands at the end of the center aisle and nods to parishioners while they leave the Mass.

When he sees Grazyna approach, he feels his stomach tighten. He's afraid she'll launch into her request for a statue dedicated to Saint Stanislaus of Krakow—and the priest would rather call bingo numbers in hell than discuss it right now.

"Father," Grazyna begins, "you putting in nice word, so I getting statue."

The priest is about to tell her that the placements will be random, but he knows the woman won't accept the fact. She'll just keep harping on and on. He decides on an easier approach.

"Of course, Mrs. Jablonski."

Grazyna grabs the priest's hand and kisses it. She smiles up at him with misty eyes, blinks a few times to spread the tears down her cheeks, then backs away in a bowed, submissive attitude.

These Poles know how to lay it on, thinks Spinelli. Well, at least she didn't mention Saint Stanislaus of Krakow.

But out of the corner of his eye, he spots the woman coming back.

✄

Grazyna is glad she'd remembered to talk to the priest about Saint Stanislaus of Krakow. She'd promised the Saint that she would discuss his monument with the priest this morning. Her mind is relieved.

Grazyna is relieved for another reason. She needs a new Virgin Mary statue—she has to return the one she'd taken from the old Italian couple down the block.

A few days before, while walking to the bus, she'd seen the old man crying in front of his house.

"What wrong?" she'd asked him.

The man explained that the Virgin statue was missing. They had two Virgins, but now there's only one. One statue is supposed to watch over him, and the other is supposed to watch after his wife. The Virgin that's supposed to watch over his wife is gone. And now his wife is in the hospital, wasting away.

"Her protection gone," the old man cried. "No one look over her now," he said, balling up his fists and covering his eyes.

His daughter came out of the house and walked up to her father. Grazyna recognized the woman as "Rosalie Palermo, your real friend in real estate." She'd seen the woman's picture on "For Sale" signs around the neighborhood.

"Come on, Pa," Rosalie said, putting an arm around the old man.

Grazyna offered a few encouraging words, nodded goodbye to Rosalie, then rushed down the street.

Grazyna knew she'd have to return the statue. But first she needed to find herself another one.

Now, this morning at Mass, a miracle! They are giving out free statues and the priest has promised to get her one.

Grazyna knows this is a sign that she should put back the old man's statue right away. She will do it late tonight. Everybody goes to bed early on Sunday. No one will be up to see her do it.

But how will she drag the heavy statue? Perhaps she can get her good-for-nothing grandson to help her. But how can she explain why they're returning the statue? Grazyna doesn't want Marek to know that she'd taken the Virgin. The ingrate will use the information against her in some way, she's sure of it.

No, she'll have to do it herself. She'll remove the sand, then put back the hollow Virgin. The old man can fill it with the sand Grazyna had left in his front yard when she stole the statue.

✄

Late Sunday night, Grazyna is on her hands and knees in her front yard, turning over the Virgin Mary to remove the sand. She lets the sand run into a large bucket she'd taken from a construction site.

For some reason, the sand has turned white. Grazyna wonders if the weather or the recent rain has caused this. It's like at those white beaches in Florida, she thinks. Maybe the Virgin had turned the sand white as a miracle.

Grazyna is over sixty, but she's still strong. She drags the bucket to her garage and covers it with a plastic lid.

Then she goes back to her front yard, eases the Virgin Mary into a green plastic garbage bag and creeps down the block to the old man's house.

The lights are out in the front window. In a few quick movements, Grazyna removes the statue from the bag and places it in the yard next to its twin. Lights snap on in the house. Grazyna sidesteps into the next yard and hides behind an evergreen shrub.

The door opens. Grazyna peeks around and sees the old man silhouetted in the doorway. He holds his face in his hands and weeps.

The man's daughter—the real estate woman—stands beside him. Rosalie puts her arm around her father's shoulder.

"I no can live. I no can live!" the old man cries.

"Pa, let's go inside."

"Whoever rob statue kill Mama!" the old man moans.

Grazyna covers her mouth with her hand, holding back a yelp.

"I find dirty bastard and kill!" the old man yells.

Rosalie leans over the porch railing and looks into the yard.

"The statue's right here, Pa," she says.

The old man bends over the banister and stares into his front yard. He sees two statues—one standing straight and the other lying on its side. He stumbles down the steps and picks up the hollow statue.

"Dirty bastard, I kill you! I kill you," he screams into the sky, then falls into the heap of sand at his feet.

Rosalie rushes to her father's side and realizes right away he's having a heart attack. She runs in the house to call 911.

From her spot behind the bush, Grazyna hears the old man groan in pain. My God, she thinks, I killed the old woman and now maybe the old man, too.

She starts to sob. She puts her hand up to her nose, wiping it back and forth. Some of the white sand from the Virgin Mary is still on her hand and seems to shoot right up her nose.

Right away, Grazyna feels happy and full of energy. This is not my fault, she thinks. It's just a plastic statue. It could not have protected the old woman or the old man. It is not my fault!

She creeps away, down the gangway, through the yard, and into the alley. Something is telling her to go home and take a big sniff of that white sand right away.

11
GIFTS OF THE SPIRIT

WHEN JERRY VALENTINO LOOKS OUT HIS FRONT WINDOW ON MONDAY AFTERNOON, he feels the blood drain from his body. The Virgin Mary statue is missing from the Jablonskis' front yard!

Could the Polish kid have figured out that the statue contained coke?

Jerry looks to the closet, where his revolver sits on the shelf. He knows he can get away with killing Marek Jablonski. There is always some reason a cop can give for shooting somebody. And he can pin at least one dry cleaning robbery on the asshole—the goose and her outfits are more than enough evidence.

Jerry will just say he'd noticed the goose on the front porch and decided to look into it. Yes, he knows he isn't supposed to investigate while off-duty, but he'll think of something, some reason for his visit to the Jablonskis. After he shoots Marek, he'll just say the kid had acted like he was reaching for a gun. Case closed.

✂

Business is so good at Redemption Dry Cleaners that Virginia has little time to visit the bathroom or eat lunch. She just stands at the counter hour after hour examining people's clothing for sins.

The variety of sins is shocking. More and more, Virginia has to use the "other" category on the dry cleaning receipt to write in something that hadn't occurred to her when she'd printed up the slip. The transgressions give new meaning to the words "original sin."

Many people have lying/cheating combinations. One obese young woman with long curly locks makes a habit of putting one of her own spirally hairs in the food when just about to finish eating at a restaurant. Then, mock horrified, she calls the waiter or waitress and refuses to pay. The restaurant staff is glad to get rid of her shrieking presence and usher her out the door without a bill. This woman hasn't paid for a meal in years.

Virginia checks off "other" and in the blank space writes "Lying/cheating/ stealing/sneakiness/gluttony." Virginia knows the woman will pull the stunt again—just as soon as she gets a chance. The woman expects to have her sins removed, then go right out and commit them again. And she isn't alone—most of Virginia's customers are deliberate repeat offenders.

At first, Virginia is annoyed. The sinners aren't grasping the spirit of her mission. Yes, she'll remove their spiritual infractions, but they should at least try to stop committing that particular sin again. Do they think her business is a revolving door?

But then Virginia sees the situation from a different perspective. If the sinners keep on sinning, it'll be good for business. Virginia will end up with millions.

She'd read about a woman in her sixties who'd given birth to a child—the result of a donated egg, her husband's sperm, and an arsenal of fertility drugs. Of course, this costs major money—and isn't covered by insurance. But if the sinners keep repeating their misdeeds, Virginia can soon afford the best fertility treatments anywhere in the world.

Jerry Valentino grabs Marek by his shirt collar and throws him against the wall of his Polish grandma's living room.

"What happened to the Virgin Mary in your front yard?" Jerry says.

Marek wonders why the cop is asking about the Virgin. He has to get rid of this lunatic—and the best way is just to answer his questions, no matter how idiotic.

"Wirgin gone?" Marek says, full of innocence and wonder.

"Where is she?" Jerry says.

"I not knowing!" Marek says, looking straight in Jerry's eyes.

The cop has a good bullshit detector. He knows the kid is telling the truth. Still, he feels incredible hatred for him. He glares at Marek, taking in his hip-hop clothes. Why would anyone waste his time on such nonsense? My God, Jerry thinks, if I'd had this moron's height and looks, I could conquer the world.

A key turns in the lock. The door opens and Marek's Busha stands there. What is she doing home, Marek wonders. Shit, Jerry thinks, she saw me.

Virginia decides she'll work hard during the coming year to make lots of cash. Then she'll retire—leaving someone else to run the business. This way, she can keep making money—but won't have to labor in the day-to-day operations.

In less than a year, she'll be sixty years old—still young enough to conceive, courtesy of the modern medical establishment. Once she has the child, she'll no longer work. Virginia will be a stay-at-home mom—she has no intention of trusting her offspring to a nanny or daycare center.

To achieve life-long solvency, Virginia needs to make as much as she can during the next few months. Soon, she finds herself checking off expensive sins—even when she isn't sure whether the person has committed them. Sacrilege is a good catchall, and nobody has complained yet—even though it's a $17.50 sin. Most people have no idea if they'd committed sacrilege—or for that matter know what it really means.

�

Grazyna forbids Marek from having visitors in the house when she isn't home. But before Marek can make up a story, Jerry introduces himself as the head of the Catholic Police Fund and tells Grazyna she was selected to receive a Virgin Mary statue.

Grazyna grabs Jerry's hand and kisses it. She looks up at him with misty eyes, then blinks a few times until the tears roll down her cheeks.

These Polskis sure know how to lay it on, Jerry thinks.

"I needing statue!" Grazyna exclaims.

"What happened to the statue in your front yard?" Jerry asks. "I noticed it when I is driving by yesterday."

"I never owning Wirgin statue," Grazyna says, feeling she's speaking the absolute truth.

"There was a statue in your yard," Jerry says.

"Maybe go away wisiting person more needing," Grazyna says, then lets out a forced laugh.

"Lady, that's a very special statue. If I don't find out what happened to it, something very bad might happen to you!"

"Maybe bad boys stealing Wirgin," Grazyna says. Then she begins to weep, covering her face with her bent arm.

Marek knows Busha. He knows she's hiding something. And, if he didn't know better, he'd also think she might be more than a little high.

✣

Virginia looks up sacrilege in the dictionary. 1. Violation of something consecrated to God. 2. Gross irreverence toward a hallowed person, place, or thing.

This way, if anybody asks, she'll just recite the definition. She knows the word can apply to a whole host of things. It can mean you failed to genuflect in church. It can mean you didn't dust your crucifix. It can mean you bit into the communion

92

wafer. It can mean you didn't give your missal or (if a non-Catholic) your Bible an esteemed spot in the house.

Never does it occur to Virginia that she might be guilty of sacrilege. Yes, she is spotting extra, nonexistent sins on people's clothes so she can make fast cash, quit her job, and pay huge sums to conceive a child. But that's part of her bargain with God—her continued work at Redemption Dry Cleaners in exchange for a child. Is she wrong to offer God a helping hand?

✄

Jerry never suspects Grazyna. He figures that maybe she's right. Some kids had stolen the statue as a prank. He decides to look around the neighborhood to see what he can find.

It doesn't take long for him to locate the empty statue in front of the Lorenzo residence. The front yard holds two Virgin Mary statues: one standing up straight, and another sitting on her side, propped up against the house—hollow, empty, without the weight to withstand the winds. Jerry knows it's the statue from the Jablonskis' yard. On the bottom is the "X" he'd told Emmett to draw in magic marker.

Jerry asks himself: If the Lorenzos stole the statue, then took the drugs, why would they leave the empty statue outside? They'd know it would be a dead giveaway.

Jerry walks up the porch steps and rings the doorbell. He waits and waits, but there's no answer. He notices something taped to the door—a death notice for Anne-Marie and Aldo Lorenzo. The double wake is scheduled for the following evening at Torretti Brothers funeral home.

Jerry figures he should attend.

✄

Each evening, after she closes up shop at nine p.m., Virginia locks the door and goes in the back to count the money. That nice Polish girl at the bank, Anna, had given her money bands for each denomination of bill. Virginia relishes stacking the cash and banding it up. Each brick of money is a stepping-stone that will take her closer to her unborn child.

After counting the cash, Virginia stashes the money in a large safe she'd had installed for this purpose. In the morning, Herb will take the money to the bank.

Virginia loves the feel and the smell of cash. She loves the new crisp bills and the old soft bills—puzzle pieces that fit together into an image of endless happiness, where she'll at long last become the mother she'd always wanted to be.

And why should she stop at one child? She can pay for the medical treatment that will allow her to conceive and carry many children—offspring she can afford to raise like River Forest royalty.

12
DIVINE INSPIRATION

WHEN HE SIGNS THE VISITORS' BOOK AT THE WAKE, Jerry scribbles an indecipherable name. If anyone asks who he is, he'll just say a member of the church, which is true anyway.

Two side-by-side coffins are at the front of the room. The place is packed with Italian women in high hair and Italian men in high-priced silk suits. They're all teary eyed—a double death, what a tragedy!

Jerry glances around to see if he recognizes anybody.

"Whaddya doin here, cop?" Jerry hears a gravely voice say over his shoulder.

Jerry turns and feels prickles move up the back of his neck. It's Salvatore (Sammy "The Psycho") Mangano, a member of the Chicago Outfit who's managed to stay alive despite repeated attempts on his life. He's worked most of the time as a bagman—and it's rumored that he was involved in a couple of notorious hits. But, as far as Jerry knows, no law enforcement agency has ever managed to pin anything on Mangano—his record is clean, without even a parking ticket.

It's common knowledge that Sammy's survival skills are the result of his prodigious psychic abilities. He just knows when his car had been wired, or somebody is waiting in a parking lot to whack him, or somebody is about to rat him out.

Now, Jerry is face-to-face with Sammy—and knows he can't hide his reasons for attending the wake. Though he figures he'll have to try, try, try.

"The Lorenzos go to my church," Jerry says.

"They don't no more," Sammy says, staring into Jerry's eyes.

"Well, they used to," Jerry responds, trying not to gulp. He feels like there's a regulation-size Chicago softball in his throat.

"So, what you doin here?" Sammy repeats.

"I was sorry to hear these poor people died," Jerry says. It's the truth.

"Yeah, they bote died, like, simultaneous almost," Sammy says.

"It's terrible," Jerry says.

"Wha's diss about drugs?" Sammy whispers.

Oh, God, no, Jerry thinks. This is the last thing I need!

"Huh?" is all he can manage to say.

"You're over here cause you wanna find out somethin about drugs," Sammy says.

Jerry takes a deep breath and arranges his face in a pained grimace. He puts his hand to his lower back.

"I pulled my back," Jerry says. "I've been taking Vicodin. Maybe that's what you picked up."

"No, diss is about coke," Sammy hisses.

"I got pulled off undercover. No more drug busts," Jerry says. "I kind of miss the work. Maybe that's what's coming through."

Sammy stares into Jerry's eyes. Reading the cop is as simple as flipping through a comic book. Sammy smiles. Jerry's former cop partner is in jail for drug trafficking—and Jerry has a huge stash of coke somewhere around his house. An image of a garage floats into Sammy's mind.

Jerry turns away from Sammy's grinning face and eyes. Without a doubt, the man looks as if he knows something.

❊

When Sammy breaks into Jerry's garage, he realizes right away that the coke isn't there. Maybe I'm slipping, Sammy

96

thinks. I was so sure about this. He takes a mini-flashlight out of his pocket, then rips out a piece of insulation. Nothing there.

Sammy closes his eyes and tries to get an image. Where's the coke? Where did the cop put it? Sammy's mind is a blank, but he hears something in his head. It's the "Hail Mary."

�֍

On his way home from the wake, Jerry curses himself for his stupidity. He'd ignored the obvious. It has to be Emmett—the only person who knew about the cocaine in the Virgin Mary statue.

Jerry figures Emmett tried to make it look as if the Lorenzos had stolen the statue. Of course, Emmett had concocted this plan after learning the Lorenzos had died. If the dead neighbors were the thieves, they took the drug's whereabouts to their graves.

Did he believe I'd fall for this, Jerry wonders. Jerry figures Emmett must take him for an idiot. If the jerk wanted to double-cross me, Jerry thinks, he could at least have come up with something more original.

Jerry parks his van in front of his own house and walks across the street to the pink brick house Emmett shares with Dennis. Jerry knows Dennis works second shift—and will get home around one in the morning. It's only 10:30—Emmett should still be up, even if he does have an early postal route.

✖

Emmett isn't asleep—but he's in no mood to be bothered. He's working on his latest painting—a portrait of his mother, which he's creating from memory. The picture isn't a literal depiction of his mother. It's meant to communicate how Emmett feels about her. To do this, Emmett has to tap into all his complex and varied feelings about the woman who'd given birth to him and raised him.

It's as if Emmett is navigating a rocky terrain, on a mountaintop, where he could slip and fall off a cliff. His feelings for his mother are so confusing and conflicted that Emmett doesn't know how to sort it all out. He gasps, feeling as if he's someplace high—where the air is thin and he can't breathe. He tries to put all these emotions on his canvas.

At first, he doesn't hear the doorbell. He's deep into his painting, deep into his feelings, deep into his past. But it's as if somebody just bounced a rubber band off his head. He snaps back to the present—cursing the person who's pulled him out of his work.

This is the only time Emmett has for himself, the few hours before Dennis gets home—after the cats have been fed and watered, after the dishes, and the yard work, and the garbage dumping, and the floor sweeping, and the other endless chores around the house.

Emmett loves these few quiet hours. He luxuriates in the silence, the solitude, the time to gather his thoughts and do some meaningful work. It's the only thing that keeps him going day after day at the post office.

But tonight something or someone has interfered, has interrupted his time. Emmett listens. Yes, he hears the doorbell. He checks his watch. It's 10:45 at night. Who the hell could it be?

❊

Virginia is tired, but she can't fall asleep. Herb snores beside her, making it even worse. Virginia feels like going into the kitchen to have a glass of warm milk. But she knows Vivaldi will be waiting for her there—demanding that she transcribe one of his compositions. No, Virginia thinks, not tonight!

She switches on her bedside lamp. Herb doesn't wake up, he never does. She opens the drawer on her nightstand and takes out some yarn and a needle. She'll crochet a while, hoping it will make her sleepy.

Virginia has no plan in mind for the crocheting. She decides to just start and figure out what it will turn into as she goes along. But she soon realizes what she's making—it's a baby bootie.

✄

Emmett lumbers down the narrow stairway from the attic and makes his way to the front door. He peeks out the window in the door and sees Jerry standing under the yellow porch light.

Emmett had shown up at Jerry's house in just this way. He'd pressed the doorbell and demanded that Jerry let him in. Now Jerry is doing the same. But why? What could the asshole want at this time of night, Emmett wonders. Shit, he's interrupted my creative time! Now I'll never get back into the groove. Not tonight, anyway.

Emmett opens the door. He stands looking down at Jerry, while wiping paint from his hands with a cloth.

"You better got a good reason to be here," he says.

Jerry pushes past Emmett, then trips over two of Dennis's cats as he barges into the house. He falls to the floor, his hands clenching his lower back.

"Ahh, Ahh," he cries out.

Emmett steps over Jerry and makes his way to the bathroom, where he washes his hands. He hears Jerry groaning and moaning under the sound of the rushing water.

Emmett looks at himself in the bathroom mirror. The whites of his eyes appear yellow—as if his recent musings about his mother have brought up toxins in his body. He has to finish the painting and be done with all this stuff about the old woman. He has to get free of these feelings—he has to face his pain and get over it once and for all. Emmett is pissed that the pain-in-the-ass cop showed up just when he was making progress.

Emmett shuts off the water and wipes his hands on a towel adorned with the faded image of a tiger. Dennis's love of cats extends to the house décor and even the dinner plates, bed sheets, and towels. Emmett feels he's the odd dog in a house full of felines.

As he steps from the bathroom, he almost trips over Jerry, who's crawling along the floor. Jerry put his hands on the bathroom doorjamb and tries to pull himself up, but keeps sliding back to the floor.

Emmett gets behind Jerry, grabs him under his armpits, and yanks him up. It hurts like hell, but Jerry doesn't let out a sound. Only his eyes tell the story—he's in an "I'm going to blow my brains out" level of pain.

Jerry drags his feet to the kitchen, and sinks into a chair as if it's a life raft.

As she knits, Virginia tries to picture what her future child will look like. Boy or a girl? Twins? Identical or fraternal? Two boys? Two girls? A boy and a girl? A blonde, like her? Or dark-haired, like Herb?

She doesn't like to admit it, but she wants a girl. If it's a boy, she will of course love him beyond words. But if she has a choice, she'd prefer a daughter. It would be such fun to make clothes for her, dress her up, take her out in the stroller.

"No, I'm not her grandmother," Virginia imagines herself saying to passersby. "I am her mother."

People are so nervy, making personal comments when they don't know what they're talking about, she thinks. What does my age matter? Whose business is it—besides mine, Herb's, and, of course, God's?

❄

Jerry glances around Dennis's kitchen. Images of cats are everywhere—on the tablecloths, the dishtowels, the potholders, framed photos on the walls, the toaster cover, cat magnets on the refrigerator.

"I ain't got all night," Emmett says.

"The Virgin with the coke is missing," Jerry says, looking for Emmett's reaction. But Emmett doesn't have one—he looks blank.

"Somebody took it?" Emmett asks.

"Yeah," Jerry says, "you got any idea who?"

"How the hell would I know?"

"You're saying you didn't take it?" Jerry says.

"You think I'm a goddamned moron?" Emmett says. "If it disappeared, the first place you goin'ta look is here."

Jerry wants to say that this isn't the first place he'd looked. But why get into a big conversation about it? He wishes he didn't have to look farther than Emmett—but a criminal, a thief never acts this way. Criminals get defensive, making all kinds of excuses and acting outraged—sometimes even crying. Emmett had just acted normal. Now, what in the hell am I going to do, Jerry asks himself.

He puts his hand to his forehead and tries to think. Where could it be? Who could have taken it?

"You better get going before Dennis come home," Emmett says.

Jerry doesn't move. Emmett wonders if he's asleep.

"I says..." Emmett begins.

"I heard you," Jerry replies.

"I got work to do," Emmett tells him.

Jerry notices that Emmett's hands are dotted with spots of yellow paint. Several paintbrushes stick out of his shirt pocket. It doesn't take a detective to figure out he was painting—and not the walls—when Jerry had pressed on the doorbell.

Jerry looks up at the wall next to the kitchen cabinets. Hanging there is a portrait of Dennis holding the orange cat that now belongs to Jerry.

"You paint that?" Jerry asks, waving toward the portrait. He isn't interested, but he's in too much pain to stand up. He wants to bide time while he gathering his physical and mental resources.

Emmett's eyes turn away from the picture. It embarrasses him. It's not his best work—or even indicative of his style. He'd painted it for Dennis's birthday—in the manner Dennis likes. Meaning, something simple and direct—even corny. That's why Emmett had insisted that Dennis hang the picture in the kitchen—it was an eyesore in the living room or the bedroom. Emmett seldom cooks, so doesn't have to look at the painting that often. He decides not to answer Jerry.

"You better get your ass movin," Emmett says.

"I need a few minutes. My back..." Jerry says.

"I can't have you hangin 'round here. What's Dennis goin'ta think?"

"Dennis won't be home for two hours," Jerry says.

Emmett opens the refrigerator and takes out a liter of root beer—the strongest thing he ever drinks.

Jerry reaches in his shirt pocket and pulls out a Vicodin. He pops it in his mouth and swallows it dry. Emmett sets a glass of root beer in front of him.

"Thanks," Jerry says, taking a drink. The foam hangs on his upper lip like a ragged mustache. He wipes it off with the back of his hand.

"So you paint that picture or what?"

"I don't like talkin 'bout my art," Emmett says.

"I was just wondering..." Jerry says.

"Wondering what?" Emmett asks, a defensive tone in his voice. He figures Jerry is going to ridicule the painting in some way or make a snide remark. Even though Emmett hates the picture, he feels protective about it. After all, he'd created it. Maybe this is how God feels about us sorry sinners, Emmett thinks.

Jerry doesn't pick up on Emmett's tone. He's too wrapped up in his own pain. He just wants to make idle conversation for a while until he musters the strength to stand up.

"If I, like, give you a picture of my kids, could you make it into a painting? Something to fit over the mantelpiece in my family room. I'd pay you."

Emmett slams his hand on the table.

"Shit damn to hell!" he says. "What you think I am? Some kind of a paint-by-numbers hack?"

"Don't get excited," Jerry says.

Jerry knows something about artistic temperaments. His father's hobby was clay modeling—tiny gnomes were his specialty—and became enraged whenever anybody interrupted him or made a derogatory comment about his work.

"You goin'ta stay here all night or what?" Emmett says.

"Who do you think took the Virgin?" Jerry asks.

He fills in Emmett on the details of his discovery, watching Emmett's face for signs of guilt.

"Maybe the Jablonskis took it, then put the statue at the Lorenzo people's house to make it look like they did it."

"I already checked out that possibility," Jerry says.

"So you believe them Polish people had nothin to do with it?"

"It doesn't seem that way."

"That old lady," Emmett says, "she always creepin 'round, taking stuff from cemeteries, out of Dumpsters. I seen her. Maybe she done it."

Jerry considers Emmett's words. Yes, it's just possible that the old lady had taken the stash. But would she even know what it was?

"That old lady take anything not nailed down—and even then not so sure," Emmett says.

"How come you're watching the old lady all the time?" Jerry asks.

"She home during the day. I'm on my route, I see her all 'round the neighborhood."

"Did you see her empty out the Virgin?"

"Shit, no. Told you just guessin, based on her other activities."

Jerry is starting to feel better. The Vicodin is kicking in—and he thinks Emmett might be right about the old lady. Anyway, it's worth looking into.

After Jerry leaves, Emmett starts to brood about what just happened. The asshole had accused him of stealing the drugs. Why is a black man always the first person suspected of anything that goes wrong, any crime, any missing item?

Emmett tosses around ideas about how he can get back at Jerry. Maybe he'll go over to the old lady's house while she's out and take a look around, see what he can find. Then he'll take the coke and leave it right on Jerry's front porch! Ha ha! That'd be a good one. The motherfreakin FBI would be on his ass for sure, just like he deserves.

As the pastel booties pile up on Virginia's stomach, they remind her of something. Then she remembers—Monet's painting of haystacks. Virginia is pleased that she'd recalled the famous work. It shows that she'll be a good mother, that she can teach her child about art and culture and all refined things.

And, of course, her child will grow up with the kind of love and care that will enable him or her to become a great person in this world—a great artist, a great musician, a great doctor or scientist. Yes, Virginia thinks, my child will change the world.

When she falls asleep at four a.m., Virginia's bed is covered in pink and blue and green and white and yellow booties. It's as if her longed-for child has left its footprints all over Virginia's bed—a pastel trail that will lead Virginia to her magical, wondrous offspring.

✄

When he gets home, Jerry sits up in bed for a long time thinking about his life. The cat never moves from his lap. It purrs, raises its head to get scratched, nuzzles Jerry's hand, then falls asleep in a lazy ball.

The cat—Jerry had named him Tony—seems to bring out buried feelings in Jerry. The prevailing feelings are remorse, guilt, and shame.

The guilt feels like a heavy weight on the back of his neck—something he's always pushing against. He's guilty that he hasn't been a better father, husband, son, brother, or friend. He's guilty that he's lied, stolen, committed violence, and in so many other ways fallen short of the mark as a human being.

The shame feels like waves of nausea in his stomach. He wishes there were a remedy he could take—a spiritual Pepto-Bismol to get rid of the sickening sensation. But Jerry knows he'll have to live with the queasiness—that it will always be there.

He experiences the remorse in his heart. A burning, grinding feeling—as if parts in his heart have come loose and just shake around in his chest, reminding Jerry of how he's failed in life.

Jerry puts his hand over his eyes. When he starts to weep, Tony sits up in his lap. Jerry looks down at the cat, then puts his hand on the cat's head. The cat sends waves of comfort through Jerry's hand. Jerry cries even harder, realizing that—at this point in his life—Tony is his only real friend.

Tony presses the top of his head against Jerry's chest, purring right into Jerry's heart. Still, Jerry cries—tears streaming down his face and snot running from his nose—thinking of how he'd fired his gun at the cat. What if he'd killed Tony? Oh, God, he cries. Thank you, God, that I did not kill Tony.

Before he knows what he's doing, Jerry bends down and kisses the cat on the top of his head and says, "I love you, Tony."

To Jerry, it looks like Tony is smiling. The edges of his lips curl up, and then the cat curls the rest of his body into Jerry's lap. Cuddled together, man and beast soon drift to peaceful sleep.

✄

Jerry wakes up when he hears banging on his back door. The cat yawns and rolls onto his back when he hears the noise, but doesn't move from the bed. Jerry eases away from Tony, trying not to wake the cat, then pushes himself up—stiff and in pain.

When Jerry looks out the glass doors to his deck, Sammy Mangano is standing there displaying the florid blue and purple hues of his famous look of death. Jerry slides open the doors.

"Where's the coke, cop?" Sammy says.

Jerry knows there's no way he can get rid of Sammy. He steps aside to let him in the house. They stand in Jerry's family room staring at each other.

"I don't know what the hell you're talking about," Jerry says.

Sammy feels something on his leg. His heart starts to kick in extra beats. He looks down. A big orange cat is rubbing against his pants.

"You got a cat?" Sammy asks.

"He comes around sometimes," Jerry says, embarrassed. He feels there's something unmanly about men who keep cats.

"He got a name?"

"Tony."

The Italian name raises Sammy opinion of the cat a couple of points—and he almost reaches out to pet him, but right now he has to take care of business.

"I know you're hiding coke for that crooked cop who's in jail," Sammy says, his eyes penetrating Jerry's.

"You're wrong," Jerry says.

"I never been wrong before."

"There's a first time for everything."

"I know you're lyin, asshole! I can always tell!"

"What are you? God?" Jerry says, trying to laugh it off.

"I am judge, jury, and executioner," Sammy says. "Don't forget that, cop."

When Sammy settles his bulk into one of the dinette chairs, Tony jumps into his lap. As Sammy strokes the cat, he starts to get impressions.

Jerry watches Sammy as his eyes roll back and forth, following the visions in his head.

Through the cat medium, Sammy intuits that Jerry has hidden the cocaine nearby. It isn't in Jerry's house, but somewhere close by. That's as specific as the cat gets—still, it's good, useful information.

psychic Mafia via cat

"Thanks, Tony," Sammy says as he sets the cat on the floor.

After Sammy leaves, Jerry is furious at Tony. He decides to ignore the cat—just to punish him.

But when Tony flops over on the floor and rolls around, Jerry reaches out and strokes the cat. He can't stay mad at him.

Jerry feels a pain shoot up his back. He smiles. He's in pain. He has to take drugs and go to bed—and forget about his problems for a while.

13

IT PAYS TO ADVERTISE

GRAZYNA EXPLAINS TO DOROTA AND BRONISLAVA ABOUT THE MIRACLE THE VIRGIN MARY HAD WORKED WITH THE SAND. Grazyna tells them how wonderful she'd felt after inhaling the miraculous powder. She offers to sell them each a quarter teaspoonful for ten dollars.

Before deciding, Dorota and Bronislava want to try it. The nerve, Grazyna thinks. They expect free samples! The Virgin, after all, had performed this miracle for Grazyna's benefit. Why shouldn't she charge others for it?

But Grazyna relents. She knows the women won't believe her until they've experienced the magical sand.

She instructs Dorota and Bronislava to dip their little fingers in the tiny metal box that contains the white powder. Then she tells them to hold their fingers to their noses and sniff.

That night, the three women finish their duties in four hours, instead of the usual eight. They thank the Virgin for their unusual energy and well-being.

Before they leave for the night, Dorota and Bronislava each purchase twenty-dollars-worth of the magical white powder. At forty dollars a level teaspoon, Grazyna realizes her bucket of magical sand could bring in thousand and thousands of dollars. She can sell it to the legions of custodial workers who clean the office buildings near the airport.

With the money, she can put a down payment on a six-flat apartment building. She can purchase the new property without selling her current house. This way, she won't have to leave Princess, her beloved pet buried in the yard.

Yes, Grazyna will buy a big apartment building and live off the rents for the rest of her life. Marek can stay in one of the apartments and do all the upkeep on the new building.

The Virgin is showering her with so many blessings!

✼

On his way home from the Lorenzos's burial, Sammy Mangano drives past Redemption Dry Cleaners and notices a long line outside the store. He figures they must be giving something away. Sammy decides to check it out. He's always up for a freebie.

Sammy ignores the line of people—and strides into the store as if he's an archbishop in ritual garb. The other customers mumble and groan, complaining that he should wait his turn. But Sammy just gives them his look of death. They all shut up.

He glides up to the counter and looks at Virginia. He thinks: the broad's got a nice head of hair. But he lets the impression pass—he goes for redheads.

"What do you want cleaned, sir?" Virginia asks.

"I thought you's givin somethin away," he tells her.

"We clean clothes and remove sins," she explains. "If you'd like to partake of our service, you must give me an item of your clothing."

"Is that why all these people are waitin?" he asks.

"That's right."

"You got a real nice racket going here, Goldilocks," he says.

Virginia doesn't get insulted or annoyed—what good would it do? If somebody doesn't understand something—especially one of God's mysteries—they just don't get it. No amount of explanations will make a difference.

"Please leave the premises," Virginia says.

But, Sammy figures, why not? After all, he's right here. He may as well try it out. He takes off his suit jacket and hands it to Virginia.

Virginia studies the spotless jacket. To Sammy it looks as if she's noticing a lot of stains. She checks many boxes on the receipt, then totals up the figures.

"That will be nine hundred and forty-two dollars, sir," she says, thrilled at how this will inflate her burgeoning bank balance.

"Almost a grand to have a jacket cleaned?" Sammy asks, his voice going up an octave.

"Six dollars to clean the coat and nine hundred and thirty-six dollars to remove the sins you committed while wearing it."

Sammy grabs the receipt from Virginia. He scans the items she'd checked: robbery, greed, calumny (he doesn't know what this is), murder, licentiousness (he has no clue), slander, hypocrisy (not sure), profanity, sacrilege, and too many others to mention.

But then Sammy thinks: Shit, if I can beat the murder rap, it's a bargain.

Aldo and Anne-Marie Lorenzo are surprised to find themselves dead. They were in their early seventies and in good health when they'd fallen ill and died. They're sure their premature ends were set in motion by the theft of Anne-Marie's Virgin Mary statue. Until they locate the robber and bring the person to justice, they can't move on.

As they walk the streets of their neighborhood, Aldo and Anne-Marie notice many things they'd never noticed before.

"Seem like everybody got a plastic goose now," Aldo says.

"Some naked, some with clothes," Anne-Marie remarks.

"Why people want a goose?" Aldo wonders.

"Maybe some kinda saint in some religion," she says.

"A goose saint?" Aldo says, shaking his head. "Only people get canonize."

"Maybe they just door stoppers."

Anne-Marie had noticed that most of the geese stand on front porches, rather than in front yards.

"Could be," Aldo says.

"Come on, we gotta find that robber, Also."

"No call me Also!" Aldo says, angry despite his lack of a corporeal body.

When Aldo had entered the United States, the authorities had listed his first name as "Also." All of his official documents are made out in this name. It had made him feel like an afterthought most of his life. He isn't about to be an afterthought in the afterlife.

They stop in front of Grazyna's house.

"I'm gettin some kinda message here," Anne-Marie says.

"Me, too," Aldo tells her.

"Let's have a look," his wife says.

✄

Grazyna needs to hide the valuable sand—she doesn't want somebody to sneak in and steal it.

She wakes Marek from a sound sleep—the slug is still in bed and it's already noon—and commands him to get up and help her. He obeys, following her up the stairs to the attic. Ziplock bags filled with white powder are stacked in the middle of the room.

"Put the bags behind the insulation," Grazyna says in Polish.

Marek decides to do as he's told, and not ask any questions.

Just then, Grazyna feels a cold breeze move through the attic. She looks at the windows. They're closed, but the wind isn't coming from that direction. It's blowing from the center of the room.

Grazyna knows enough about the spirit world to be afraid. She realizes ghosts are in the room.

"What you wanting?" she asks in English.

"To going back to bed!" Marek replies.

"I not saying by you," Grazyna says.

She turns around and sees two small tornadoes.

"Look," she says to Marek.

Marek doesn't see the funnel clouds. He shrugs and continues to hide the plastic bags behind the insulation. Whatever Busha says or does, he plans to ignore her. He wants to go back to sleep.

"Who you are?" Grazyna says to the two clouds.

"You murder us, evil woman," one of the tornadoes says. Its shape shifts until it looks like an old man. Grazyna recognizes it as the old dead man from down the block.

"How I am killing you?" Grazyna asks.

"You rob Virgin Mary," the other spirit says. It looks like an old woman.

"God telling me is okay to taking statue. You having two, I having nothing," Grazyna says.

"You must pay for sin," the old man says.

"Pay?" Grazyna says, spitting out the vile word.

"You need buy two saint statue, large statue for church," the old woman says.

"I having no money for large statue," Grazyna says.

"We haunt you then," the old woman says, snarling and making a scary motion with her hands.

"What name of saints?" Grazyna asks.

"Antonio and Lucia," the old man says.

Italians, Grazyna thought. Enough Italian saints already in church.

"I promising statue for Saint Stanislaus Krakow. I not can helping you," Grazyna says.

"You gonna be sorry, cheapskate!" the old man says before he and the old woman disappear.

Grazyna decides that rather than sell the magical sand, she'll start her own housecleaning business. Why allow the workers to do such fast work for somebody else? Grazyna can capitalize on her commodity in two ways—by direct sale, and by reaping the fruits of the buyers' labor. They can clean an entire house in an hour. Since Grazyna will charge day rates, an endless flow of cash will be hers.

To enhance her prospects, she'll add a religious spin to the enterprise—drawing inspiration from Virginia Martyniak's success at Redemption Dry Cleaners. She christens her housecleaning service "Spotless Souls."

As an inaugural move, the new president of "Spotless Souls" will put her bum of a grandson to work.

She clomps into Marek's bedroom and swats him on the shoulder with a dishtowel. He covers his face with his hands as she outlines his new duties.

Since Marek is unemployed and has no hope of further robberies or other forms of income, he accepts her offer—but demands that she pay him a living wage. He'll help her start the housecleaning service, but she has to hire him as a supervisor—making twenty dollars an hour. Grazyna trusts no one—but figures if Marek tries to rob or cheat her, she can have him deported.

"You will have to work hard for that kind of money, Marek," she says.

Marek has no problem with working hard—he'll put in the hours, and make sure everything is done just right. He won't do any manual labor himself—it's beneath him—but he knows how to supervise others, knows how to make sure they do their jobs. He had plenty of related experience with the animal handlers in the circus.

With the aid of a Polish/English dictionary, Marek writes an ad for the neighborhood newspaper. He decides on a competitive approach.

SPOTLESS SOULS
HOUSEKLEENING SERVICE

We removing sin right away on premises. No waiting for dry cleaning to coming back! We giving fast/immediate result! We washing floor/ window/ bathtub and taking away lifetime spiritual grease/ grime. We vacuuming rug/curtains/ furniture and removing generation of sinful dust/dirt/lint. And we can doing all this in just one morning/ afternoon/ evening. Price depending on number and type of sin (mortal/venial). Don't delaying your response/ answer/ reply—calling us today. Your eternal life (heaven/hell/ purgatory) may depending on it.

After reviewing the ad copy and making some edits—changing rug to carpet, and curtains to drapes—Grazyna sends Marek to the neighborhood newspaper office. She wants the ad to start running right away.

14

SEEK AND YE SHALL FIND

WHILE MAREK IS AT THE NEWSPAPER OFFICE AND GRAZYNA IS ON HER WAY TO WORK, Jerry decides to take a look around their house. He can't believe his luck—the Polish duo is seldom gone at the same time, as if their little shack were Fort Knox. Well, maybe it is, Jerry thinks, if they've got the coke in there.

✂

After leaving the dry cleaners, Sammy decides to take a spin around the neighborhood and see if he can pick up any vibes about the missing cocaine. Thanks to Jerry's cat, Tony, Sammy knows the stash is somewhere near Jerry's house—it's just a matter of pinpointing the location.

Sammy wants out of the Outfit, and the cocaine will be a nice peace offering for his boss—a parting gift that might put the big man in the mood to cut Sammy loose. Sammy is tired of the life, he's bored—and he's feeling something even more foreign: guilt about what he does for a living.

Before, he'd been almost unconscious about his actions. He did something, it was over, he did something else, went someplace else, ate, drank, went home, went to bed, got up, and started all over again.

But now it's different. He's aware of each and every thing in his day: if he has to shake somebody down, if he has to muscle somebody, lie, cheat, steal. These things, Sammy now tells himself, are sins. Sins. They are wrong.

God, if anybody in the Outfit knew what he's thinking and feeling, they'd call him a traitor or a coward or worse. Nobody questions what they have to do—never, ever.

Then his Aunt Anne-Marie and Uncle Aldo had died within hours of each other—and something broke apart inside Sammy. He just can't keep on living the way he's been living.

And he feels so sorry for his cousin Rosalie, the Lorenzos's daughter. She'd not only lost both parents on the same day—she'd lost her husband only a few months before. On top of it, she has two rowdy teenage boys to look after, plus her real estate agency.

Sammy wants to quit the Outfit and join Rosalie in the business. The coke stash is his way out.

As he drives down the block, Sammy sees Jerry sneak into the back door of the house across the street from where he lives. Interesting, Sammy thinks.

❁

When Giovanni comes in with his shirt, Virginia asks him to watch the counter for a few minutes while she attends to some business in the back. The lovelorn Italian is ecstatic—his muse has singled him out, put him in a position of honor!

"Customer, please," he says, on tiptoes behind the counter, "stand please straight line, clothes fold by left arm, keep ready for Virginia."

Giovanni waves his hands, directing people into an arrow-straight line. Then he tidies the pens and dry cleaning receipts on the counter. He aligns some hangers on a hook. He takes out his clean, ironed handkerchief and with great care dusts Virginia's beloved icon of the Black Madonna.

After he's exhausted his straightening and dusting possibilities, and Virginia has still not returned, Giovanni isn't sure what to do next.

Since he's in charge, he feels he should do something. He's more than just a classroom monitor—watching for unacceptable behavior such as line breaking and loud talking. No, he's not just there to stop bad behavior—he should initiate good behavior. He has an idea.

Giovanni lifts the Black Madonna, holds her up high for all in the room to see, then says: "Please, kneel and we pray."

Many in the crowd are non-Catholics, so they're not used to kneeling in church, let alone in a dry cleaning establishment. But no one gives it a second thought. It's just part of the procedure.

There's a loud shuffling of shoes and purses as the customers fall to their knees. When everyone is in the proper position, Giovanni says: "Say like I say, please."

Giovanni makes the sign of the cross, then begins: "Hay Mary."

"Hay Mary," says the crowd.

"Fulla graze," Giovanni intones.

"Fulla graze."

"Delorid iz wit dee."

"Delorid iz wit dee."

❅

Jerry uses a master key to open the Jablonskis's back door. Jerry's basement and garage are jammed with crook's tools—but his favorites are the master keys that can open any lock.

He only wishes he had something like it to figure out his life. Why have things turned out so bad? Why is he a middle-aged man whose only friend is a cat? Why is he so miserable? Why does nothing bring him joy anymore? And, most of all, why does he have to suffer each and every day with his screwed up rotten back?

As soon as he enters the Jablonski kitchen, Jerry's nose is assailed with an array of smells—cabbage and Lysol pine scent and bleach. God, these Polskis are clean, Jerry thinks—but they stink like hell. He prefers Italian aromas—garlic and tomatoes and bay leaves and oregano and olive oil. Even the cleaning solutions in an Italian home smell of lemon and sweet basil.

Jerry wishes he was in his mother's warm, fragrant kitchen right now—instead of in this sterile, Clorox-smelling place. He's glad he won't have to spend a lot of time in the kitchen— he doesn't think the Jablonskis hid the drugs there.

Jerry decides to start with the obvious—he'll look in the attic. After all, if somebody has a large stash of drugs, that's the only logical place to hide it.

❋

Sammy parks a few doors down, and walks to the house he'd seen Jerry enter a short time before. Sammy decides to go in through the front door—he can jimmy the lock—and launch a surprise attack on Jerry.

If somebody stops him before he gets inside—say, if the occupants arrive home or if a neighbor wants to know who he is—Sammy will whip out some raffle tickets from his pocket and say he's selling them for Saint Francis of Assisi Church, which is true anyway.

None of the neighbors stop Sammy—but the thingamajig on the porch stares at him: a plastic goose dressed like Betsy Ross. Sammy knows all about these geese—his wife has one on the porch at home. Only Theresa's is a boy—and at present is dressed as Uncle Sam.

Sammy checks the name on the mailbox: Jablonski— Polacks, Sammy thinks. The neighborhood is getting overrun with them.

While he's taking a credit card from his wallet, the Lorenzo ghosts drift into the yard.

"Look who here, Aldo," Anne-Marie says, pointing to Sammy.

"He put on weight," Aldo says.

"He always sittin in cars," Anne-Marie says. "Don't get enough exercise."

Sammy pushes the credit card into the space between the door and the lock. He turns the knob and the door opens.

"What he's doin?" Anne-Marie says.

"Maybe he know woman steal our Virgin and he gonna get revenge," Aldo says.

"Lucky for us Sammy a mind reader," Anne-Marie tells her husband.

In less than a minute, Sammy is inside the Jablonski living room. His quick scan of the room—with its plastic-covered furniture and parade of framed sepia relatives on the wall—is enough. These people for sure have no taste. Still, it doesn't seem like the home of cocaine thieves. But, these days, who knew?

Sammy stands still and listens. He hears noise coming from the attic. This is turning out a lot easier than he'd expected.

✄

Virginia hears the praying in the front of the store. She figures that Giovanni is biding time while she's away. She smiles, thankful that the little limousine driver is so resourceful.

Now, she doesn't have to rush. The customers are occupied. For that matter, Giovanni can lead them in an entire rosary. She has one on the counter—and maybe her helper will notice it after saying a few Hail Marys.

Virginia is happy to have a respite from her endless service to her customers. She has to go to the bathroom more and more often these days—feeling that she has to pee again as soon as she's finished peeing.

Virginia hopes that she doesn't have a bladder infection, or some kind of female disorder, or, God forbid, cancer. But would God give her cancer when she's spending endless hours doing His work? She doesn't think so—but even saints had been afflicted with horrible diseases. That's why they're now the patron saints of those diseases. Saint Alphonsus Ligouri and arthritis, Saint Peregrine and cancer, and so many others.

What's worse, sometimes Virginia feels a frightful urge to urinate and nothing will come out. What if she has a tumor impeding the flow? But if she waits long enough, just sitting and relaxing, she can make water. Oh, this is a disturbing, embarrassing problem. She has to wait on the public for most of the day, and can't keep excusing herself to go to the bathroom.

Virginia has no choice—she will have to hire an assistant.

Jerry lifts the exposed insulation, and soon finds the stash. He stuffs the baggies of coke into the athletic bag he's brought along.

This has turned out a lot easier than he'd expected. Jerry decides he'll rent a storage space—under a fake name—and put the coke in there. These things are confidential. No one will ever have to know. When Frank gets out of jail, and enough time has passed, Jerry will take out the coke and give it to him.

In the middle of Jerry's daydream about how he's going to work out his problems, he senses something and turns around. There, right behind him, is Sammy Mangano holding a gun. Jerry's dream of salvation drifts away like so much steam from a summer sidewalk.

Emmett, too, had seen Grazyna and Marek leave the house. He intends to look around for the coke—and leave it on Jerry's front porch, as he'd decided the night before.

After delivering a priority package a few houses away, he stands on the Jablonski front porch, another package in his hand. If they come home while he's looking around, he'll say he needs their signature.

Of course, the package isn't theirs. When he realizes his fake mistake, he'll bid them good day and leave. Why should they suspect anything? Even if they find him in their attic, he'll just say he's looking for them.

These Polish people won't know that a postal worker isn't supposed to enter someone's abode. How could they know—unless they look into it? And if they do, Emmett will flat-out deny it. He has a spotless record, so there's no way he can get in any trouble. The United States Post Office will take his word for it. After all, he's an American, and these other people are foreigners.

Emmett is surprised to find the door open. Could the two Jablonskis have forgotten to lock it? He pushes his bulk through the door and skulks into the living room—a glance at the décor gives him a stabbing sensation in his stomach: plastic-covered furniture, decorated eggs on a shelf, and landscapes painted on glass. He hears voices upstairs. One is Jerry Valentino's, and the other—a deep, thug-sounding voice—belongs to a stranger, maybe one of Jerry's goon friends. Most of the cops, Emmett feels, are mixed up in the mob—none more so than Italian cops.

Emmett wonders what to do. He'd planned to stuff the coke in his mail pouch and deliver it to Jerry's house. But he can't do that now—because Jerry and his buddy have already found the stash.

Still, Emmett is curious. And then he starts to feel something else: Envy. Why should the rest of the world get easy money? Why does he have to slave his life away? He has the potential to become a great artist—if he ever had any real time for his work.

Emmett thinks it only fair that he get a share of the coke. He'll just tell Jerry and the other guy that if they don't cut them in he'll blow the whistle. If they threaten to kill him, he'll say he'd left a detailed letter in a safe deposit box that implicates Jerry Valentino. Of course, it's a lie, but the cop will have no way of knowing that.

✄

As he gazes at Sammy's gun, Jerry can't believe his bad luck. How can he lose the coke not just once, with the Jablonskis, but now twice, with the Outfit bagman?

Jerry and Sammy turn when they hear footsteps on the stairs leading to the attic. Jerry figures it's Marek Jablonski coming home.

When Emmett's face appears at the foot of the stairs, Sammy wonders what the mailman is doing here. The mail never arrives when you want it, Sammy thinks, but always shows up when you don't.

"I want in on this deal," Emmett says, taking an offensive approach.

"There ain't no deal," Sammy says.

"If you know what's good for you," Jerry says to Emmett, "you'll leave right now, and make like you haven't seen nothing."

Sammy turns his gun toward Emmett. When he does, Jerry jumps up and hits Sammy's hand, sending the gun flying across the room.

"Get the gun," Jerry says to Emmett.

Emmett complies, then turns the gun on the two men. He strides across the room and picks up the athletic bag filled with cocaine.

Emmett sees an image of himself in front of him.

"What you doin, fool?" the other Emmett says.

"Shuddup," Emmett says.

"You gonna get your ass in jail."

Since childhood, Emmett had often battled with his conscience this way. Most often, his conscience had won—

that's why Emmett had wasted his life in a dead-end, repetitive job.

Yes, he had been honest and hardworking his entire life. But where had it gotten him? Sure, there's his government pension. But, by that time, he'll have cataracts or glaucoma—or both—plus arthritis, and won't be able to paint worth shit.

No! He has to do something with his life while there's still time. He needs money. He needs to paint! With money, he can quit the post office—and do the work he loves for the rest of his life.

"Fool, what you doin with a gun?" Emmett's conscience says.

"I told you, shuddup!" Emmett says and pretends to shoot his alter ego. He sees a cartoon balloon that says "Pow"—then his conscience blows into a thousand bits.

Emmett backs down the stairs, the gun aimed on the two men.

Jerry and Sammy laugh as if this is the funniest thing they've ever seen. They make high-pitched squeals and hold their arms across their stomachs.

Emmett figures it's some kind of Italian thing—maybe Dagos laugh like this when they're scared or pissed off.

"Where you goin?" Sammy says.

"I'll figure it out," Emmett tells him, backing down the stairs.

"You better kill us." Sammy says. "Otherwise, you're dead."

Emmett has no intention of killing anyone. The gun is little more than a prop. In a few seconds, he realizes what's so funny. How could he get away with this? Jerry and the other guy will come looking for him, take back the coke, and then pop him. What in the hell is he doing? Is this what they call temporary insanity?

Emmett crowds his way back up the stairs.

"I want my share, then," he says.

"Your share?" Jerry asks.

"Yeah, for helpin you hide it in the first place!"

"Let's get the hell out of here before these people come home," Sammy says.

"We gotta talk this over," Emmett says.

"I know just the place," Jerry replies.

15

THREE DIVINE PERSONS

JERRY KNOWS THAT DENNIS LEAVES FOR WORK AT FOUR IN THE AFTERNOON. It's now 4:15. They can go over to Emmett's house and discuss the situation.

At first, Emmett resists. What if Dennis comes back for something? How will he explain why he's in the house with two other men? Dennis is the jealous type and will think the worst.

Emmett calls Dennis on his cell phone just to make sure he's on his way to work. He starts with some chitchat about whether the lawn needs mowing. Dennis mentions that he'd left a nice lasagna in the oven.

"I got a taste for lasagna," Emmett says, trying to make sure he says the right thing so Dennis will stay in a good mood.

It's so easy to upset Dennis by saying something wrong—and half the time Emmett doesn't even know what he'd said to set Dennis off.

Before Dennis hangs up, he says: "I love you." Emmett has no choice but to respond, even though Sammy and Jerry are standing right next to him.

"I love you, too," he says. Emmett knows if he doesn't say it, Dennis will get pissed for sure.

Soon, the three men are in the house Emmett shares with Dennis. A throng of cats greets them in the kitchen. The cats flop in front of Sammy, rolling at his feet. He bends down and pets the animals, saying: "Nice kitty, nice kitty."

Sammy doesn't have a cat of his own—he'd vowed never to own one again, not after what had happened to his childhood pet. When Prince had been murdered, Sammy had almost died of grief. He never wants to feel that bad about anything again.

But he loves to run into cats at other people's houses or on the street. It gives him a chance to get his cat fix, without any personal responsibility or emotional liability.

Sammy is surprised that, with all the cats, Dennis's house doesn't smell like cat piss. This guy Dennis is a neat freak—the whole place is spotless, not a piece of lint or a strand of cat hair anywhere. And the place smells good—as if somebody has just made a pot of marinara sauce. Sammy's stomach starts to growl.

"Let's go in the basement," Emmett says.

Sammy is disappointed—he was hoping Emmett would offer to serve the lasagna that's sitting in the oven. But Emmett isn't Italian—and doesn't understand that the deal would go off a lot better if he gives his guests something to eat and drink.

�

When Virginia gets home from work, she's exhausted. She doesn't even have the energy to eat. But she knows she has to—she needs to be in good health for God to answer her prayer and help her conceive.

It's ten at night. Herb is already asleep. Virginia sees the note on the kitchen table: *Dinner is in the oven.*

Virginia takes out the little casserole of stew, sets it on the table, pours herself a glass of milk, then sits down and shovels the food into her mouth.

She glances at the pile of mail on the kitchen table. A bright blue envelope catches her eye. She looks for a return address, but the space is blank. She opens the envelope with her butter knife and reads the letter.

> Dear Mrs. Virginia Martyniak:
> Perhaps you are unaware of the historical significance of your current business venture at Redemption Dry Cleaners. Nearly five hundred years ago, in 1517, Martin Luther posted his Ninety-Five Theses on the door of the Wittenberg Cathedral. He refuted the Catholic Church's selling of indulgences. His principal contention is that man is justified

126

by faith alone, and not by works. Over the years, the Catholic Church has realized the absurdity of selling salvation. But now you have reverted to many of the Church's most primitive practices—promising to get rid of sin for a price! Even the Catholic Church no longer sells indulgences! But you and your business would take us back to a primitive, foolish time. Repent, Mrs. Martyniak, have faith in God—and cease your sham.

Sincerely,

A Concerned Believer

✂

Sammy and Jerry follow Emmett down the stairs to the finished basement. This, too, meets with Sammy's approval. It's a beautiful space—blonde paneling on the walls, terra cotta tiles on the floor, a beige sofa and matching chairs with blonde legs. It is all very simple and tasteful—with a light, airy atmosphere that makes Sammy feel good. It would be a nice, comfortable, relaxing place to sit and drink coffee and pet cats—two of Sammy's favorite pastimes.

"Who did the remodeling work down here?" Sammy asks.

"Dennis did it himself," Emmett says.

"Dennis must be handy," Sammy remarks.

Emmett lets the comment pass—he figures it might be a reference to his and Dennis's sexual preference, but isn't sure. Anyway, he doesn't want to get into a needless argument or, worse, a fight.

"Yeah," he says.

Jerry, too, likes the basement. He's handy himself, but doesn't have any decorating sense—as his wife has never hesitated to point out. Not that Annette has any great taste herself—she collects those stupid ceramic statues of giraffes. Thank God she'd taken them with her when she moved out.

The three men sit down—Emmett on one of the chairs and Sammy and Jerry on the sofa. Emmett sets the athletic bag filled with coke on the coffee table in front of them.

For some reason, Jerry thinks of a line from his catechism, "One God in Three Divine Persons." He'd thought about it when Emmett had appeared at his door, and now he's thinking about it again.

Jerry amuses himself by wondering which of them could play each role. Sammy as God the Father, himself as God the Son, and Emmett as the Holy Ghost. What does this mean? Why does he keep thinking about it?

Virginia puts the letter back in its envelope. Well, she thinks, there are always cranks.

She closes her eyes. Dear Lord, she prays, inspire and guide me. Teach me Your ways. Show me Your path.

Virginia sees an image in her mind: A fluffy white lamb. Then she hears the words: *Lamb of God who takes away the sins of the world.*

From her Catholic catechism, Virginia knows that Jesus Christ was the sacrificial lamb sent to earth to redeem mankind from sin. Mankind was too far-gone to achieve this on its own.

To Virginia, it's akin to getting in over your head with credit cards. After a while, there's no way you can pay it off. To get out from under your debt, you need somebody to come in and pay the bill.

Jesus had paid the bill.

But now the bill has built up again. During the two thousand years since Christ's death, mankind had once again racked up a huge debt of sin. That's why God had inspired Virginia to offer the sin removal services. But it only goes so far. People need their clothes cleaned over and over.

What the world requires is a new redeemer, Virginia thinks.

The mystery of God's Divinity had perplexed Jerry throughout his childhood. His tiny mind had tried to grasp the huge implications—how can God be three persons? But Jerry hadn't wondered about this in decades. Why does he keep thinking about it now?

Why is he thrown together with these two other men? Who would have thought things would turn out this way? It's as if his life has a will of its own, beyond his control.

"I want my share," Emmett says, breaking the silence.

Jerry shakes his head, and Emmett understands every silent word. Jerry is saying: *Nobody promised you anything. You helped me out because you didn't want me to turn you in for the dry cleaning holdup. You got no part in this. Nothing is owed you. You got no business horning in here. Are you crazy, thinking you can deal with me this way?*

But then Jerry starts to nod his head up and down. Emmett understands his unspoken message. I was an idiot to involve anybody else in this, Jerry is thinking. I should have handled it myself. I should have kept my mouth shut. I should have hidden the drugs myself. But I didn't, and now I have only myself to blame that I'm sitting here with these two people who want in on the deal. I did this. Me, me, me. I am an asshole and an idiot. I deserve everything that happens to me. I have no choice but to go along with this.

Father Spinelli decides to write Virginia a threatening letter every day until she either closes her business or he drives her crazy.

Until Virginia came into his life, the priest had considered himself free from sin—even immune to it. He's charitable, does his duty, is thoughtful, kind, and loving.

The only sin he can ascribe to himself is the minor selfishness he feels about his time. Yes, he needs time for himself and his musical work. But is that a crime? Even Jesus took time for Himself—going to weddings and socializing with friends.

But Virginia has unleashed a rash of sinful, hateful feelings in Father Spinelli: envy, pride, vengeance, hatred, anger, even sloth. The priest doesn't feel like doing anything anymore—except getting revenge on Virginia.

How he hates that woman! There, he's said it. He's admitted it. He hates her! But should a priest hate anyone—even the vilest criminals? So be it, Spinelli thinks. I am only human.

Spinelli spends so much time brooding about Virginia and harboring ill feelings toward her that he knows it isn't healthy—and he could end up with cancer or a heart attack.

He admits something else: in face and body type, Virginia resembles his own Polish mother—the mother who'd prayed to God that her only son would become a priest.

How he resents her for it! Yes, at last he's confessed it. He'd never had the desire to become a priest—instead, he wanted to pursue his musical inclinations. Now, here he is fifty years old, a slave to his parishioners—never a moment for himself or his talent.

He's too old to start over in another profession. What could he do? Teach music at a high school? Deal with disrespectful, ill-mannered teenagers every day? There's no prestige in that—nothing like the fear and respect he inspires in his parishioners. If he renounces the priesthood, he'll end up as a nobody. He's stuck. He hates his job—but, even more, he hates to give it up.

All the priest's rage and disappointment have erupted in his loathing for Virginia Martyniak. He'll exorcise his demons with one quick explosion.

"And what do you think is your share?" Jerry asks Emmett.

"There's three of us," Emmett says.

"You want me to give you a third?"

"Yeah, a third for each of us."

"What about the guy who it belongs to?" Jerry says.

"Give him your third," Emmett says.

During all this, Sammy sits back on the sofa, with a white cat on his lap. Sammy imagines the cat's name is Snowball. He pets and scratches the animal while Emmett and Jerry blabber away. Sammy figures he'll just wait until the two men have talked themselves out. Then he'd tell them what he wants.

✂

Father Spinelli gets the facts he needs over the Internet. It's amazing how much subversive information—germ warfare, munitions, explosives—is available to anybody with a computer.

The priest isn't at all handy. He can't even find the right end of a screwdriver. But the bomb instructions are detailed—with clear, simple illustrations. An illiterate half-wit could follow them.

✂

"What about you, Mangano?" Jerry asks.

Sammy snaps back to the present—he'd been thinking about Prince, the black cat he'd had as a child. The memory always makes Sammy weepy and sad. He sniffles for a second, as if he's allergic to the cat on his lap. He takes a deep breath before speaking—he doesn't want to start bawling in front of the other men.

"What's this cat's name, anyway?" Sammy asks.

"That's Frosty," Emmett says.

Well, I was close, Sammy thought. Still, he considers Snowball a better name.

After Sammy unzips the athletic bag and takes out a plastic Ziploc bag, he shoots Jerry a dirty look.

"This stuff ain't even wrapped right. It's gotta be wrapped up tight, with duct tape, or it'll disintegrate," Sammy says.

Emmett gives Jerry an I-told-you-so look.

"The Jablonskis wrapped it up like that," Jerry says.

Sammy opens the baggie, dips his little finger in the coke and puts his fingertip on his tongue. The cat rolls over in his lap and reaches out his paws in a "let's play" gesture. Sammy strokes the cat's stomach as he samples the coke.

"This is pure, uncut," he says.

"Yeah," Jerry says, "the guy it belongs to, he got it straight from Colombia."

"Well," Sammy says, "if we cut it, the stuff will be worth a lot more. Nobody sells coke this way."

"I have no idea how to cut cocaine," Jerry says. "I don't know anything about drugs or any of this. I was just doing somebody a favor."

Again, Jerry feels like kicking himself in the ass for getting involved in this huge, giant mess that has cost him his marriage and is threatening to land him in jail for years.

"You gotta cut it with baby formula," Sammy says, "the powdered kind."

"Who's gonna do it? That's an art, for Christ's sake," Jerry says.

"Youse two can do it. I'll tell you how," Sammy says.

"So, you're the supervisor now?" Jerry asks.

"You ain't cuttin no cocaine here," Emmett says.

"Let's go back to your place," Sammy says to Jerry.

"The fricking FBI is watching my house night and day. No effin way."

"So, we'll rent a hotel room," Sammy says.

"Shit no," Jerry says. "That sure as hell will be an effin disaster. The housekeeping staff will barge in on us, we'll leave something behind, they'll trace it to us. No! Shit no."

"Looks like it's your place, cop," Sammy says. Then he turns to Emmett and says: "Bring the lasagna."

16
GIVE US THIS DAY

AFTER JERRY IS SURE THAT NOBODY IS WATCHING HIS HOUSE, Sammy and Emmett sneak through his backyard and enter the house through the basement door.

Beforehand, Sammy had made a quick stop at a nearby location to pick up a fifty-pound bag of baby formula. Neither Jerry nor Emmett asks where he got it.

While Sammy and Jerry eat lasagna, Emmett ducks out on an errand. The other two voted him to pick up boxes of heavy-duty plastic Baggies and rolls of duct tape. Emmett has to stop at the ATM to get enough cash for these purchases. He sure as hell ain't gonna to charge the stuff.

Emmett thinks it's damn unfair that he has to do the dirty work—and use his own money on top of it. Still, Emmett doesn't argue. Soon enough, he'll be rich. Of course, he has to figure out how he's going to unload his share of the coke. But he'll worry about that later.

When the cocaine-cutting operation gets started in Jerry's basement, it's eight o'clock.

Emmett knows they won't be finished before Dennis gets home at one a.m.. He suggests that they continue the following day. But Sammy won't hear of it.

While he barks out orders to Jerry and Emmett, Sammy lounges on Jerry's La-Z-Boy and cuddles Tony in his lap. He's amazed at how beautiful the cat is—a gorgeous reddish orange with symmetrical stripes.

"Where's Tony's toys?" Sammy asks as Jerry and Emmett sweat and struggle at their task—cutting the coke and the baby formula with playing cards on Jerry's Ping-Pong table and then bagging it up and taping it tight.

"Sorry, I haven't had time to visit Cats 'R' Us," Jerry says.

"Ain't he got a toy mouse or some bouncy balls or a piece of yarn or something?"

Jerry opts for a slow-burning silence.

"You're some caregiver," says Sammy, who knows from a daytime talk show that people aren't supposed to call themselves pet owners.

He pulls his key chain out of his pocket and dangles it in front of Tony, who swats at it a few times. But Tony is more interested in cuddling and getting scratched and petted. He reaches with his paw and gives Sammy a gentle touch on the cheek.

"Tony, macaroni" Sammy croons. "What a sweet kitty baby boy cat Tony baby is." He kisses the cat on top of his head and hugs him tight.

"Since when is that cat called Tony?" Emmett asks.

"Since he started living over here," Jerry says.

"Dennis find out you got that cat, he out call the National Guard. It his favorite," Emmett says.

"Tony belongs to Dennis?" Sammy asks.

"Dennis call him Punkin. He love that cat to pieces," Emmett says.

"Then what's the cat doin over here?" Sammy asks.

"He always runnin off every time he can," Emmett says.

"So maybe he don't wanna live with Dennis. Cats got rights, too," Sammy says.

Jerry throws one of his cocaine-cutting playing cards—a Queen of Hearts—onto the Ping-Pong table.

"This is effin impossible. It could take years," Jerry says, brushing the white powder from his hands.

"Watch that dust," Sammy says. "I don't want Tony to inhale it and get sick."

"Take him upstairs then," Jerry says. "You're sure as shit not doing nothin down here."

"I gotta go home soon," Emmett says. "Dennis call the cops if I ain't home when he get there. He the worryin type."

"Call that asshole Dennis and pick a fight. Then say you're goin out drinkin," Sammy says.

"I never touch a drop," Emmett says.

"Say you're goin drinkin for the first effin time, then."

"I gotta go to work early in the morning. I can't work all day if we stay up all night."

"So call in sick tomorrow. After this, you can quit your effin job."

"What Dennis goin'ta think if I stop goin to work all of a sudden?"

"Tell him you won Publisher's Clearing House or the lottery or some effin thing. Ain't you got no creativity?"

✄

Virginia wakes up in the middle of the night, and goes to the kitchen for a glass of water. When she turns on the light, she sees Father Antonio Vivaldi sitting at the table.

"Virginia," Vivaldi says, "you promised to spend half an hour each day transcribing my compositions."

"I've been so busy, Father," Virginia says, covering her face with her hands.

"But I must get my work into the world!" Vivaldi tells her, then he begins to hum a new tune.

Virginia sinks into a chair and begins to sob. The dead priest thinks she's crying for joy—realizing she's privileged to assist one of the greatest geniuses the world has ever known.

"I can't do it," Virginia cries. "It's too much. I'm only human!"

"But it is such an honor I am bestowing on you!" Vivaldi tells her.

"I'm a fifty-nine-year-old woman who's doing God's work over eighty hours a week! I simply don't have the time."

"You'd better find some time," Vivaldi says in low, ominous tones.

✣

Emmett shoots Sammy a mad-dog look, whips his cell phone out of his pocket, and dials Dennis's number.

"That lasagna you left in the oven, it's bad. You tryin to poison me?" Emmett says into the phone. He decides to show Sammy just how creative he can be.

"Don't say you're sorry," Emmett says. "You must be related to that Lucretia Borgia woman! All you Eye-talians got poisoners in your background. You're probably related to one of those crooked Popes, too. Maybe he your great-great-great grandpa. You Catholics all a bunch of hypocrites. Criminals, murders, liars, thieves, poisoners! I got stomach pains from hell, I'm doubled over with diarrhea, and I'm vomiting like a volcano."

Sammy acts like he doesn't even notice that Emmett's on the phone. He wiggles his fingers in front of Tony, and the cat paws at his hand. Jerry struggles to scoop a batch of cut cocaine into a bag.

Emmett says into the phone: "I'm tellin you the food is poisoned. I'm goin to the emergency room and have my stomach pumped! I'll probably be there all night! Maybe I'll die. Maybe I'll end up in the cemetery. I'm leavin a note that it's all your fault. No, I ain't tellin you what hospital!"

Emmett clicks off the phone and goes back to his task. He knows Dennis will see his car in front of the house when he gets home. Emmett will say he'd called a "friend" to take him to the hospital.

All is silent for a minute, until all three men look upward—hearing the footsteps on the floor above.

Jerry figures it's the FBI with a search warrant taking a look around—or, worse, his ex-wife looking for something she'd left behind. He puts his finger to his lips, indicating for Emmett and Sammy to stay quiet.

❋

"Why should I channel your works," Virginia asks, "when I can go directly to the spirit for inspiration? You may be great, but you're still just a go-between."

Vivaldi gasps. The ingratitude!

"If you don't give me some of your time," Vivaldi threatens, "I can make things very difficult for you."

"That doesn't sound very Christian, Father," Virginia tells the priest.

"I can make you feel like you're going mad," Vivaldi says. "I'll talk in your head twenty-four hours a day, seven days a week. See how long you can take that!"

"You don't scare me!" Virginia exclaims, standing up. "Now get out!" she says, pointing to the back door.

"Virginia, please, don't be hasty," Vivaldi counters.

"I only serve the spirit!" Virginia says.

The dead, dejected priest knows that no matter how much he begs, the woman will not budge. He'll have to find a new channel.

❋

Jerry takes the basement stairs two at a time, trying not to cry out from the pains in his back. He steps through the door just as Annette is about to open it.

The first thing he thinks is how fantastic Annette looks, as if she's just come back from a party. Black dress, black high heels, black stockings. He feels flushed.

"What's going on?" he asks. He decides not to act defensive, not to say: "Don't you knock?" It'll be best just to find out what she wants—in a calm way—then get her the hell out of here.

"I been lookin all over for that album with my Grandma's pictures. The last day of the wake is tomorrow, and I wanna have the album to show people," Annette says. She takes a tissue from her pocket and blots her eyes and nose.

"Your Grandma died?" Jerry asks.

"Uncle Enzo died, but he's in a lot of the pictures. The album's in the basement," Annette says, then lets out a loud sneeze. She blows her nose.

"Got a cold?" he asks.

"I have allergies, remember? September is the worst."

Annette's eyes and nose start to run. Her tissue is sopping wet.

"What'd Enzo die of?"

Jerry can't believe that he didn't know about Enzo's demise. Then again, nobody calls him anymore. And he's been too busy to read the obituaries.

"Hit and run," Annette says, squeezing past Jerry. Again, she sneezes.

Jerry stands in front of the basement door, trying to figure out how to handle the situation.

"Where'd it happen?"

"He was crossing Harlem Avenue when a truck hit him. It was a guy who'd paid off the Secretary of State to get his license."

"Harlem and what?"

"Harlem and Irving."

"That's a bad corner," Jerry says.

"Will you get out of my way!" Annette yells.

"How come you don't invite me to the wake?"

"Nobody on my side wants to see you. Now get out of my goddamned way."

"Let me get it," Jerry says.

"I wanna get it myself."

"Annette, please, don't go down there."

"What'sa matter? You got Frank Czmanski's coke down there?"

For months before she'd walked out on him, Annette had confronted Jerry about the cocaine. She was sure he'd hidden it for Frank. But Jerry never wavered. He said he didn't have it. She knew better. When she couldn't take it anymore, she left.

"I got a cat down there, and I know you're allergic," Jerry says.

Annette laughs so hard that her false eyelashes stick to her cheeks.

"That'll be the day when you get a cat. You won't even feed goldfish."

"Wait right here," Jerry says, holding up his finger.

In a few seconds he's back with Tony in his arms, cradling the cat like a baby.

"He stays mostly in the basement. That's why you better not go down there. It's all full of cat hair."

Annette starts to sneeze nonstop. Jerry takes the cat back to the basement, into Sammy's waiting arms. He hops back up the stairs.

"Just tell me where it is and I'll get it."

"I put it in your workroom on the shelf," she says. "Bring it outside. I'll wait in the car."

Thank God, Jerry thinks, that I have a real fricking cat for my fake fricking excuse.

While Jerry searches for Annette's photo album in his workroom, he stops and glances around as if paying a visit to a foreign country. It's been a long time since he'd spent any time here.

He used to like to build things. When he and Annette were newlyweds, he'd made a coffee table and a cabinet. But they weren't to Annette's tastes. He was crushed when he came home from work one day and learned she'd given the furniture to the Salvation Army.

Jerry is handy. He's proud of it. He can fix things, build things, rewire a house, and install paneling and drywall. He'd wanted to go into construction work, but Annette felt he should have a real profession. The best he could do with a high school education was the police department.

He'd never liked it, but had stayed for over twenty years. He hopes he can remain on sick leave for a few more months. When Jerry thinks about going back to work, he feels as if there's an icy finger is sliding around his stomach.

As he searches for the photo album, Jerry feels a pain shoot up his back. He pats his pocket and detects the comforting bulge of his Vicodin bottle. He takes out a pill and swallows it dry.

He thinks he hears something. He turns and sees a man sitting at his worktable. The man wears a flowing white robe with a green cape. He has long hair and a beard. He holds a wooden staff in one hand and a hammer in the other. Jerry thinks the man looks like Saint Joseph, the carpenter.

"Yes," the man says, reading Jerry's thoughts. "That's who I am."

"What do you want?" Jerry asks. He's trembling.

"I need devotion," the Saint says. "You must help me."

"Devotion?"

Saint Joseph explains how the saints are in competition to see who can get the most devotion. It counts for a great deal in the afterlife. The more devotion, the higher the saint is elevated in the spiritual realm.

Jerry figures he's fallen asleep and is having a dream—or he is in a drug-induced delirium. In the dream or vision, he's sitting in his workshop talking to Saint Joseph.

"I'm like a middle child," Saint Joseph says.

As a middle child, Jerry knows what Saint Joseph means—he gets lost in the shuffle between people's wild devotion for Jesus and Mary.

"Even my feast day, March nineteenth, gets overlooked. After Saint Patrick's Day, everybody forgets about me."

"It must be tough," Jerry says.

"So, you will help me?" Saint Joseph says.

"How?"

"Put some statues of me around the neighborhood. And not buried ones, either. That Rosalie Palermo has me underground in yards all over the neighborhood!"

Saint Joseph is referring to the Italian-American custom of burying a small Saint Joseph statue in the backyard to bring about the quick sale of a piece of real estate.

"Where should I put the statues?" Jerry asks the Saint.

"In every yard where there's a Virgin Mary statue, put a statue of me right next to it."

"Why's that?"

"I miss my wife."

Jerry understands. He, too, misses his wife. He can't wait to go outside and see her again.

✂

By nine the next morning, the cocaine is cut and packaged. Sammy had spent most of the night sleeping with Tony on his lap.

While Sammy had pleasant dreams of leaving the Outfit, Tony had nightmares that he was back at Dennis's house with a gang of other cats. When Tony wakes up, he's relieved to find he's the only cat on the scene and snuggles into Sammy's ample lap with gratitude. When Sammy wakes up, he lifts Tony and looks into the cat's yellow eyes, then kisses him on the top of his head.

"Tony, baby, did my big boy kitty cat have a nice sleepy-time?"

Tony smiles and nuzzles Sammy's cheek.

Sammy looks around and sees that Emmett and Jerry are stacking the bags of coke into three piles.

Jerry can't wait to get the two men out of his house. He doesn't know what he'll say to Frank when and if his ex-partner gets out of prison. He doesn't know how he'll explain why there's less coke and why it was cut.

Jerry will just have to tell his former partner that he has a bad memory about how much coke he'd handed over—and that somebody had played a trick on him and had delivered cut coke in the first place. But Jerry decides to think about all this later.

For now, he just wants to divide up the stash and get Sammy and Emmett the hell out of his house. More than anything, he wants to take a Vicodin and go to bed with Tony snuggled up beside him. His back is killing him from bending over the Ping-Pong table all night.

Emmett has already called his supervisor at the post office, saying he's sick. Now he has to figure out what he's going to tell Dennis when he gets home. But no matter what he says, Emmett knows the day holds a giant fight. Then he gets an idea.

If he brings Tony—or Punkin, as Dennis calls him—home, there won't be a fight. Dennis will be so happy to see his beloved cat that all will be forgiven and forgotten. But Emmett knows it'll be almost impossible to take the cat without Jerry noticing.

Jerry shoves Sammy's portion into a doubled-up Jewel shopping bag. Emmett stuffs his own share in his mailbag. Jerry knows he'll have to hide Frank's stash again—but where? He decides to put it in the root cellar under his workroom—praying that the FBI doesn't show up with drug-sniffing dogs.

Before Sammy leaves he gives Tony one last kiss, then turns to Jerry and says: "Make sure you take real good care 'a Tony." It sounds like a threat.

Emmett looks for an opportunity to grab the cat, but Jerry stands by the door as he leaves the house.

"Don't ever let me see you over here again," Jerry says.

"Do you know how I can get rid of this stuff?" Emmett asks, indicating his mailbag.

"No fricking idea," Jerry says and slams the basement door.

As soon as Sammy and Emmett are gone, Jerry shovels the bags of coke into his root cellar, disguised by a trapdoor that looks like the rest of linoleum. It's a not bad hiding place. Not as secure as under the floorboards in the attic, but a lot more accessible.

✂

After he sneaks from Jerry's backyard, Emmett has to pass the Jablonski house. There she is on her front porch: "Mailman, you having letter for me?"

The mailbag feels heavy on Emmett's arm. He wants to say, "No, I not having letter for you, but I having your motherfreakin cocaine in my mailbag."

But he opts for an easier approach: "Sorry, Mrs. Jablonski."

Grazyna places her plastic goose—dressed as a fairy princess, complete with magic wand—on her porch and waves to the mailman as he walks across the street. She watches him open his trunk and put his mailbag inside. Then she sees him walk up the front steps of the house he shares with the little Italian.

Before the mailman even opens the door, Grazyna hears the Italian yelling from inside the house. She doesn't want to listen —arguments are so distressing, even more so early in the morning. But she can't help feeling sorry for the mailman.

✂

When Sammy gets home, his wife doesn't say a word—she's used to him staying out all night on business. But when she sees the reddish-orange hair on his black pants, she starts to get suspicious—all-too-aware that her husband goes for redheads. Sammy notices her looking at his pants and reads her thoughts.

"I was holding a cat. The cat is orange. That's why I got hair on my pants," he tells Theresa.

"I never saw a cat with hair that shade of red," she answers.

"Well you seen it now," Sammy says.

"I see the hair, but not the cat," she snaps back.

"Take my word for it."

"Whose cat is it?" she asks.

"Don't ever ask me about my business, Theresa."

"What? Now you're working for the anti-cruelty?"

Sammy dismisses the remark, but it sticks in his head. Yes, he wants to say, I'm working for the anti-cruelty.

He can't stand the thought of committing a violent act ever again—and hopes that soon his former life will fade into memory. But he doesn't want to let his wife in on his plans. First off, she'll think he is crazy. And, second, she'll think he has no balls.

Sammy needs to figure out how to broach the subject of getting out of the Outfit to his boss. He doesn't have that much contact with the big man. It's like getting an audience with the Pope—or even God.

Then Sammy opens the mail and falls to his knees. He thanks God, Jesus, Mary, and all the angels and saints. It's an invitation to the boss's mother's hundredth birthday party. This is a big, big deal—and the boss is going all out, throwing the bash in the grand ballroom of the Four Seasons Hotel in downtown Chicago. Sammy's sure the boss will invite at least five hundred people.

Sammy figures he can get at least one minute with the boss

to discuss business. Sammy views the party as a miracle—without it, he'd have no chance of getting any one-on-one time with his boss.

Sammy decides to go right over to church and light some candles and pray—he has to show his proper thankfulness to God for this miraculous blessing.

Emmett has no idea how he's going to unload his share of the cocaine. And he can't keep it in the trunk—as he knows, cocaine needs to remain under cool, dry conditions.

He wonders if he can sell his share to Sammy, offer it to him at a bargain price. The coke is worth a million bucks. They'd doubled the volume—making it worth two million. Emmett's share is one-third—valued at $666,666.

Emmett doesn't like these numbers. They remind him of his mother—how she's always talking about the "sign of the beast" from the Book of Revelations. The sign of the beast is, of course, the number 666. She often uses the phrase on Emmett.

Emmett wonders if Sammy will buy his coke for, say, two hundred thousand dollars. This is a nice chunk of money that will set up Emmett for years. While he's figuring out what to do with the rest of his life, he can take a leave of absence without pay from the post office.

Emmett realizes he should have brought this up with Sammy while they were cutting the coke. He has no idea where Sammy lives. He's sure the thug has an unlisted phone number. Besides, he doesn't even know the man's last name. How can he find him?

Then Emmett remembers that Sammy belongs to Saint Francis of Assisi Parish, where Dennis attends Mass on Sunday. Dennis is always asking Emmett to go to church with him. If Emmett says he wants to go to Mass, Dennis will be thrilled—and it will help prevent arguments for a good long while.

17
FILLED WITH THE SPIRIT

HERB SHOWS VIRGINIA THE AD FOR "SPOTLESS SOULS" AS SHE'S GETTING READY FOR WORK. He's outraged. Virginia has discovered this new approach to sin removal, and now somebody else is trying to horn in. A cheap imitation!

But Virginia just shrugs and says: "You've got to expect competition, Herb. This is America."

"But what if they undercut our prices? They're already offering immediate results! It'll be months before we can clean clothes on the premises."

With their substantial earnings, Virginia and Herb have purchased property at the other end of the mall—a huge discount store that went out of business several months before.

Herb hired contractors to turn half the facility into a dry cleaning plant. The other half of the building will be a church—with a stage, organ, and theater-style seating. As soon as the building is completed around Christmas, Virginia will begin to hold services on Sunday mornings—and they'll start to clean the clothes on the premises.

But until that happens, they're vulnerable to competition.

"Herb," Virginia says, patting his hand, "none of these impostors can offer the real thing. We'll just have to let the spirit take care of it."

Then Virginia goes off to work.

His wife's words do nothing to alleviate Herb's fears about the competition. After Virginia leaves the house, he sits down and writes his own newspaper ad.

The next afternoon, the Jablonskis's phone starts to ring—calls from people who want to enlist the services of Spotless Souls Housekleening.

Grazyna feels like doing backflips—her old forte in the circus—but it's been years since she's tried it. She can quit her job this very day. After a lifetime of bondage as a time-clock-punching employee, Grazyna will at long last be her own boss.

Before she leaves for work, she and Marek sit down for a late lunch of ham sandwiches and vegetable soup. They discuss how they'll organize Grazyna's new business—and where they'll find their staff.

The plastic goose sits in one of the chairs. The goose is dressed in a turquoise taffeta formal, with a blonde braided wig on her head, and a tiara on top. A dish of raw oatmeal is in front of her.

Grazyna has put the goose at the table for each meal since Marek had brought her home—almost four months now. It hadn't bothered him that much before. But he isn't in the mood right now.

"Please putting goose on porch!" he says in English, knocking the tiara from the goose's head.

"The goose is not your business," Grazyna replies in Polish, swatting Marek on the head with a dishtowel.

"I stealing goose from blonde at dry cleaner!" Marek blurts out, then bursts into a fit of hysterical laughter.

Grazyna gasps. She turns and stares at the goose. Bronislava and Dorota have told her all about Redemption Dry Cleaners and how it's dedicated to Gertrude, the goose stolen at gunpoint.

"You kidnapping goose?" Grazyna says in English.

Marek, still laughing, nods.

"Is bad luck! You must taking back!" Grazyna says, remembering what had happened when she'd stolen the Lorenzos's Virgin Mary statue.

"If I taking back, woman knowing I am robber!"

Marek then confesses everything—telling Grazyna of all the robberies he'd committed. He reveals how he'd worn a black ski mask and had imitated the voice of a black man.

After his confession, Marek feels so relieved. He wants to light a cigarette, but is still maintaining his Lenten sacrifice. Each day, he believes this gains him extra points with God.

Grazyna is appalled that Marek has committed such flagrant crimes. She's sure that God did not give him permission to take money from the stores. What kind of a grandson is he? Where did he come by such dark traits?

But Grazyna knows where—from his fire-eater devil of a grandfather, that disgusting pig! Yes, you stinking swine, you are dragging us through the mud, even from the grave. Look at your grandson—a common thief!

Grazyna glares at Marek, and sums up her thoughts in a few simple words: "Boy, you'd better go to Confession!"

That night, as Virginia is about to go to bed, she hears a voice in her head. It's a soothing female voice, telling her to find a pen and a tablet of paper. Virginia is used to these spiritual experiences. She doesn't hesitate.

After just a few seconds, she's sitting at the dining room table, pen poised above the paper.

"In the beginning," the voice says, "is the spirit of the sky. The spirit of the sky spread her wings and soft feathers drifted through the heavens..."

Virginia writes down every word. By the next morning, she has three chapters of *The Book of Spirit*, the holy manuscript that the spirit told her to use in her work at Redemption Dry Cleaners.

When Herb gets up the next morning, he sees Virginia slumped over the writing tablet. He shakes her by the shoulder. She sits up, then leans back and stretches. Herb stares at Virginia's stomach. It looks as if she has a cantaloupe inside. He's worried that something is wrong with her.

"Your stomach, Virginia..."

She looks down at her belly and puts her hands across it.

"Yes," she says.

"Is something wrong?" Herb asks. He knows she hasn't been eating any more than usual.

During her nightlong marathon of transcribing the spirit's words, Virginia had learned that she's carrying a child. She's beyond blissful! She can't wait to tell her husband—and now here he is right in front of her.

"I'm pregnant!" she says. "Herb, I'm expecting a child!"

Then Virginia weeps with utter abandoned joy. This is the answer to a lifetime of prayer. It's a miracle. And now she won't have to spend all that money with the fertility doctors!

Herb sinks into a chair. It isn't just the fact that Virginia is fifty-nine years old. They haven't had sex in what seems like a year.

"Who got you pregnant, Virginia?" Herb asks.

"I've been praying for a miracle!"

"But who is the father?" Herb says.

"The Virgin Mary gave me a miracle!"

"This is a virgin birth?" he asks.

"Of course," she tells him.

"Well, all right, then," Herb says. He looks in her eyes. He believes her.

�

Father Spinelli has been up all night assembling the bomb he intends to plant at Redemption Dry Cleaners. Now he's keyed up—and feels as if he'll never fall asleep again.

He decides to play the piano for a while. Maybe compose something, if anything comes to him.

When he enters his study, Father Spinelli doesn't see Antonio Vivaldi seated at his piano. He almost sits in the dead priest's lap.

Vivaldi is certain that he can channel through the conceited priest. But Vivaldi knows if he does, Spinelli will take credit for the compositions.

Still, Vivaldi's artistic drive is so strong that he cares more for creation than he does for credit. He just wants to get his music into the world.

✻

After he gets over the shock, Herb is excited about Virginia's pregnancy. He's always wanted a baby, and, even at the age of sixty-two, is still young enough to see the child grow up.

Herb wants to tell somebody, anybody, everybody that his dear wife is pregnant. But Virginia convinces him that it's best if they keep the news to themselves for a while.

Herb busies himself turning Virginia's sewing room into a nursery. Virginia tells him not to bother—that they'll soon buy a beautiful new home in River Forest, the classy kind of place where Virginia wants the child to grow up. The rich suburb also has good schools—but Virginia won't trust her offspring to the school system. She feels it best to educate the child at home.

Still, Herb wants something to do. He decides to make a rocking cradle from the best maple. As he works, Herb often thinks of Saint Joseph. Herb feels a special kinship to Jesus's stepfather—they share a love of carpentry. They also, at first, may have doubted their wives' faithfulness. But Herb knows Virginia. She never even looks at another man. No, there is only one explanation for it. His saintlike wife is carrying a divine child.

✄

As soon as Father Spinelli sits before the piano keys, a beautiful melody enters his head. He plays it, savoring the nuance of each note. His heart fills with rapture. This is what he's been waiting for all these years. Divine inspiration! Maybe assembling the bomb has released something in me, he thinks.

He grabs paper and a pen—he won't need a pencil!—and writes down the notes. Vivaldi stands behind Spinelli feeling both pleased and distressed. It is as if he's turning over a beloved child to a stranger. He feels both joy and sorrow—joy at the wonderful birth, sorrow at not giving the child his name.

Spinelli squeezes his eyes shut and listens for more music. Vivaldi sends the notes to the priest, who jots them down. Beautiful, beautiful, beautiful, Spinelli thinks, his chest expanding with pride.

✄

As she looks at the results of her home pregnancy test, Virginia feels ashamed. There, in the middle of the square white test is a big pink plus sign. Proof positive that she's pregnant. Her faith had been too weak to trust God's word— she had to be like Saint Thomas and see for herself.

I don't deserve this blessing, she thinks. Oh ye of little faith, she berates herself. Oh, Dear God, why did you choose me—a flawed, frail human being?

Why me, she wonders. Why has God picked me to write inspired scriptures, like Moses? Why did God choose me to compose inspired music, like King David? Why did God pick me to take away sins and perform miracles, like Jesus? And, most of all, why did God pick me to conceive by the Holy Spirit, like Mary?

Have I done something to deserve these blessings? Am I better or finer than other people?

Dear Lord, I'm just a humble dry cleaning clerk, Virginia prays. Why did you choose me? Virginia tries to listen for God's voice, but no answer arrives.

But, it's fine. God doesn't need to tell her. She just wants Him to know that she's a willing servant, and will do whatever He asks her to do.

18

THE SIN BUSINESS

GRAZYNA HIRES TWENTY WOMEN TO WORK IN SPOTLESS SOULS HOUSEKLEENING SERVICE, and tells them to come to her house on Saturday afternoon at two o'clock to get their work orders for the following week.

Grazyna decides to hire only women because she believes they are better workers. Many men had applied for the jobs—but Grazyna doesn't trust men. She thinks you have to watch them all the time—or they'll be off taking cigarette breaks, stealing from the customers, or demanding higher wages.

When several of the male applicants accuse her of discrimination, Grazyna laughs right in their faces. Men have all the advantages in this world. If she owns a business and wants to hire only women, that should remain her choice. America has all kinds of crazy laws that protect people who don't need protection. She isn't about to go along with any of it.

No, Grazyna will have an army of women—platoons of females who will make everything sparkling clean. Men are slobs by nature. They have no concept of what "clean" means. Grazyna thinks of her dead slob of a husband—God how she hates that man, even in his grave. Not only a slob, but lazy, too. Yes, all men are lazy slobs—even her grandson. She's stuck with Marek, but is going to make blasted sure he does his job.

Around noon, Grazyna goes up to the attic for her secret weapon—the magical sand that will allow her cleaning ladies to work at top speed. But when she looks behind the insulation, the magical sand is gone.

"Marek," she yells. "Marek!"

Marek is getting dressed for his first day as a supervisor, when he hears Busha's cries. He hopes she doesn't have a chore for him. From now on, she'll have to hire people to work on her house. He has a job!

When he climbs the attic stairs, he finds Busha sitting on the floor.

"Magic sand is gone."

"Gone?"

"Where did you put it?" she asks in Polish.

"I haven't touched the stuff since we hid it behind the insulation," he replies in his own language. The sentiment is too complicated to express in English—and he doesn't know the English word for insulation.

Grazyna knows Marek is telling the truth. He has one of those open, read-me-like-a-book faces. She wonders what could have happened to her valuable commodity. Then she recalls the Lorenzo ghosts. The vindictive dead Italians no doubt had made it disappear, she tells herself.

Now what will she do? She'd started the business because she figured she could make a lot of money—selling the magical sand to her workers and getting them to do the work fast. She knows she can't survive, can't compete without an angle.

Then she remembers the name of her business: Spotless Souls. Yes, her advertisement had boasted that her workers could clean away spiritual blight. But she had considered this a mere marketing trick. Now, she'll have to play up this distinction.

�֍

Jerry wakes up to banging on his back door. He looks at the clock. It's noon. He feels like a bum lounging in bed half the day. Still, he isn't ready to get up. He glances around for Tony, but the cat isn't around.

Jerry hopes the person at his door will just go away. But the racket keeps up—getting louder and more insistent with each bang. He rubs his eyes and begins the painful process of getting out of bed. He curses himself and his bad back, he curses his rotten luck, and all the things he's done to deserve to live in constant agony.

"Ahhhh," Jerry screams, rising to his feet.

Bang! Bang!! Bang!!! BANG!!!! Jerry figures maybe the FBI has at last come to pay a visit.

As he steps into his family room, Jerry looks through the sliding glass doors leading to his deck. He sees Sammy Mangano standing there with brown paper bags in his arms. Tony is sitting on the floor, looking up at Sammy.

Jerry slides open the door.

"What now?" he asks.

"I brung over a few things," Sammy says.

"Don't you have a family? It's Saturday, for Christ's sake," Jerry says.

Sammy marches into Jerry's house. Tony follows him, rubbing on the legs of Sammy's black wool pants.

"Wife went shopping. She's going out with her girlfriends tonight to see Tony Bennett."

"Don't you have any kids?" Jerry asks.

"Away at school."

Sammy sets down his bags and picks up Tony. He gives the cat a big hug and kiss.

"How's Daddy's little baby?" he croons to the cat. "How is my big boy kitty cat?"

Tony rubs his face against Sammy's cheek.

"What a sweet kitty boy cat Tony baby is," Sammy says.

Jerry decides to leave the two lovebirds alone for a while.

After he gets out of the shower, Jerry makes his way back to the family room. When he steps through the doorway, he slips on something and falls flat on his back. The pain is beyond anything he's experienced before—searing, tearing, excruciating, jabbing, stabbing pain.

Grazyna decides to pay a quick visit to Redemption Dry Cleaners. She doesn't wish to partake of the services, but only wants to take one of the dry cleaning receipts. This way, she can make out her own receipt—with the same sins.

She'll offer to remove the sins from people's houses—charging a fee for each sin, and undercutting Virginia's prices. But she doesn't know the English words for different sins—and she doesn't have time to flip around in a dictionary. It's much easier to steal the names of the sins from Redemption Dry Cleaners.

"Ohhhhh! Ahhhh!" Jerry says. He moves his head to see what he's slipped on—a small stuffed mouse.

As Sammy rushes over to help him, Jerry looks at the minefield of cat toys on the floor—little fuzzy balls, a stuffed bird, mice in all colors, string, something that looks like a feather duster.

"What happened?" Sammy asks.

Jerry can't answer. He just keeps screaming in pain. Tony watches him with large worried yellow eyes.

"You wanna go to the hospital?" Sammy asks.

"Oh God! Oh God! Oh God!" is all Jerry can say.

Jerry scans the room. There's a set of silver bowls on the floor, a large bag of *Science Diet* cat food in the corner, plus at least fifty cans of cat food on the counter. There are cat treats, cat brushes and combs, a large wicker cat bed with a plush pillow, and a pale blue cat carrier.

After Sammy helps him up, Jerry grabs the Vicodin bottle from the pocket of his robe and swallows a couple of pills. He lowers himself onto the sofa until he's lying down.

Tony stands beside Jerry and stares straight in his face, as if he's a doctor about to diagnose a patient. Jerry looks at the cat's neck. Around it is a thick purple collar with a red heart-shaped nametag. Jerry reads the tag. It says: ANTHONY and lists Jerry's address and phone number.

✻

Grazyna ties a faded babushka under her chin and borrows Marek's sunglasses on the way out the door. Grazyna doesn't want Virginia to recognize her—they belong to the same church. Grazyna believes she's well-disguised and looks like many of the other sixty-something Polish women in the neighborhood. Besides, she's wearing sunglasses to hide her eyes—a person's most distinguishing feature.

When she reaches Redemption Dry Cleaners, she sees a line of people over a block long. Grazyna has to get back home soon—the cleaning crew is coming—and doesn't have time to wait. She tugs the sleeve of the man in charge at the front of the line. She holds up a sweater filled with holes and begs the man: "Please, emergency. Please! Please!" Then she looks up at him, blinks a few times, and glossy tears run down her face, below her sunglasses.

When Giovanni—now Virginia's full-time assistant—nods for her to go ahead, Grazyna grabs the man's hand and kisses it.

These Polish people sure know how to lay it on, Giovanni thinks.

✻

"The cat's name is Tony, not Anthony," Jerry says, managing to squeeze out a few words between shooting pains. But the double dose of Vicodin is starting to kick in. Jerry knows that soon he'll drift off to sleep and forget about the pain.

"It's like, you know, when you get baptized," Sammy says. "You gotta have a saint's name. His real name is Anthony, but we call him Tony."

"So you're saying the tag is like the cat's baptismal certificate?" Jerry says, as if talking in his sleep.

"Sorta."

"But you get baptized to remove original sin from your soul," Jerry says, again remembering his catechism. "Animals don't have original sin."

Sammy doesn't say anything. He hasn't thought about original sin since he was a kid. The Church says you're born with sin on your soul. If a baby dies before baptism, the child can never go to heaven. Sammy has never believed this. It's just too cruel.

"Has Tony been to the vet?" Sammy asks.

"I been busy, Mangano."

"He needs to have his shots and get his teeth cleaned. Maybe a bath. There's a cat groomer on Irving Park Road that says it takes away fleas and sins."

"Animals can't commit sins," Jerry says. "They act out their nature."

"What about people?" Sammy asks. "If somebody commits sins, are they just actin out their nature?"

"People have free will," Jerry says. It is another thing he remembers from his catechism lessons.

❀

While Virginia attends to Grazyna, Giovanni corrals other customers behind velvet ropes and shows them how to hold their clothing and stand in straight lines. He marches up and down the waiting area like a stormtrooper.

"Yes?" Virginia says when Grazyna approaches with her sweater.

Even though both women attend services at Saint Francis of Assisi Church, Virginia doesn't recognize Grazyna. They've even exchanged the "sign of peace" at Mass on several occasions. But Virginia never looks into the other person's face or eyes when she fulfills the obligation.

At church, Virginia's thoughts were always on one thing—praying to God to conceive a child. But now Virginia is pregnant! Pregnant! Pregnant! Her thoughts explode with how happy she'll be when she becomes a mother, how happy she is with her wonderful secret: she is with child. She doesn't even mind working—she'll need money to support the child in style, and give her precious offspring everything in the world and more.

✄

Besides the cat stuff, Sammy has brought a large sack of groceries. He starts to prepare dinner.

While Sammy cooks, Jerry sleeps on the sofa. Tony curls up in his new bed and also naps. He holds a mouse toy between his paws as he dozes.

Sammy turns on the radio—low, so as not to wake Tony or Jerry—and listens to *The Marriage of Figaro* as the manicotti bakes. Sammy plans to keep the food warm until Jerry wakes up. He hates to eat alone.

Sammy spots the orange hair on his pants—and makes a mental note to brush it off before he goes home. Why give Theresa another reason to doubt him?

But Sammy will think about that later. For now he enjoys the Saturday afternoon stillness, the rich good cooking smells, the soothing strains of Mozart, the steam at the windows, the autumn leaves outside the sliding glass doors, the misty glow of sun through the overcast sky.

Sammy starts to think about what Jerry said about sin—about how people have choices. Sammy doesn't like to think about the sinful things he's done. He pushes these thoughts away, telling himself he did what he had to do.

But, Sammy thinks, if I get out of the Outfit and promise to sin no more, can I get forgiveness for all the bad things I already done? Is Confession enough? Or do you have to, whichacallit, do penance or at-one for it? Sammy has always pronounced "atone" as two words, "at one."

Sammy hopes Jerry will wake up soon. He doesn't want to sit around and think about his sins. He needs to get his mind on something else. He opens a bag on the counter and starts in on a nice, mindless task.

✄

When she looks at Grazyna, Virginia sees only one thing— the potential for making money. She doesn't care a bit about the woman's sins and salvation. No, she's only concerned about her unborn child—and making money for him or her.

Grazyna hands Virginia the sweater and looks for an opportunity to make her next move. She watches as Virginia checks off boxes on the dry cleaning receipt.

"That will cost you $7,082.58," Virginia says, hoping the woman will leave the item.

With all the construction work on their new facility, Virginia is under pressure to make more and more money—and this time, she doesn't have to spot extra sins. The woman has over seven thousand dollars worth of sins on her holey sweater.

"Please, Missus, can I seeing cost?" Grazyna asks, reaching for the receipt.

Virginia turns the receipt so Grazyna can take a look at it.

"As you see," Virginia says, "it's not the number of different sins, but the quantity of each individual sin. Your infractions lie in just a few areas—stealing, cheating, and lying. But you have committed each of these sins time and again while wearing this sweater."

160

When Jerry opens his eyes, he sees Sammy at the kitchen table rolling red yarn into a ball. The ball is already the size of a coconut.

"Holy Christ," Jerry says.

Sammy puts down the yarn and rushes over to Jerry.

"Need to go to the bathroom?"

"What the hell you doin?" Jerry asks.

"About what?"

"With that string?"

"It's for Tony."

"You're starting to scare me, Mangano," Jerry says.

Grazyna grabs a corner of the receipt, but Virginia holds it tight.

"Can I seeing closer, I having eye problem," Grazyna says, tapping on her sunglasses.

"Many of our customers find that their physical infirmities disappear once their sins are removed," Virginia says.

"Can I seeing sin closer?" Grazyna says, tugging on the receipt.

"I can read it to you, if you like," Virginia says, turning around the receipt.

"No, I must seeing by myself," Grazyna says.

Virginia knows that other businesses are in competition with hers—she's seen scads of ads in the local newspaper for hair salons, housecleaning services, carpet cleaners, house painters, and others that boast of removing sins for a price.

Virginia realizes that her list of sins and their removal fees are a vital part of her operation. This is proprietary information—the very essence of her business. She can't risk exposing the information to a potential competitor.

"I'm sorry," Virginia says, "it's against company policy."

Grazyna throws her sweater at Virginia's head, and Virginia reaches up to catch it—letting go of the dry cleaning receipt.

By the time Virginia disengages herself from the ragged sweater, Grazyna is gone.

"Stop! Thief!" Virginia says.

When they're almost finished eating, Jerry hands a piece of meatball to Tony. In a blink, Sammy is out of his chair, grabbing the meatball from Jerry's hand.

"You freakin nuts?" Sammy says. "There's garlic in that!"

"So?" Jerry says.

"So, cats can die from garlic, idiot!"

Jerry can see by the Tony's expression—a slight downturn of his mouth and eyes—that the cat knows he almost poisoned him. Jerry pats Tony on the head, and right away Tony forgives him—nudging against Jerry's palm.

"How come you know so much about cats?" Jerry asks.

Sammy sits down and proceeds to tell Jerry a long, involved, sad story about his childhood pet—a black and white cat named Prince. The family wasn't supposed to have pets. The landlord had forbid it. They already had too many people living in the apartment—the parents and seven kids in a four-room flat on the West Side.

Sammy takes a deep breath and goes on with his tale. One day, Prince got out and the family looked and looked for him. While six-year-old Sammy was out searching for Prince, something told him to look in the trashcan. He found Prince there, shot through with a hunting arrow. The dead cat was covered in blood, his face paralyzed in a death mask.

Little Sammy started screaming, then looked up and saw the landlord—who laughed and held a bow and arrow high above his head. Then Sammy blacked out. He didn't speak for weeks—but during those weeks of silence, Sammy discovered the psychic abilities that would save him so many times in years to come.

"It was like a gift from Prince," Sammy says, near tears. "He was takin care of me, even after he was gone."

Jerry shakes his head. It's a horrible story. He'd like to kill the landlord right now.

Sammy swats tears from his eyes. Tony, sensing the visitor's sad mood, jumps in his lap and rubs against his chest. Sammy hugs Tony and kisses his head.

"This is the first cat since Prince I ever bonded with," Sammy says. He puts a hand over his eyes and weeps.

"Is that how you got into your...business?" Jerry asks.

Sammy wipes his eyes on his shirtsleeve and says, "You mean, like for revenge against louses? The first louse being my landlord, Franco LaRussa?"

"I heard your specialty is shaking down real estate guys," Jerry says.

Sammy looks at Jerry as if he's just had a revelation.

Giovanni hears Virginia's screams and runs into the store from outside. Virginia is slumped in a chair, trying to catch her breath.

"That woman," she gasps.

"Woman with sweater?" Giovanni asks.

"Yes," Virginia says, just about fainting. "She stole my proprietary information."

Giovanni doesn't know what this means—and tries to puzzle out the words, so he won't appear stupid in Virginia's eyes. "Proprietary" sounds close to "proper" and information sounds like "invitation" when combined with "proper." Maybe it's an invitation to an important event. Perhaps Virginia has an invitation for an audience with the Pope. Yes, that has to be it, Giovanni thinks. Virginia is on equal level to Pope, for sure.

Giovanni races from the store, but Grazyna is already halfway home.

As she runs, Grazyna realizes she's the second person in her family to rob Virginia. First, Marek had held up the store and had stolen money and a plastic goose. Now she's stealing Virginia's secret business information. Well, Grazyna thinks, some people just have bad luck.

�֎

"Jesus, Mary, and Joseph," Sammy says when Jerry, in a confessional mood enhanced by Vicodin, finishes telling him the whole story of how he got involved with the coke.

When Sammy says the three holy names, Jerry hits his head with his hand.

"What?" Sammy asks.

Jerry tells Sammy about his dream—more like a vision— where Saint Joseph had instructed him to set up statues around the neighborhood, next to the Virgin Marys.

"But you're supposed to bury Saint Joseph," Sammy says. "My cousin Rosalie does it all the time. She's in real estate."

"That is the point," Jerry tells him. "Saint Joseph doesn't want to be buried anymore. He wants to be next to his wife."

"I don't think they make big Saint Joseph statues," Sammy says. "Just Virgin Mary, Saint Anthony, and Saint Francis."

"I guess that lets me off the hook," Jerry says.

"If I was you," Sammy advises, "I'd try to do like he says— or you might run into a streak of even worse luck."

19
MASS HYSTERIA

EARLY SUNDAY MORNING, Emmett is already dressed in his good pants and a nice pressed shirt when Dennis gets up.

"Where you going?" Dennis asks.

"I thought I'd do what you been askin," Emmett says.

"That's a long list," Dennis replies.

"I thought I'd go to church with you this mornin," Emmett says.

Dennis puts down the two cats he's cuddling, then rushes up to Emmett and gives him a big hug and kiss.

"It's like an answer to prayer," he beams.

"Come on, let's get goin," Emmett tells him.

"But it's only 7:30. I don't leave for Mass until 10:45."

"The first Mass is at eight, right?"

"So?"

"So, I want to go to it."

Emmett figures that Sammy Mangano might be at the eight o'clock Mass, and he doesn't want to take the chance of missing him.

"Can't we go later?"

"I'm already dressed," Emmett says.

✄

As they approach the Gothic-style gray stone building, Emmett has to admit it's beautiful. Then again, he knows how rich the Catholic Church is—they can afford big splashes like this, unlike the little ramshackle Pentecostal storefronts in his own South Side neighborhood.

As he and Dennis climb the stairs, Emmett thinks about the crazy-looking stairways to heaven painted by Max Escher. He hopes he'll have some time to paint today—he needs to make some headway on the portrait of his mother.

When they walk through the church's heavy wooden door, right away Emmett notices the smell. Not a bad smell, just an unfamiliar one. It smells like burning wax, floor polish, and some kind of incense—Emmett figures it is frankincense, that's what the Wise Man had carried to the Christ Child.

He watches as Dennis dips his right hand in something that looks like a birdbath. Then Dennis makes the sign of the cross. He nods for Emmett to follow his example. Emmett gets too much water on his fingers, and splashes himself in the eye when he crosses himself. He hopes he doesn't get an infection—that birdbath must be loaded with germs, he thinks.

They walk midway down the center aisle. Before Dennis enters the pew, he kneels on one knee and bows his head. He nods for Emmett to do the same. Emmett makes a halfhearted attempt—not quite kneeling, just giving the indication of the gesture.

Emmett notes that there are two altars. One is a table surrounded by a white satin skirt with decorations on it; another, on the far wall, has a little golden case on it. Above the case is a giant crucifix.

Emmett gazes around at the different statues. He recognizes the Virgin Mary, Saint Francis of Assisi, Saint Joseph, and Saint Anthony. He looks at the stained glass windows that feature more saints and angels. Along the walls are images of Christ depicting the events leading up to the crucifixion. And all around are candles in green glass holders.

Emmett finds all this visual imagery stimulating. He has to give the Catholics one thing—they give you something to look at.

The pews hold just a few scattered people—and the Mass is about to begin in a few minutes. Emmett figures most Catholics must get up late on Sunday morning—after drinking, gambling, and carousing on Saturday night. The people in the pews are mostly old folks—and elderly people usually get up early—and, of course, all are white.

❦

For the first time in years, Father Spinelli doesn't mind spending his Sunday saying Mass and mingling with parishioners. The day holds some personal enjoyment for him—after Mass, he'll stand at the back and sell CDs of his recent compositions.

He's already set up a card table with a sign that reads: "Now available...*Romantic Interludes* by Louis R. Spinelli." A few days before, the priest had recorded the tunes at a music studio—and the place had given him a starter supply of fifty CDs. The priest is awaiting the remaining thousand CDs he'd ordered. Spinelli figures if he sells out his supply today, he'll take additional orders—he has the forms ready on the back table.

The priest is so enthralled with his new compositions that he gave sheet music to the church music director and instructed her to play the songs at the beginning and end of the Mass.

Never has Spinelli felt so good about being alive, so right with the world, so happy. These days, he can't wait to get up in the morning. He no longer resents his duties. He knows that whenever he sits down at the piano, he'll compose beautiful, satisfying music. This music will achieve world renown—and place Spinelli's name in the annals of musical history. He'll be the greatest priest/composer of all time.

Father Antonio Vivaldi is aware of Spinelli's thoughts and aspirations. Still, he can't allow himself to care about such petty matters. He needs to get his work into the world—because the world needs this music. It can bring people joy, heal weary souls, move people closer to God. If Vivaldi has to use the arrogant Spinelli to achieve his aims, so be it. Vivaldi considers Spinelli no more than a ventriloquist's dummy—and should the master resent such a vital part of his act?

❈

Compared to services at black churches on the South Side, the Mass at Saint Francis is like a coming attraction. Emmett is surprised that the whole thing is over in less than forty-five minutes.

The Catholics cram a whole lot into that brief time—readings from the Gospel, music, a sermon, announcements, the priest fooling around with chalices and communion wafers, altar boys ringing bells, people traipsing up in long lines to get communion, songs, handshakes, kneeling, standing, sitting.

Emmett figures Catholics must be afflicted with attention deficit disorder, and need a lot of activity and stimulation to keep them occupied.

When it's all over—and the priest and the altar boys parade up the aisle with tall candles—Dennis gets up to leave. But Emmett continues to sit there. Throughout the Mass he'd kept a lookout for Sammy, but the gangster hadn't shown up. Maybe he'll be at the next one, Emmett figures.

"Let's go out for breakfast," Dennis whispers. "I'm starving."

Emmett shakes his head and remains in his seat.

"So let's go home, then," Dennis says.

Emmett doesn't budge.

"What'sa matter?" Dennis asks.

"You go home," Emmett says. "I gotta pray for a while."

❈

After Mass, Father Spinelli stands in the back of the church at a card table that features his CDs. As people leave, he shakes their hands and foists his music at them. Then he points to the sign: "ONLY $10!"

Many parishioners reach into their pockets and purses for the cash. Spinelli's wad of bills gets fatter by the minute.

As Emmett watches the priest hawking his wares, he thinks of the moneylenders in the temple—the ones Jesus drove the hell out of there. Emmett wonders what Jesus would think about Father Spinelli's business dealings. After all, the priest has a captive audience—people who feel that God wants them to buy the CDs.

At first, Emmett doesn't think this is right, then he feels something else: sympathy for the priest. After all, most artists can't sell their work—they have to peddle it whichever way they can.

Emmett wonders where he can sell his paintings. He'll try to get a gallery to show them—someplace nice and classy, like the ones in Wicker Park or downtown on Superior. But what if nobody will take him on—and if they do, what if nobody buys a painting? Maybe he can start going door to door in the neighborhood. The neighbors are so scared of him that they'll buy something just to stay on his good side.

✄

Dennis can't figure out what's up with Emmett. What does he need to pray about? Dennis is a devout Catholic, but he has never in his life stayed through two Masses in a row. He thinks about going home—but figures if Emmett is so taken with the church in just one visit, he should stay with him.

While he's waiting for the next Mass to start, Dennis purchases a CD from Father Spinelli—which the priest autographs with a flourish—then lights some candles, praying for the return of his beloved orange cat, Punkin. With the cat gone, Dennis has a huge hole in his life. Sometimes he cries about it—he misses Punkin with an aching heart.

Before the nine o'clock Mass begins, Dennis rejoins Emmett in the pew. Emmett sees Mrs. Jablonski and her grandson walking up the aisle. The twosome sits a few rows in front of Emmett and Dennis.

Dennis notices Emmett watching the Jablonskis and feels his jealousy flare up. Does Emmett have a crush on the Jablonski kid? Sure, the kid is young, tall, and handsome—it's impossible not to find him attractive. But does Emmett have designs on the Polish stud, Dennis wonders.

Dennis decides to let the whole idea pass away. He has to pray for Punkin's return and doesn't want to taint his pleas with a jealous heart and mind.

Please, Dear God, Dennis prays, *bring Punkin back to me. Like the prodigal son, lead him home. Please God, let no harm come to my precious cat, Punkin, while he is away. Protect him from all harm. Don't let him get hit by a car, mauled by a raccoon, eaten by a coyote, or beat up by another cat. Wherever he is, make sure he is well fed and safe from the elements. I humbly pray with all my heart. Amen. Oh, and please return him to me before the winter weather sets in. Amen again.*

The nine o'clock Mass is just like the eight o'clock Mass—even the same sermon. Still, Emmett never gets bored. There's so much to look at—even the ceilings have ornate murals to peruse. Plus there's all the standing, kneeling, and sitting and shaking hands, and other stuff to keep your mind from wandering.

Emmett watches the Jablonskis. With folded hands and bowed heads, they both seem to be praying hard—probably for the return of their coke, Emmett figures.

Emmett is right. Marek is praying hard. Tomorrow is the first day of Spotless Souls Housekleening Service. Busha printed up a form with lists of sins and rates for their removal. The cleaning ladies are supposed to check off sins when they enter the abodes, then tell the occupants how much it'll cost to clean away their spiritual blight.

It's Marek's job to visit the houses—twenty to thirty stops per day—and collect the fees. At the end of each week, the cleaning ladies will receive a salary—a percentage of whatever they'd booked in business that week. The cleaning ladies love this new arrangement—for the first time in their lives, it gives them a chance to free themselves from hourly wage servitude.

Marek doesn't feel right about this sin business. How can anyone but God decide who has committed sin, and of which type and quantity?

Still, Marek has no other job prospects. Busha has agreed to pay him a good salary—he can make at least a thousand dollars per week—and not charge him room and board. If he watches his expenses, he can return to Poland with a nice bankroll in a few months.

Marek wonders if every job in the world presents ethical or moral dilemmas. Even in the circus they'd inflated their claims. They'd boasted that their pitiful menagerie had played before Kings—giving the impression that they had entertained royalty. But, in truth, they'd once played for a family named King. Marek laments that there's so much like this in the business world—deception, downright lying, and worse.

Marek has to laugh at his moral misgivings over his current situation. Here he is feeling squeamish about deceiving people with Busha's bogus sin removal services. And just a short time ago, Marek had been robbing dry cleaners at gunpoint.

Still, he believes outright robbery is more honest than corporate deceit. In the former case, people know they're getting robbed—unlike the business world, where they're swindled, but don't realize it. Marek decides it's worse to rob an unsuspecting suspect. This is his own ethical code, where he draws the line between right and wrong. He figures each person must have such a moral compass.

As he sits in the pew, Marek prays that God will guide and forgive him. He believes his only choice is to go along with Busha one last time—and then get his ass back to Poland once and for all.

※

After Mass, Grazyna grills Father Spinelli about the statue of Saint Stanislaus of Krakow. When will the priest install the monument? Honoring this saint is important to the Polish parishioners, she tells him. It will be a good investment, encouraging Poles from other neighborhoods to join the parish, fattening the church coffers. The Polish people will pay for lighting many candles to the esteemed bishop and martyr. The church will recoup its investment within a short time.

Spinelli nods as Grazyna chatters on about the statue. It doesn't even faze him. He has no intention of fulfilling her request, but isn't about to tell her as much. He just wants to get rid of her. He tries to interest the old woman in one of his CDs, but when Grazyna notes the price, her eyebrows shoot up like sparrow's wings. Soon enough, she breezes out the door—flying away from the pompous priest and the pressure to spend money.

※

After the nine o'clock Mass, Dennis gets up to leave, but Emmett bows his head and acts as if he doesn't notice.

"Come on," Dennis says.

Emmett shakes his head and says: "I still gotta pray."

Sammy Mangano wasn't at the Mass. Emmett has to stick around until the thug shows up—he needs to get a word with him, set up a meeting to talk about the coke.

Dennis doesn't know what to think of Emmett's behavior. Is he already turning into a religious fanatic? For a long time, Dennis has tried to get Emmett interested in Catholicism, but this is too much. He sits next to Emmett and tries to project pure annoyance. Emmett gets the message.

"Go home," Emmett says.

"No," Dennis snaps back.

Emmett always tells him he's stubborn, and Dennis has to admit it's true. He just has to stick around and find out what's going on with Emmett. Is he in trouble? Is that why he needs to stay in church and pray?

Dennis has his doubts about the episode a few nights ago, when Emmett had picked a fight about the so-called poisoned lasagna. Dennis knew this was a ruse—a way for Emmett to stay out all night. Where had he been? What had he been doing? Who had he been with? But Dennis had been so glad to see Emmett that he'd decided to let the whole matter slide—for the time being. Sooner or later, the truth always comes out.

❈

The eleven o'clock Mass is just like the ten o'clock Mass, the nine o'clock Mass, and the eight o'clock Mass. Emmett is starting to feel bored. He has the whole thing memorized. He's kneeling before he's supposed to kneel, standing before he's supposed to stand, extending his hand in the sign of peace a few seconds before the appointed time.

During the first three Masses, Emmett only shook hands with Dennis because nobody was sitting near them. But this Mass is better attended.

A young couple with two small children sits in front of Emmett and Dennis. They turn around to shake hands. Emmett tries to read their eyes to see what they think about a black man in their white church. Their eyes look blank, no response at all. But the two little blond boys grab Emmett's hands—one each—and hold them for a while. They look at him as if he's a superhero—which he does resemble in height, build, and shaved head.

For a while after this, Emmett imagines what he'd be called if he were a superhero. But every name he thinks of is already taken.

From time to time, Emmett turns, looks this way and that and scans the gathering. Dennis follows his gaze, wondering what or who Emmett is looking for. Dennis is getting hungry—Emmett got up early and ate breakfast before they'd left home. But Dennis always fasts before communion, which he'd taken at eight o'clock Mass.

He's so hungry that he's tempted to go to communion again at this Mass, but he pushes back the thought—horrified at it.

Imagine, taking communion because you're hungry, Dennis thinks. The Body of Christ should never be consumed for this reason, Dennis knows. He forgets about Emmett for a while, thinking about how he's just sinned in thought. And it's a bad, bad sin on top of it. Right away, he repents—but knows he'll have to go to Confession some time very soon.

Emmett can't believe Sammy Mangano is still not at the Mass. Well, he'll just have to sit through one more.

�֎

After the eleven o'clock Mass, Dennis springs from his pew with relief.

"Now, let's go!" he says to Emmett through his teeth.

But Emmett just shakes his head and says: "I gotta pray."

Dennis sinks into his seat. He's too bullheaded to go home. But he'll have to make a trip to the restroom or he'll never make it through another Mass.

During the interval between the eleven o'clock and noon Masses—about ten minutes—Spinelli sells his remaining CDs and starts to take orders. He instructs the parishioners to fill out the forms and pay in advance. He'll give them the CDs as soon as they arrive—in about two weeks.

Dennis leaves his seat and waits in line at the restroom. Afterwards, he goes outside and bums a cigarette from a woman old enough to be his grandmother. It's the first cigarette

Dennis has smoked in years. But he's going crazy sitting through all these Masses.

As he smokes, Dennis thinks about running two blocks to the convenience store, buying a package of Little Debbie cakes and eating them on the way back to church. But he knows the sweets will spoil his appetite for a good breakfast—brunch, at this point—plus give him a sugar headache.

He throws down his cigarette, stamps it out, then picks up the butt and carries it to a nearby trashcan. He feels lightheaded from the cigarette, as if he's about to pass out. He needs something in his stomach right away. He asks another old lady if she has any mints or gum.

While Dennis is outside, Emmett bobs his head around to see who's coming into church. He figures if Sammy Mangano shows up early, he'll say a few words to him, set up the meeting, then he won't have to sit through another Mass.

But when the Mass starts, Sammy has not arrived. Still, Emmett sits in his pew. He'd kick himself if he left—and could you walk out of a Mass?—and found out Sammy had arrived after his departure.

Emmett turns and sees a tall blonde, around sixty, enter with a man Emmett assumes is her husband. Emmett perceives a sort of aura around the woman, as if she's rich or famous.

It might be her hair—Emmett has never seen another shade like it, and he's great with colors. That's the best part of his paintings, the colors he uses together. He's studied Matisse's work over the years for this. He wants to go home and start painting. Thank God, this is the last Mass for the day.

When Emmett turns around, he thinks he sees the priest sneer at the big blonde as she takes her seat. But he dismisses the thought. Priests aren't supposed to sneer, even if somebody does come in late for Mass.

Virginia doesn't know how much longer she can keep coming to Saint Francis of Assisi for Sunday Mass. She'd hoped that the parish would get a new pastor—they should have been able to find one by now. Well, when Redemption Dry Cleaners starts holding Sunday services around Christmas, she'll no longer be available to attend Sunday Mass. God will understand that she can't be in two places at once.

She rests her hand on her growing belly and smiles. Virginia thinks of all the years she's spent in this church praying for a miracle. Now, here she is pregnant. She's living the miracle.

Now she has new things to pray for: a successful pregnancy, a safe birth, a healthy baby—a child who will bring honor on his or her parents. Virginia wants the world for her offspring—and she expects God to come through with His most abundant blessings.

✂

After five Masses, Emmett gets around to doing what he'd told Dennis he was doing all along—praying. He prays that Sammy Mangano will come to church so he can have a little conversation with him.

Emmett is praying not to God—but to himself. He knows it'd be wrong to ask God to assist with the cocaine sale. Emmett isn't crazy. He knows God wouldn't go for something like that.

He doesn't feel guilty about getting involved in the cocaine. He didn't rob anybody for it. He didn't sell any to schoolchildren. He just wants to make some money and not hurt anybody in the process—just have the thug give him some cash so he can stop working and do what he's meant to do on this earth: paint.

Right before Communion, Emmett turns and sees Sammy Mangano enter the church accompanied by a small woman with streaked blonde hair. He assumes this is Mangano's wife. She is all dolled up in a fur coat—and it isn't cold enough for such a garment.

Emmett reaches in his shirt pocket for the note he'd placed there: "Need to talk to you about important matter. Where and when can we meet?" The note includes Emmett's cell phone number.

Right after Communion, Emmett turns and sees Sammy and his wife leaving the church. He stumbles over Dennis in the pew, attempts to genuflect, then speeds down the aisle—with everybody's eyes on him.

He races out of the church, down the steps, and scans the parking lot. He sees Sammy Mangano opening a car door.

Emmett runs across the parking lot and stands behind Sammy's car as he's backing out. Sammy slams on his brakes and opens the window.

Sammy wonders what in the hell Emmett wants and what he's doing at church. But he decides to act like he doesn't even know him.

"Where's the closest bus stop?" Emmett asks as he slips the note through the window. It falls in Sammy's lap and Sammy palms it, glancing over at his wife.

"No idea," Sammy says and screams out of the parking lot.

Dennis has followed Emmett from church. He sees Emmett race after Sammy and bend down to talk to him. Dennis tries to read the license plate—to check out later—but it's too far away to make out.

Dennis now knows why Emmett had sat through five Masses. But who's the man? What's Emmett's business with him? Why didn't Emmett just call the guy if he wanted to get in touch?

But then, all of a sudden, Dennis doesn't give a damn. He just wants to go home and get something to eat. His whole day has been wasted sitting at Mass, where desire for food had caused him to commit one of the most horrible sins he can imagine—temptation to take Communion because he was hungry. He wishes he'd stayed in bed.

20
MARY AND JOSEPH

SAMMY KNOWS WHAT EMMETT WANTS—to sell his portion of the coke at a bargain price. What a chump, Sammy thinks. Does he think I'm getting involved in buying and selling drugs?

Sammy decides he won't even place the requested phone call—the jerk will have to figure out he's not interested in dealing with him for any reason whatsoever.

Sammy feels bad about where he's hidden his share of the cocaine. He doesn't like to involve his family in his business—but if this all works out, he won't be in this particular business too much longer.

After the Lorenzos died, Rosalie needed to clear out their house, go through all their clothes and possessions—then put the house on the market so she could divide up the money with her siblings. But she just isn't up to doing it right now. She tells her relatives she'll take care of it after Thanksgiving.

In the meantime, she has to keep up the property—mow the lawn, rake the leaves, take in the mail. When Sammy offers to pitch in until Rosalie is ready to put the house on the market, she gives him the keys.

Sammy decides to hide the cocaine above the drop ceiling in the Lorenzos's basement. He'll only have to keep it there a short time longer—the boss's mother's birthday party is just a week away. After he makes a deal with his boss, Sammy will deposit the coke with an intermediary—and he'll be out of the Outfit for good.

Jerry pulls up in front of "Goodbye Wishes"—a rambling storefront with a gravel-covered lot populated with plastic deer, ducks, gnomes, flamingos, squirrels, as well as the Virgin Mary, Saint Francis (bird on shoulder), and Saint Anthony (baby Jesus at chest).

Since the neighborhood is close to the city's major cemeteries, many stores on the edge of town sell funeral wreaths and lawn ornaments.

Jerry doesn't see any Saint Joseph statues in the outside area. He's tempted to drive away—telling himself he at least made an effort—but decides to do the right thing and go inside and ask. If he fulfills Saint Joseph's request, Jerry figures he can get forgiveness for some of his sins.

❀

Sammy's boss's mother's birthday party is a black-tie affair. Sammy decides to buy a new tuxedo—an Armani. He considers this a business expense—the business of his future.

Then there's the matter of the gift. What do you give the boss's mother for her hundredth birthday? What can the old bird use? But that isn't the issue—it's a question of what kind of gift will impress the boss, make him feel that Sammy is respecting his mother.

It can't be money—too crass. And how much money would be enough? Sammy doesn't think Big Mama would want jewelry. He doesn't know about her taste in clothes or what size she wears. He knows she lives in a retirement home—so a big TV or other major appliance isn't practical.

Then Sammy gets an idea—he believes it's divine inspiration, and thanks God for it.

❀

A bell rings when Jerry enters "Goodbye Wishes." All around—on shelves that form a dusty maze throughout the place—are statues, cemetery wreaths, plastic flowers, as well as birdbaths and plastic geese. Jerry thinks back to the woman at the dry cleaners. He wonders if she'd bought herself a new goose.

He meanders around the store, but doesn't spot Saint Joseph.

"Can I help you?" he hears a voice say—the voice of a very old woman.

But when Jerry turns around, he's facing a very old man. The man isn't much bigger than some of the plastic gnomes that sit around the room. He has a bald head edged with tufts of white hair. He wears a starched white shirt, red suspenders, and black pants. He has on a red bow tie. All in all, he looks quite natty and projects a vitality that belies his years.

"I'm looking for Saint Joseph," Jerry says.

Sammy pulls into the parking lot of "Just Mary," a store that sells one thing: statues of the Blessed Virgin. For such a specialized business, it's a rather large store—and still bears the architecture of its former inhabitant, a Walgreen's Drug Store.

Before getting out of his car, Sammy stares at the sign on the facade. It says "Just Mary" in Gothic lettering and bears an image of the Virgin's smiling face. Sammy wonders if "just" means "morally right" or "only." He knows the word "just" is used in two different ways. Then he figures that's the reason the owner had picked the name—it can work both ways.

When Sammy enters the store, he's surprised. He'd assumed the store would display the statues around the perimeter of the room, with a large open space in the middle. Instead, the statues are in aisles, on shelves—the same shelves and aisles from when the store had been a Walgreen's.

Sammy looks up at the signs that indicate what's in each aisle: Aisle 1: Fatima; Aisle 2: Lourdes; Aisle 3: Guadalupe;

Aisle 4: Immaculate Conception; Aisle 5: Immaculate Heart; Aisle 6: Madonna and Child; Aisle 7: Perpetual Help; Aisle 8: Mt. Carmel; Aisle 9: Black Madonna; Aisle 10: Misc.

It's overwhelming—there are so many to choose from. Sammy wants to buy the most expensive twelve-inch statue in the store. He figures anything bigger wouldn't be practical. In the retirement home, he boss's mother likely doesn't have a lot of space for statues and whatnots.

Sammy hopes he can find a nice, expensive-looking, impressive statue—one that features ivory and gold—for about five hundred dollars.

The man reaches under the counter, pulls up a six-inch statue of Saint Joseph, and thrusts it at Jerry.

"I was looking for something bigger. Say, this high," Jerry says, indicating two feet with his hands.

"It'd take a lot of digging to bury a statue that big," the tiny man chuckles.

"I don't want to bury it," Jerry says. "I want to put it in my yard."

"Saint Joseph only comes in this size," the man says, pointing to the small statue.

Jerry gets an idea.

"Do you know anybody who could make one?" he asks.

"Make one?"

"You know, like somebody who molds things."

The man shakes his head.

As he's leaving the cemetery supply store, Jerry hears the high-pitched voice say: "Do you ever think about your own death?"

As Sammy speeds up and down the aisles, the Virgin's face becomes a blur. All the images of Mary seem to merge into one benevolent face and smile.

Row after row, aisle after aisle, Virgin after Virgin greets Sammy. They seem to emit soothing waves. Sammy pushes his shopping cart around the store a few times, soaking up the pleasant vibrations.

He glances around for a clerk, but nobody is around—and there aren't any other customers in the store. Sammy figures the storeowner doesn't worry about thieves—who'd steal a religious statue?

Then Sammy remembers reading about how thieves pillage churches in Latin America—stealing statues that are centuries old. But those are poor countries where people struggle to stay alive. Here, on the Far Northwest Side of Chicago, few people have such problems.

Still, Sammy wishes he could talk to a clerk—and tell the expert what he's looking for in size and price. As it is, each time Sammy spots a statue that looks right, he picks it up, sees the price on the bottom—and is disappointed that it's too cheap. He doesn't want his boss coming over here and finding out he'd only spent a few bucks on the gift.

Sammy closes his eyes and calls on his psychic powers to lead him to the right statue. He takes a deep breath and rolls his eyes back in his head. He senses a movement in his midsection, like a rope tugging at him. He follows the sensation until he's face to face with a statue. The Virgin is black. Sammy looks at the overhead sign. He's in the Black Madonna aisle.

❀

Jerry feels prickles run up the back of his neck. He turns around, but can't see the man. After a while, he spots his elfin form in a corner, next to a shelf of green plastic wreaths.

Jerry walks over and looks in the man's eyes. He is oh-so still, staring into space. After a few seconds, the old man shakes his head as if waking from a dream.

"Sorry," he says, "I have these little lapses from time to time. Now, what was I saying?"

Jerry remembers what the man was saying—he was talking about death, something Jerry doesn't like to think about.

"Sorry for drifting off like that," the man says, as Jerry leaves the store.

As he heads to his car, Jerry thinks of his own "little lapses." He's sinned so often and in so many ways that he has no idea how to make it right. He hopes to get some spiritual points by performing this duty for Saint Joseph—but even that's proving hard to do.

�֎

Sammy figures maybe these statues were intended for black people—the way toy companies manufacture black baby dolls. Then he thinks again. Most black people aren't Catholic—and those that are, say, Haitians, don't live in this neighborhood.

He picks up a leaflet on the counter. It tells about the mystery of the Black Madonna—how the image has been found in all countries and cultures. Sammy realizes this will be a unique gift. There's the off-chance that another partygoer will give the boss's mother a Virgin Mary statue—but he doubts anyone else would think of giving a Black Madonna.

Sammy picks up the statue he's drawn toward. The tag on the bottom says: $500, ebony and gold leaf, replica of Our Lady of Loreto.

The statue features a large tubular dress with gold designs and black wood showing through. The Virgin's head emerges from the garment with baby Jesus's head next to hers. Each wears a tiered crown that looks like a large thimble. Sammy thinks the statue very unusual—he's never seen anything like it.

He wonders if his boss will take offense—wondering why Sammy gave his mother a black statue. But Sammy decides to leave the tag on the bottom about Our Lady of Loreto—it's in Italy, after all. He'll peel off the section with the price. He's still undecided, but opts to follow his instinct. If he can ever find a clerk, he'll tell the person to wrap it up.

21

HAPPY BIRTHDAY, DEAR MOTHER

AS HE SIPS HIS AFTER-DINNER COFFEE AND NIBBLES ON HIS BIRTHDAY CAKE, Sammy tries to figure out how much his boss had spent on the bash. Prime rib sit-down dinner, full orchestra, well-known singer, expensive wine, gifts for each guest, the best venue.

The decorations are incredible. Since the boss's mother's birthday is on Columbus Day, the theme of the party is "Follow Your Dream," and the decorations include large-scale papier-mâché replicas of the Niña, Pinta, and Santa Maria. Sammy guesses the tab must be at least a thousand dollars per person— or about a half a million dollars all told.

Sammy is still looking for a chance to get a few words with the boss. The big man has hovered near his mother all night, without even a trip to the men's room. Now it's time for Mama to open a few random gifts. Since there are so many, it'll just be too tiring for Mama to open all of them right now. They'll cart home the gifts in vans and Mama will see them later.

Anticipating this, earlier in the evening Sammy had slipped one of his cronies a few hundred bills to make sure his package is one of those the boss's mother opens.

Mama points to a few packages and the boss's underlings tote them to the old lady's lap. The first one is a small box. The old lady's ancient, gnarled hands fumble with the wrapping, so a helper removes the paper and ribbons.

Inside is a blue rosary that shimmers in the dim light. Sammy is sure it's made of sapphires. He tries to calculate how much a sapphire rosary would cost. About sixty beads on a rosary, at about fifty bucks per sapphire, the rosary would cost three grand—much more than Sammy had paid for his gift. He kicks himself. He should have bought a ruby rosary for about five Gs. He'd figured the old lady wouldn't want jewelry, but hadn't thought about buying a rosary.

The old lady manages to open another small package. Inside is a rosary made of red glimmering beads—rubies, Sammy figures. He's happy he didn't buy one. Two rosaries in a row— the givers must feel like idiots.

The next package is another rosary—a green one. Sammy figures it's made of emeralds—and cost at least ten grand. Next, a pearl rosary (maybe six bills).

The old lady points to a larger package on the table. Soon, it's on her lap. The boss himself helps her open it. Inside is the statue that Sammy bought—the Black Madonna.

The old lady gasps, kisses the statue, then clutches it to her breast. Tears roll down her cheeks. She says something to her son in Italian. Sammy understands. She's from Anconda, on the Adriatic Sea, just a short distance from Loreto. She'd grown up praying to the sacred image. She tells her son this is the best gift in the world.

The boss looks at the tag on the box: "Happy Birthday with love from Sammy and Theresa Mangano." The boss nods to Sammy. He has tears rolling down his cheeks, happy that his mother is so happy—happy that the birthday party is a hit.

❀

These days, Virginia finds it hard to fall asleep. Even though she works long, long days and is exhausted, Virginia can't coax her body and mind into slumber. She's up most of the night, lying awake in bed thinking about her life.

Her initial ecstatic joy about her pregnancy has evaporated. She thinks it odd how soon a person can become accustomed to even the most astounding circumstances.

Even though for decades she'd prayed to conceive, now that it's happened, the pregnancy no longer seems so miraculous. It has come to pass. Virginia starts to take the situation for granted, the way she takes the sun for granted.

The overwhelming responsibility of parenthood starts to press down on her. She's pregnant with a divinely conceived baby. What will the child be like? What will he or she need? Will Virginia be an adequate mother for such an offspring?

�֍

Sammy feels his knees about to buckle. This is beyond his most vivid dreams. It's better than perfect. He's so thankful, so grateful that he'd heeded his intuition about which statue to buy.

This is the ideal setup for the request he's about to make.

As the guests are departing, the boss shakes everybody's hands. When Sammy's turn arrives, the boss embraces him and pats him on the back. Sammy whispers something in his ear. The boss nods.

Soon, they're in a corner speaking in hushes. After listening to Sammy for a minute—Sammy tells his story and makes his request fast, he's rehearsed it many times—the boss says: "I need you with me."

Then Sammy brings up the business about the cocaine.

"To make it work, what you're offering gotta be worth at least a mil, maybe two."

Sammy knows his share is worth about half a million. But he nods to his boss. He figures he'll return Emmett's phone call, after all.

✖

As she rests in bed with her hands over her belly, Virginia realizes she has everything she's ever wanted. She's pregnant. She's rich. She's successful. She's in a position of power.

She's beloved, adored, idolized. But her fulfillment creates a vacuum in her life—in a strange way she longs for her life of longing.

Before all this, things had been so simple. Back then, she knew what she wanted—and had prayed and prayed for it. But now that she has everything she'd dreamed of and more, she feels deflated.

What will she wish for now? Yes, there's the desire for a wondrous life for her child—but she has no doubt that this will happen. She longs for more children—and has no doubt that this will come to pass.

This knowing, this certainty that she'll have everything she wants, takes the spirit and the fun out of Virginia's life. She's ashamed to admit how depressed she feels. How can I feel this way, she wonders. What is wrong with me?

Could I have been happier when I was unsatisfied, unfulfilled, and longing for what I couldn't have? Is the desire, the hope of something better, the real source of happiness?

❀

On his way to his evening meeting with Sammy, Emmett notices Punkin sitting on Jerry's deck railing—his orange fur glowing in the last rays of sunshine. Emmett can't believe his luck. Jerry seldom allows the cat outside—and Emmett has been looking for an opportunity to grab the animal for days.

If he brings Punkin home, Dennis will be so grateful, so easy to get along with, so agreeable. Emmett needs that kind of domestic peace—never more than now.

❀

When Emmett pulls into the shadows of the church parking lot, Sammy Mangano is already there in his dark blue Cadillac DeVille. As soon as he sees Emmett, Sammy gets out of his car.

"You got the stash?" he whispers into Emmett's window.

"Show me the money," Emmett says.

Sammy opens his trunk and nods toward an open briefcase on the floor. It's the sum he and Emmett have agreed on—$212,414.

While the two men are looking at the money, Tony jumps out Emmett's half-open car window and trots up to Sammy.

"What're you doin with Tony?" Sammy asks Emmett as he picks up the cat.

"Takin him back to Dennis," Emmett says.

Sammy gives Emmett his look of death and tries to decide what to do. Should he get involved in this cat custody battle?

Emmett says, "I ain't got all night" after Sammy is silent for at least a minute.

Tony nuzzles Sammy's shoulder. Sammy reaches over and strokes the cat, whose purrs sound almost musical—like the strings of an angel's harp.

As if on cue, piano music erupts from the rectory next to the church.

Sammy looks up at the clear black sky and takes in the stars and the crescent moon overhead. He lets the music flood through him. The cat is draped over his shoulder, purring in time to the music. A tear flows down Sammy's cheek.

Emmett senses the music all through his body, like tingles going up and down an invisible circuit. He feels dizzy, giddy, light, as if he could float up into space.

Just as fast, the music stops. The back door to the rectory flings open and Father Spinelli runs into the parking lot. He jumps and leaps, kicking his heels and saying what sounds like "whee, whee, whee." He's in a euphoric trance because he's just composed an amazing piece of music.

But after spotting the two figures, he snaps back to the present.

"What are you doing here, Sammy?" the priest asks,

holding his arms across his body to fend off the night chill.

Sammy looks at his companion. He knows they don't blend. What reason can he give for their pairing?

"We're prayin for world peace," Sammy says. "We met on the Internet."

✖

Virginia's thoughts turn to Gertrude, her beloved lawn goose. In the previous months, Virginia has been so busy that she's nearly forgotten about Gertie. But right now she starts to remember all the good times they'd shared.

All of a sudden, happiness floods into Virginia's heart. She's missing Gertrude. The goose is something she doesn't have, something she can pray for and long for—and serve as the focus of fervent prayers.

Please, Oh God, Dear Lord, bring dear Gertrude back to me. Lead her to my door. Have her return post haste. Amen.

✖

As Father Spinelli plays an enchanting tune on the piano, Sammy and Emmett sit in upholstered chairs in the priest's study. Each holds a cup of hot chocolate. Tony enjoys the music from the comfort of Sammy's lap.

The final note of the song echoes in the cozy room. The priest turns to the two devotees to world peace. They set down their cups and clap. Tony sits up straight in Sammy's lap and smiles—like all cats, he loves good music.

Spinelli bows his head, trying to seem humble. But he's proud, ever so proud.

"Please, please," the priest says, holding out his hands. "It's a gift from the spirit. I can take no credit." Though, of course, that's what he wants most of all.

"Well, thanks a lot," Sammy says, rising to his feet. He slings Tony over his shoulder.

Emmett also stands up.

"Please, just one more," the priest says.

"Really, Father," Sammy tells him, "we gotta get back to our duty."

"Yes, yes," the priest replies, "I understand."

Then Spinelli whips out two CDs—he's been saving them for special occasions until the shipment arrives in a few days.

"Only ten dollars," the priest says.

Sammy tosses the priest a sawbuck, and Spinelli hands each man a CD—with the reverence he reserves for baptized infants and communion wafers.

When they get back to the parking lot, Sammy eases Tony into the back seat of his car. Then he makes the exchange with Emmett—his money for the mailman's share of the coke.

"I want that cat!" Emmett says. "I need that cat. I gotta have that cat. My life at home is a living hell without that cat."

"I soon as shoot you as give you Tony," Sammy says, though he doesn't want to shoot anybody.

He doesn't want to sin at all anymore. He's proud that he's made his latest pronouncement without using even one profane word.

Sammy gets in his car and glides away—he doesn't want to jar Tony in the back seat. As he drives, Sammy starts to do some calculations. His stash is now worth over a million bucks. But the boss had said a million or two. Will this be enough?

What if he turns over the stuff and the boss says thanks and oh by the way you're still in—it isn't enough to get out. Sammy knows that if he has the whole load—Jerry's share included, he can clinch the deal.

Sammy doesn't want to return Tony to Jerry—but believes that stealing somebody else's pet is about the lowest form of crime. Until he's sure Tony no longer wants to live with Jerry, Sammy feels obliged to return the cat. Besides, it'll give him a chance to nose around and find out where Jerry hid his share of the coke. Sammy figures he can always come back another time and make off with it.

22
GIVE AND TAKE

EMMETT CAN'T PUT THE $212,414 IN THE BANK.
He doesn't trust a safe deposit box. Few spots in the house are beyond the reach of Dennis's all-seeing eyes. There's only one place where Dennis will never look—amid Emmett's art supplies.

Dennis encourages Emmett to engage in his "hobby," as he calls it—to Emmett's annoyance—but he's jealous of the time Emmett spends with his paints and canvases. He avoids Emmett's avocation and its accoutrements as if they're rivals for Emmett's affections, which they are.

Emmett stashes the cash at the bottom of a big art box, which he covers with a shelf filled with tubes of acrylic.

He decides to wait until the end of the year to ask for a leave of absence without pay. He can't quit his job right away. It will look suspicious to Dennis, who knows that Emmett isn't that great about saving money.

✂

Late at night, as Emmett works on the painting of his mother, he feels hateful judgment and scorn coming right out of her flinty eyes and hard-set mouth. Yes, his mother has always disapproved of Emmett—no matter what he's done. He remembers how he got revenge on her one time.

"Where's my lottery tickets?" his mother had barked.

Emmett played five dollars in Quick Picks for his mother each week, then turned the tickets over to her. But this time, he waited a day. He found out the winning numbers, bought a ticket with the same numbers for the following week—and put it in with his mother's tickets for the previous week.

He waited while she checked the numbers in the paper. Soon, she was hooting and hollering and kicking up her heels.

"I won, I won!" she crowed.

Emmett intended to play along with the joke for a while, but he couldn't keep from laughing and snorting as soon as she started up.

When he confessed what he'd done, his mother looked as if the weight of her unhappy life had come crashing down on her—crushing her features into a look of total shocked despair.

"You're the evilest man that ever drew breath," she says.

She'd wept over it for days, then fell into a speechless strangeness. She seemed to give up hope. Emmett almost felt sorry for her—and that took a lot.

As he looks at the painting of his mother, he hears her say again: "You're the evilest man that ever drew breath."

Well, maybe I am, he thinks. Maybe I am. He decides to play the same trick on Dennis.

✄

Herb seldom visits Redemption Dry Cleaners. He spends most of his time going to and from the bank, supervising the construction of the new facility, and overseeing the interior design in their new River Forest home.

Giovanni is relieved that Virginia's husband seldom shows up at Virginia's place of business—because he resents the man's existence. Giovanni likes to believe that he and Virginia have a unique and special relationship—sort of a spiritual marriage. Herb's all-too-real presence bursts this fantasy.

More and more, Virginia relies on Giovanni. He likes this just fine, too. There's nothing he wouldn't do for Virginia. She is all-woman and all women to him.

She could ask him for the sun, the moon, the stars and he'd try to get them for her—yes, it sounds like something from an

Italian song. She could also ask him to do the most mundane, off-putting chores—cleaning the restroom, sorting customer's smelly socks, sweeping the floors. It doesn't matter. Whatever Virginia wants, Giovanni is ready and more than willing to provide.

❈

Yes, Emmett will tell Dennis he'd won two hundred thousand dollars in the Illinois lottery. He'll show him the ticket—Dennis will never think to check the drawing date.

This way, Emmett will have a good excuse for taking off from work. He'll even give Dennis a chunk of money—the little guy deserves it. He's allowed Emmett to live in his house for the past year without charging him one dime in rent.

Dennis's house is paid off—he'd inherited it from his hardworking Italian immigrant parents—and he only asks Emmett to chip in for half the utility bills. He wants Emmett to save up money so he can take time off and paint.

But Emmett hasn't saved any money. Painting is an expensive avocation—canvases and paints and art books and all of it cost a lot. Well, he doesn't have to worry about that anymore. He has $212,414 in his art box. He decides to give Dennis twenty thousand dollars—ten percent of his haul. He figures this will keep Dennis in cat food for quite a while.

❈

Virginia is moody these days. Often, she seems close to tears. Her heart isn't in her work. More and more, she asks Giovanni to pitch in and help.

Virginia tells Giovanni that she needs him to work by her side. She'll examine the clothing, call out the sins, and Giovanni will check off the spiritual infractions on the dry cleaning receipt.

"I need you, Giovanni."

Yes, she relies on him as she relies on no one else. He, Giovanni Gammeri, has been singled out by the Queen of Women. He would rather die than let her down.

Emmett's little trick with the lottery ticket works just as he'd hoped. Dennis is elated—and asks Emmett when he'll receive the money. Emmett tells him around the end of the year. He also mentions that he intends to give Dennis twenty thousand dollars.

A sob catches in Dennis's throat. Nobody—other than his parents—has ever given him anything. He's always been the giver in his relationships—and doesn't know how to feel about the news.

Dennis is good at giving. But the idea of taking something from anybody is so foreign that he's confused—is he happy or sad? It's as if his whole identity goes through a shift. If he's on the receiving end, he can no longer think of himself as a martyr. He can no longer consider himself put upon and taken advantage of and unappreciated.

At first, Dennis acts glad about Emmett's newfound wealth and the gift he's offered. But the more Dennis thinks about it, the worse he feels. He wonders if Emmett intends to give him the money as a guilt offering, a parting gift, and then take off and take up with somebody else.

Sammy decides to wait until around Christmas to decide what to do about his boss. In the meantime, he's busy. He's doing all his regular work with the Outfit—mainly, collecting street tax from real estate agents—taking care of the Lorenzos's house, and paying regular visits to Tony, Jerry's cat.

Sammy knows that Jerry's getting fed up with his frequent and impromptu visits. But Sammy can't help it. He loves Tony. It's the best kind of situation—a cat he loves that somebody else is responsible for. He's like Tony's godfather—there when the cat needs him, a bringer of treats and hugs and kisses. Then he can just go home to his cat-hair-free home.

Sammy plans to check in on Tony after he hides Emmett's share of the cocaine in the drop ceiling of the Lorenzos's basement.

But as he stands on a stepladder and shoves the bags of cocaine under the Fiberglas tiles, Sammy feels as if he's not alone.

✻

If Emmett walks out, Dennis doesn't know if he has the emotional wherewithal to start up again with somebody else. Relationships are just so draining.

The two men had met a few years before, when Emmett rang Dennis's doorbell to deliver a certified letter. Dennis struck up a conversation—telling Emmett that he, too, worked for the Postal Service, as a night supervisor in the facility near O'Hare Airport.

After that, Dennis opened the door each day as Emmett arrived with the mail—engaging him in conversation, inviting him inside for coffee. One thing led to another and now here they are: A couple.

Dennis hates dating, hates going out and trying to meet people. He hadn't been with anybody in years before he'd met Emmett. And, even then, Emmett had just shown up on his doorstep. If Emmett takes off, Dennis will live the rest of his life alone with his cats. Dennis cries just thinking about this. It seems so pitiful.

He decides then and there that he won't take Emmett's money. If Emmett leaves, so be it. But he'll have to depart with a guilty conscience. He'll have to leave knowing that Dennis had been the one to give, give, give during the relationship, while all Emmett had done was take, take, take.

If Dennis has to live the rest of his life alone, at least he'll have the satisfaction of knowing that he's never taken anything from anybody—and that Emmett had taken advantage of him. These bitter thoughts will warm many a long, lonely winter night.

✂

"What Sammy up to?" Anne-Marie Lorenzo's ghost asks her dead husband.

"He hidin somethin, look like," Aldo says.

"Probably not so legal, what he doin," Anne-Marie says.

"He musta got a good reason," Aldo tells her.

Then the two ghosts settle into their twin recliners and remember all the time they'd spent together in the chairs— talking, eating, watching television. Really, they think, life goes by so fast. And, after all, what is it all for?

There must have been more to it than eating and talking and watching television. Then they remembered that they had loved each other. They had spent many hours holding hands across the small space that separated their two chairs.

Even though Anne-Marie and Aldo no longer have their bodies, they still have the love. Even now, they sit next to one another and hold hands, watching Sammy as he hides the cocaine in their basement ceiling.

Again, Sammy senses something. He looks around, wondering if he was followed or if someone's watching him. But then he figures it's just a case of nerves.

He's more nervous than usual these days—just thinking about his upcoming deal with the big man makes him start to shake. There's always the chance the boss will take the coke, and then have him whacked. Sammy doesn't want to die, but can't go on living the way he's been living.

He wants to start over, erase his past. He wants a chance to lead a good, decent, honest life. He wants to look his future grandchildren in the eye and tell them to follow his example and lead a virtuous life.

It'll all get settled one way or the other around Christmas.

23
TOMORROW TIMES THREE

GRAZYNA IS MAKING WADS OF MONEY WITH SPOTLESS SOULS HOUSEKLEENING SERVICE—but knows her income is meager compared to what Virginia Martyniak rings up at Redemption Dry Cleaners.

It's now early December—three months since Grazyna stole the dry cleaning receipt from Virginia. She feels enough time has passed that it's safe to again spy on Redemption Dry Cleaners—and see if she can gather some moneymaking information from the business.

Dorota and Bronislava have invited her to attend the grand opening—the discount store remodeled into a massive new operation for Redemption Dry Cleaners.

After nine o'clock Mass, Grazyna ambles home and waits for Dorota to pick her up. While waiting, she dresses her plastic goose in a red velvet evening gown and cloche hat. With an endless supply of clothing, the goose has never worn the same ensemble twice.

❧

Grazyna can tell by their smug smiles that Dorota and Bronislava feel special because of the clothes they're wearing——garments that were cleaned, pressed, and sin-removed at Redemption Dry Cleaners.

Dorota pulls into the crowded parking lot and finds a spot a block from the building's entrance. During the five-minute walk, Grazyna has time to study every aspect of the facade. There's a huge marquee, like for a movie theater. On it, in square black capital letters, is written: WASH YOUR SINS

AWAY. Above the marquee is a large sign with light bulbs around the letters: REDEMPTION DRY CLEANERS.

To Grazyna, everything looks first-class. She's sure they'd spent a load of money on the renovations. As she moves toward the building, Grazyna sees lines of people crowding into the place. This is an operation on a grand scale, she thinks—on par with the Catholic Church, for sure.

✄

Jerry gets an inspiration—he's sure it came from Saint Joseph. Christmas is just a few weeks away. They sell nativity scene lawn ornaments all over the place—and the Saint Joseph figures in the sets are about the right height.

When Jerry stops off at the K-Mart garden center, there they are: Saint Joseph, Mary, Jesus in the manger, the Three Wise Men, shepherds, plus angels. The plastic statues are hollow to accommodate light bulbs.

Jerry grabs a shopping cart and piles it with Saint Joseph statues. He plans to make multiple trips until he's purchased all twenty on the shelves.

But when he gets to the checkout, the cashier refuses to ring up the sale.

"These are part of a set," the chubby-as-Santa teenage boy tells him. "You can't buy them alone."

"But I only need Saint Joseph," Jerry says. "Mine is missing."

"They why do you need six?"

"On my block..." Jerry stammers, "...in my neighborhood, somebody stole all the Saint Josephs. I took up a collection and I'm the one who got elected to go out and buy them."

Right away, Jerry sees the problem: he's lying about a spiritual matter. But what other choice does he have?

"I've heard of people stealing baby Jesus, but not Saint Joseph," the cashier says.

"I can't afford to buy six whole sets," Jerry says.

"Sorry," the teenager tells him, yanking the basket of Saint Josephs away from Jerry.

Jerry tries to figure out what to do. He realizes he'll have the same problem at every store. He decides to buy one complete Nativity set.

✂

When Grazyna and her friends enter the lobby of Redemption Dry Cleaners, they feels a hush. Grazyna looks down at the dark pink carpeting—she's vacuumed many, many rugs in her life, and knows this is the best quality. The walls are painted a pale pink that looks like the inside of a shell. It feels very cozy—with a wonderful, light mood about the place.

Three oak doors lead to the main worship area. When the women walk through the center door, they hear celestial music coming from the loud speakers. The theater-type chairs are in a dark pink that matches the carpet. The ceiling is painted like the sky in a sweet fairy tale blue, with clouds and stars and suns and moons and planets spinning through the sky.

At the front of the room, in the altar area, stands a large painting of Gertrude the goose. She's wearing a gown and cape reminiscent of the Virgin Mary. On her head is a golden crown. Under the painting, it says: *The Goddess Comes in Many Guises.* Grazyna decides to look up "guises" in her English/ Polish dictionary first thing when she gets home.

Grazyna and her two friends find seats near the back of the room. The place swells with people—and everyone wears sparkling clean, pressed clothing.

Set up high in the walls are stained-glass windows that depict the goose in various scenarios. Grazyna figures this is a goose version of the Stations of the Cross. She tries to make out what's happening in the windows: a baby goose in a straw manger, a goose flying, a goose swimming, a goose walking, a goose sitting on a nest.

Toward the end of the wall, the windows show a goose getting abducted by a man in a black ski mask. Grazyna feels a mixture of emotions—shame that the window depicts Marek committing a crime, and pride that Marek has been commemorated in this public way.

Grazyna notices a wire pulley that runs the length of the room on either side—and half-expects to see Marek doing his high-wire act up there. But she knows the lazy slug is in bed snoring like a bear—and will still be that way when she gets home.

✂

Jerry buys mold-making materials from a hobby shop. He plans to make a mold of the Saint Joseph statue, then create plaster duplicates from the mold.

Figuring he'd better do something with the other statues, he sets up the Nativity scene—minus Saint Joseph—in his front yard.

It's a good thing I'm still on sick leave, Jerry thinks. This project is going to take a lot of time. Good. What else have I got to do, except play with Tony?

✂

At eleven o'clock, Virginia Martyniak steps onto the platform at the front of the room. The crowd erupts into applause. Virginia smiles and smooths the folds of her pink choir robe. The color sets off her golden hair and makes it look even more enchanting.

Grazyna notices the bulge in the front of Virginia's robe. She wonders if the woman has a tumor. She's too old to be pregnant. She's got to be about my age, Grazyna thinks.

"Good morning, customers," Virginia says in her usual straightforward manner. "Thank you for joining us this morning at Redemption Dry Cleaners."

The crowd murmurs its pleasure at attending the gathering.

"Please turn to Hymn Number Ten in *Songs of the Spirit*."

There's a shuffling sound as people pull books from pockets in the seats in front of theirs and flip open the pages.

Virginia sits at an orchestra-sized Hammond organ and begins to play, leading the crowd in song. It's one of the tunes she'd received from Father Antonio Vivaldi. She'd written the lyrics herself—to Vivaldi's chagrin.

"Wondrous spirit, set us free, let us ride on your heavenly breeze," Virginia sings in a shaky soprano.

She can't even rhyme, Vivaldi fumes from the aisle. It's a travesty! He marches out of the premises.

✄

When Jerry's ex-wife, Annette, drives by Jerry's house, she feels the roots of her hair stand up like porcupine quills. She can't believe Jerry would go to the trouble of setting up a Nativity scene.

During most of their marriage, Jerry had shown little enthusiasm for anything domestic—other than that God-awful furniture he'd made in the early years. After Annette had dispatched the eyesores to the Salvation Army, Jerry had ignored anything related to the house and the furnishings. He always claimed he was preoccupied with his job.

Annette slams on her brakes and backs up until she's parked across the street from the house. She stares at the makeshift Bethlehem in Jerry's front yard. Right away, she spots the missing Saint Joseph.

Is he trying to send me a message, Annette wonders. Is he trying to say that I've eliminated him from the picture, that it's just Mommy and kids now?

Jerry has always been good at sending silent messages— he's never liked open confrontations.

Annette only lives a few blocks from Jerry, but she may as well reside in Nazareth for how often she or the kids see him.

As she meditates on the Nativity scene, Annette decides to have it out with Jerry. He has a lot of goddamned nerve airing their domestic problems for everybody in the neighborhood to interpret!

✻

Grazyna finds the service at Redemption Dry Cleaners rather humdrum. A song, a reading from the *Book of Spirit* (like the Bible, only it features the exploits of a goose), a sermon on redemption (what else?), another song, a prayer to the Spirit, another song. It isn't so different from a Catholic Mass.

"Now, it's time for communion. Please have your receipts ready," Virginia announces.

Grazyna watches as people form lines on either side of the room, and offer their pink receipts to the preacher and her husband.

Virginia and Herb press buttons and a line of clothes flows into the room on the pulleys—as if arriving from a holy of holies behind the altar. The couple gives the clothing to the communicants, and the people return to their seats holding their dry cleaning.

✻

Annette jumps out of her car, tears across the street, and lets herself in with a key. She doesn't care if her ex-husband has a cat whose dander will cause her face to swell up and her eyes to water. She's going to have it out with him right now.

She finds Jerry in the basement. He's mixing a large bucket of something that looks like plaster.

When Jerry glances up and sees Annette, his heart goes thwomp. He feels hurt and happy at the same time—just realizing how much he loves and misses his ex-wife.

"What the hell's going on?" Annette says, blowing her nose and wiping her eyes.

"I'm doing a project," Jerry tells her, turning his face away. He's blushing!

"I mean, about the Nativity outside," Annette says, letting out a loud sneeze.

She steps closer to him. Jerry can smell her perfume, her shampoo, even the lingering scent of Wisk on her clothes.

"It's Christmastime," Jerry says.

"You trying to send a message?"

"Message?"

"No Saint Joseph in the Nativity scene means no father and no husband in the picture anymore, right?"

Jerry laughs. Annette is a genius when it comes to reading messages where there are no messages.

"You think it's funny?"

"Annette, come on, it's just a Christmas scene, for Christ's sake," Jerry says.

Annette notices a wooden box on the floor. It looks like a small coffin.

"What's in the box?" she says. "Frank Czmanski's coke stash?"

"I told you, I haven't got any coke," Jerry says.

"You're gonna wind up in prison yet, Jerry!"

"No wonder I left you!" Jerry yells.

"I left you!" Annette screams back.

Since their divorce, the only thing they discussed is who had left whom. As Catholics, they couldn't get divorced. But they had. Then Annette had gone to the Chicago Archdiocese Metropolitan Tribunal Office and requested that the Church recognize the divorce—and grant her an annulment. The case is pending.

Jerry continues to mix the plaster. If he doesn't pour it soon, it's going to set up in the bucket, and he'll have to start over.

"What the hell you doing anyway?" Annette asks.

"Annette, please, it's a long story. It's just a project, okay?"

Annette struts over to the box and opens it. Inside, there's an indention of Saint Joseph.

"St. Joseph in a coffin, Annette says. "This is sick!"

"I'm making a statue, okay?" Jerry explains.

"For what?"

"I had a dream, okay? Saint Joseph told me to do it."

When all the clothes are off the rack, Virginia moves to the center of the platform, closes her eyes, folds her hands, and prays.

"Dear Spirit, you have removed the sins from our clothes. Thank you for redeeming our transgressions. Let us go from here today and vow to sin no more. Thank you, dear Spirit, who guides us and cares for us all the days of our lives."

"Amen," says the crowd.

Annette doesn't argue back. She often has dreams where saints tell her to do things.

"So, why's Saint Joseph want you to make statues?"

"He didn't ask me to make them. He just asked me to put his statue around the neighborhood, next to the Virgin Mary. Only there aren't any statues for sale. Except in Nativity Scenes. Only you can't just buy Saint Joseph, you have to buy the whole set, which is too expensive. So I decided to buy one, use it as a model and make some more. Okay?"

"Why didn't you just say so in the first place?"

As she leaves Redemption Dry Cleaners, Grazyna feels conspicuous. She's the only one not carrying a hanger of clothes covered in plastic. She knows members of the congregation are looking at her as if she's a black, black sinner.

But, on the plus side, she's gathered some useful business information for her work in Spotless Souls Housekleening Service. Virginia, she realizes, gives the customers something to take home with them. This is a powerful method of reinforcing ties to her customers.

Grazyna decides to start selling her own line of sin-removing sponges, dish cloths, towels, brooms, mops, and perhaps—if she can make a good deal with a manufacturer—vacuum cleaners. She can also sell dishwashing liquid, window cleaners, kitchen cleanser, and all the other items that people use each day around the house.

Grazyna doesn't worry that customers will think they can clean away their own sins with these do-it-yourself products. She'll advertise the items as interim tools—good only for between cleaning sin removal.

She realizes there's no end to ways you can make money—once you get started with a good, solid business concept.

24
THE HOLY FAMILY

A FEW DAYS LATER, Annette returns as Jerry is removing a Saint Joseph statue from the mold. Five completed statues stand in the basement.

"You've been busy," Annette says, as she sets down what looks like a toolbox.

"It kills the time," Jerry says, as he sneaks a look at Annette's tight black pants and red sweater.

Tony comes out of a brown paper bag, stretches, then strolls over to Annette and rubs on her legs.

"You hate cats, Jerry," she says, brushing off her pants.

As she bends over, Jerry takes in the view.

"He's more like a dog," Jerry says.

"You hate dogs, too."

"Not as much as cats."

Tony stares at Jerry as if he understands everything the man just said. He looks annoyed.

"Sorry, Tony," Jerry tells the cat, then asks Annette: "How come you're not sneezing today?"

"Before I came over, I got a shot from Dr. Zuppa," Annette says, referring to her allergist.

As Annette counts the statues with her eyes, Jerry can't take his eyes off his ex-wife.

"They dry yet?" Annette asks, referring to the statues.

"Take a couple days," Jerry tells her.

"Oh," Annette says, sounding disappointed.

"What'sa matter?"

"I was gonna help you paint them. I had a dream. Saint Cecilia told me to do it."

�

It's after three in the afternoon before Virginia leaves Redemption Dry Cleaners. The Sunday service was over at one o'clock, but afterwards customers had waited in line to speak with her.

People wanted to ask Virginia for advice, counsel, a sympathetic ear. They wanted to pour out their troubles and have her give them answers. They wanted to hold onto her hands, have her hug them. They wanted her to nod in understanding and compassion. They wanted her to tell them how to live, what to do, how to act.

When she managed to get away, Virginia felt drained—and resentful. What do people expect? Can't they appreciate what she's doing for them? Why do people always want more and more and more?

If this keeps up, Virginia fears she'll have no life of her own anymore. She'll get sucked dry by her dry cleaning customers, and become overwhelmed with their demands and problems.

Virginia will have to put some distance between herself and her customers. Yes, she wants to continue her business. It's her livelihood. But she isn't about to let it take over her life.

✻

Even though the statues aren't dry enough to paint, Annette opens her art box and removes tubes of acrylic.

"What color you gonna paint his cape?" Jerry asks.

"I usually see it in green, in holy pictures."

Jerry's sitting on the floor, stirring plaster. When he tries to stand, his back seizes up again.

"Sonofabitch!" he screams.

"So, you want the cape blue?" Annette says.

"No, my back. I hurt it on the job."

"Carrying coke?"

"I told you, Annette…"

"Yeah, Jerry, but I don't believe you."

Herb drives Virginia home in their new gold Lexus sedan. They travel in deluxe silence toward their new showplace house in River Forest—they'd moved in just a few days before.

The house has fifteen rooms and five bathrooms. It's a gray stone Tudor-style dwelling that had once belonged to a famous member of the Chicago Outfit, a man bumped off in a restaurant parking lot on Harlem Avenue.

Virginia has no misgivings about buying a former Mafioso's home. She doesn't believe that the man's spirit will haunt the place, or his lingering vibrations will taint the atmosphere. After all, he didn't die at the location.

It's a well-built, semi-mansion on a beautiful tree-lined street in a wonderful neighborhood. It's surrounded by a tall wrought iron fence. It's private. It has a lovely, large garden. It's well maintained. Everything was in move-in condition—Herb only had to oversee the painting of the rooms in lighter, more cheerful colors.

He'd hired an interior decorator to select the furnishings—instructing her to do up the place as if it belonged to Jacqueline Kennedy Onassis. The decorator had complied with simple, elegant, expensive furnishings.

Virginia is pleased with the results. She feels that she's more than the wife of a president—as Jackie had been—she's like a president herself in power and influence.

Virginia only wishes her mother could see her now. Mama, I made good, Virginia thinks. Mama, you would be proud of me. Mama, I wish you were here so I could share this with you. Mama. Mama. Mama. Mama.

As they sit in their exquisite living room, Herb wonders why Virginia is clutching her Black Madonna icon and crying. But he figures she's thanking the Virgin for all her blessings.

It's too much. Jerry can't keep lying any more. He confesses everything to his ex-wife.

"So, just go to the cops and tell them."

Jerry coughs out a bitter laugh.

"Better you tell them before they find out," Annette adds.

Jerry shrugs. She's right. It would be better.

"Either way, I'll go to prison."

"Yeah, but if you tell, you'll go for less time."

"Yeah," Jerry says, "but if I tell, when Frank gets out he'll kill me."

"Trust me on this, Jerry," Annette says, "Frank's gonna rat you out. Better you do it first."

Jerry shakes his head and says, "I'll just have to take my chances."

�

When Virginia moved into the new house, she felt she'd stepped into the life she was always meant to live. Yes, she's sad that her mother isn't around to share in the opulence. But sometimes she imagines her mother is right there with her, by her side, basking in the riches.

During these times, Virginia feels as if her new home is a haven, a fortress—a welcome respite from her draining work at Redemption Dry Cleaners.

While Virginia loves the way people treat her—as a star, an inspired individual, a near-goddess—she wants to manage the acclaim.

This is a business, she thinks—just that, nothing more. I have no responsibility to these people. I have my own life, my own goals. And as long as my personal plans coincide with the customers' needs, fine. When the two diverge, changes will have to take place.

Virginia wonders if she can appear via closed circuit television, or prerecorded video. To be frank, she doesn't like interacting with the customers—and what a relief it would be if she could avoid all personal contact.

�֎

"What if I tell?" Annette says. "Then Frank won't think it's your fault. I'll say I found the stuff in the house."

"Annette, I'll go to prison!"

"You're going to prison, either way."

"I'm gonna ride it out."

"If you let me turn you in, I'll remarry you when you get out."

Jerry feels as if he's just scratched off a winning lottery ticket that he can't cash in. It's the thing he wants most of all—but not this way. Anyway, he can't believe she'll wait—it could take years before he gets out.

"Let me think about it," he says.

25
TRUTH BE TOLD

JERRY DECIDES TO LET ANNETTE TURN HIM IN AFTER HE'S FINISHED THIRTY-ONE SAINT JOSEPH STATUES—the number of days in March, the month that marks the Saint's feast day.

Jerry has never felt closer to Annette than during their time working on the statues. He has to admit she's done a beautiful job.

"Here's what we gotta do," Jerry says to Annette as she paints Saint Joseph's brown eyebrows with a tiny brush.

Annette has always been good with cosmetics. She's one of the top Mary Kay representatives in the area, and is close to getting a pink Cadillac.

"Yeah?" Annette asks as she fills in the Saint's eye pupils.

"I take the coke. I put it in the attic where it was in the first place…"

"Yeah…"

"So you go up there. You're looking for some old photos. Your Mary Kay ring gets caught on the quilt that's draped over the chair. You take off the ring, then try to get it loose from the quilt. The ring falls on the floor. You crawl around on the floor looking for it. While you're searching for the ring, you look at the cracks in the floor. You think you see the ring, so you take a screwdriver—I'll leave one up there—you put it down in the crack. But then you notice the floorboards are loose, then you try to pull them up, thinking maybe the ring is under there. But when you lift up the floorboards, you find the coke. See what I mean?"

"Why I do have to do all that? Why can't I just say I found the drugs?"

"Annette, this way, your story will sound real—because it will be real. It really happened. So you can picture it in your mind as you tell the story. Cops can always see that. Plus, if they give you a lie detector test, you'll pass. It will be a true story."

"A true story that's made up," Annette says.

"A made up story that will sound true because it really happened."

"So, I find the ring, too, right?" Annette asks.

"No, you forget the ring, you're just thinking about the coke. So, next thing, you come down and confront me about the drugs. You say you know I hid them for Frank. You say I'm an idiot and you're not gonna let me see the kids anymore, then you leave. While you're gone, I hide the coke somewhere else. You come back—you forgot your Mary Kay ring—and you see that the coke is gone. You ask me where it is, but I won't tell you."

"So why do I go to the cops if the coke is gone?"

"Because you know about it—you'd be an accessory if you didn't turn me in."

"So I have to turn you in because we're divorced and the 'don't testify against your husband' thing doesn't apply?"

"Right."

"So where you gonna hide it?"

"That's something you won't know. If I tell you something I don't want you to tell the police and they ask you about it and you try to lie, they'll know it. Believe me, Annette, I have good reasons for doing it this way."

"When you wanna do this?"

Jerry looks over to his workshop where he hid the coke.

"Might as well do it now," he says.

✂

Jerry sits on the living room sofa and waits for Annette to come down from the attic. He's trying to act as if it's a normal day. She'd come over to look for something in the attic. While she's up there, Jerry's reading the newspaper. The cat's asleep on the sofa next to him. It could have happened this way.

He hears Annette's footsteps on the stairs. When she steps into the room, she shoots him a hateful look and screams: "You rat!"

Jerry knows she's improvising. Annette has always wanted to act—and sometimes takes part in amateur productions at the Chicago Park District.

Annette's loud voice wakes Tony from a sound sleep. He raises his head and stares at the interloper.

"Whaddya talkin about?" Jerry asks Annette, trying to play his part.

Annette drapes one arm across the stair railing and raises a hand to her forehead. "I found it!" she says, spitting out the words.

As the couple argues, Tony's head darts back and forth from Jerry to Annette.

"Found what, for Christ's sake?"

"The cocaine in the attic!" Annette says, the collapses on the bottom stair. "You hid it for that low-life creep, Frank Czmanski!"

"You're crazy!" Jerry tells her, setting the newspaper on the sofa and standing up.

Tony stares at Annette, his yellow eyes wide and unblinking.

"Crazy, huh? I seen it with my own two eyes!" Annette says, pounding her fists on her knees.

"It's just some salt I put away up there. Supposed to keep away evil spirits. My ma always used to do it."

"Liar!" Annette says, standing up and stalking across the room to face Jerry. It looks as if her hips are on hinges.

"Get the hell out of here!" Jerry tells her, pointing to the door.

Tony jumps up, runs over to Annette, and chomps on her heel—a warning bite, not enough to break the skin. Annette swats away the cat and covers her heel with her hand.

"Cat from hell!"

She grabs her woolen hat and yanks it onto her head.

"Get the hell out of here!" Jerry repeats, jabbing his finger toward the door.

"Gladly!" she says as she thrusts her arms into her coat and pulls on her boots—all the while keeping an eye out for Tony, who sits on the coffee table like an Egyptian ceramic.

Annette storms over to the front door, turns, glares at Jerry over her shoulder, and says: "You'll never see the children again!"

Then she grasps the doorknob and starts to open the door.

"Wait!" Jerry says.

Annette turns around and looks at him.

"That last line," he says, "didn't sound real. You should say: 'You'll never see the *kids* again!'"

Annette backs up a few steps.

"Where should I take it from?"

"Take off your boots. Put them on again. Walk to the door, turn, look at me, and say the line."

Annette follows Jerry's suggestion. From her amateur dramatic endeavors, she understands about taking direction.

Again, she turns to him at the door—this time saying: "You'll never see the *kids* again!"

She leaves with a dramatic slam of the door.

Jerry peeks out the window and watches Annette get into her car and drive away.

Now he has to hide the drugs. But he's figured out the perfect place.

❄

As Annette drives home, she feels like sparklers are going off in her chest. She hasn't had this much fun with Jerry since they'd started dating, more than twenty years before.

It's just lousy luck, now that they're getting along so well, that Jerry is headed to prison. Annette decides to make the most of their final days together. She has a few other skits in mind that they can act out together.

Annette knows she'll have to go back and get the Mary Kay ring. But she has to give Jerry time to hide the drugs someplace else. He didn't mention when she should come back.

She figures she'll return after the kids are in bed. Since she lives with her mother, Annette never has to worry about a babysitter.

❈

After hiding the drugs, Jerry goes back to the basement. Only one more Saint Joseph to finish. Then his duty to the Saint will be complete. He feels sad that the project is almost over. It's the way he'd felt when he graduated from high school. It's a "now what" feeling? But Jerry remembers "now what"—prison.

After he takes the statue out of the mold, Jerry sits on the basement floor and studies it for a while. Jerry feels as if he's communing with the Saint, telling Jesus's stepfather all about his life and his problems.

Of course, he has to apologize, too. He'd hidden the cocaine in the Nativity scene Saint Joseph—the model for the other statues—and had placed the statue with the rest of the Holy Family on his front lawn.

After spending what he considers a respectable amount of time asking for the Saint's forgiveness, Jerry goes upstairs. He's exhausted—in every possible way.

He takes a long, hot shower and falls into bed with Tony snuggled beside him.

Jerry wakes up as if he'd been shot—and hears somebody walking through the house. In recent weeks, his house has been a regular O'Hare—Emmett, Sammy, Annette, and Tony traipsing in and out. Could the FBI have finally arrived?

Jerry reaches for the revolver under his pillow, but stops when he spots Annette shadowed in the doorway. He can see the curves of her body through her negligee.

Tony rolls over and lets out a short meow.

Annette slinks over to the bed, grabs the cat, then sets him outside the bedroom and closes the door. She places something on the table and strikes a match. The match lights up her face and the candle she'd put on the table.

Annette then sets a boom box on the night table. She pushes a button and sweet piano music starts to play.

"What's all this?" Jerry says, finding it hard to believe this is happening.

"A tape I bought from Father Spinelli. Some music he just composed. Romantic, huh?" she says, sliding next to Jerry on the bed.

All of a sudden, Jerry feels deflated—and he doesn't know why. Annette looks beautiful in the candlelight. He wants her more than he'd ever wanted her. Just a moment ago, he was so excited. What's wrong?

He reaches over and takes her hand. He raises it to his lips and kisses it. He notices that she'd retrieved her Mary Kay ring.

"You came back for your ring," Jerry says. They have to finish this part of the previous skit before they can continue with other activities.

"Yeah," Annette says, "and I looked and the coke is gone!"

"It was never there," Jerry says. "You're imagining things."

"Bullshit! You hid it someplace else, didn't you?" Annette says as she slips her hand under the sheet.

"I never had any coke!" Jerry says, trying to act mad, the way he's supposed to in the script. But he's feeling sort of woozy, as if he's taken a Vicodin, which he hasn't.

The music catches Jerry's attention. Annette is right, Jerry thinks, it is romantic. So, why am I not feeling romantic right now?

There's a good reason. The couple has a spectator. Drawn to the scene by his latest compositions, Antonio Vivaldi is eager to hear what the man and woman think.

Jerry, sensing the dead priest's presence without realizing it, can't concentrate on what he's been fantasizing about for months—his ex-wife in bed with him.

Annette knows Jerry is distracted, but, for once, doesn't take offense.

"You're worried about going to prison, right?" she says.

"I guess," Jerry replies.

Vivaldi is disappointed. He wants them to talk about the music. The dead priest has composed some of the most romantic music ever written—and he's sure thousands of people had been conceived while their parents were listening to his works.

Annette puts her arms around Jerry and rests her head on his chest. It feels wonderful to Jerry—much better than sleeping with Tony.

As if sensing what Jerry's thinking, the cat starts to howl outside the bedroom door. After a minute, the bedroom door flings open. Sammy Mangano stands in the shadows cuddling Tony. Jerry figures that the cat's screeching had covered the sound of Mangano's footsteps.

"Sorry," Sammy says, glancing away from Jerry and Annette. "I didn't know you was shacked up."

"Shacked up!" Annette says, insulted.

"This is my wife," Jerry says.

"You ain't married."

"My ex-wife, okay? What the hell you doin here?" Jerry says.

"I come over to check on Tony. And good thing, too," Sammy tells him, stroking the cat.

Tony nuzzles Sammy's chest then throws Jerry and Annette the disgusted look he reserves for toy poodles.

Sammy notices the music.

"Father Spinelli?" he asks, pointing to the boom box.

"Uh-huh," Annette says.

Vivaldi feels like crying. Yes, he knew Spinelli would take credit for the work and had steeled himself for this, but it still hurts.

Sammy manages a sideways look at Tony, who's draped around his neck and purring in his ear.

"How come you got Tony outside the door?" Sammy asks.

"We're busy," Annette spits out.

"That ain't no way to treat a cat," Sammy says. "If you don't wanna take care 'a Tony, let me have 'im."

"Who the hell are you, anyway?" Annette says, sitting up and pulling the sheet over her chest.

All of a sudden, Sammy realizes something. The last couple of trips to Jerry's, he's had no psychic impressions. He now understands that Tony had put a psychic block on him—so he wouldn't argue with Jerry.

But now Tony is pissed that Jerry had locked him out of the bedroom. Right away, Sammy gets filled in on everything that Jerry and Annette are planning.

"You're out of your motherfreakin mind, cop!" Sammy says. "You're gonna let her turn you in? You're gonna give up the drugs? Maniaco!"

"Get the hell out of my house," Jerry says, aiming his revolver at Sammy.

"Never let a broad know your business. That's rule number one!" Sammy says.

Then he does a quick pivot—careful not to disturb Tony, balanced on his shoulder—and heads toward the back door.

After a few moments, Jerry hears Sammy rummaging around in the kitchen. He pulls on his shorts and follows him.

Jerry sees Sammy throwing stuff into a box.

"Now what the hell you doin?" Jerry asks.

"Packin Tony's things," Sammy says. "He's movin in with me."

�֎

After filling his trunk with Tony's food, cat bed, toys, and other paraphernalia, Sammy goes back into Jerry's house, sets the cat into the pale blue carrier, and stomps out.

He slides the cat carrier in the back seat—feeling as if he's just rescued Tony from the penitentiary. Through the wire grating, Tony looks up at Sammy with a little smile on his face.

Sammy can't wait to get home and prove to his wife that it was cat hair on his pants. See! Here's the freakin' cat!

Theresa isn't fond of cats—she's a fussy housekeeper—but too goddamned bad. They're keeping him! After all, who pays the bills? Sammy does, damned sure!

As he's about to pull away from the back of Jerry's garage, Sammy starts to pick up impressions. He turns and looks at Tony, who gazes at him with knowing eyes. Sammy gets the message.

He drives around the front of the house to pay a visit to Saint Joseph.

26
MOVIN ON

AFTER SAMMY RETRIEVES THE COCAINE FROM
JERRY'S SAINT JOSEPH STATUE, he arranges a meeting
with his boss. The boss tells him to come over in an hour.
Though the two men exchange few words, they understand
each other. Sammy is to deposit his load with an intermediary,
then come over to talk about it.

When Sammy hangs up the payphone, he wonders if he
should drop off Tony at home first, or just take him along. If he
stops at home, Sammy knows he'll get into an argument with
Theresa over the cat.

He has to get the rest of the stash from the Lorenzos's place,
then drive over to River Forest right away. He has no choice—
he has to take Tony with him.

Sammy prays that he won't find his cousin at the Lorenzo
house. She's still too distraught to sell the place—and has told
her relatives she'll put it on the market in the spring. But
Sammy often finds her wandering through the rooms, crying
and talking to herself.

He thanks God that Rosalie isn't there when he removes the
stash from the basement ceiling—and he's more than relieved
to get the drugs out of his dead aunt and uncle's house.

As he drives down Thatcher Road, winding around the
forest preserves, Sammy worries about his cat. It's cold
outside. Tony could freeze in the car. Sammy could leave the
car running, but that might look suspicious to his boss.

Sammy figures he has only one real choice: Take the cat
inside with him, even if it makes him look like a fool. His boss
knows he's a pushover when it comes to animals.

✤

Sammy double-parks in front of the wrought-iron gate to his boss's semi-mansion. He gets out of the car, and presses the intercom to announce his arrival. In a few seconds, the tall black gates swing inward and Sammy drives up the winding path to the gray stone building, where a couple of standard-issue Outfit guards are positioned on either side of the door.

All around are sculpted grapevine reindeer covered in Italian lights. Even the tall elm trees have been draped in lights. Tasteful, Sammy thinks—a single theme, understated and elegant—in contrast to the hodgepodge of plastic Santas, toy soldiers, candy canes, Rudolphs, and Nativity scenes in his own neighborhood.

That's the difference when you have money, Sammy muses. You don't have to be splashy. You have the confidence to keep things simple.

Approaching the house, Sammy nods to the guards and makes some holiday chitchat. As he stands on the stone steps with the pale blue cat carrier in one hand, he detects the smell of baking cookies.

The big man himself answers the door. It's after seven o'clock and he's spending the evening with his family.

The boss looks Sammy in the eye, then glances down at the cat carrier. Sammy is quick to notice his boss's raised left eyebrow—and knows he's thinking, "Why the eff did you bring an effin cat wit'you?"

"Let's go downstairs," the boss says.

The finished basement is decorated with simple, expensive furnishings—as if lifted from the "Home and Garden" section of the *Chicago Tribune*. Sammy imagines an article entitled, "Mob boss modernizes River Forest home."

Sammy sets Tony's cat carrier on the floor, then hands his boss the coded receipt he'd received from the intermediary that says, "Apostle's Creed+4 Our Fathers+3 Hail Marys." Sammy knows this stands for $1,550,000.

The boss raises both eyebrows. It's more than he'd expected.

"What about the cat?" the boss asks.

"Nuttin's in de cat," Sammy says.

"So why you bring 'im?"

"I haddem in de car when I cawd," Sammy says. "I din wanna leavum in de code."

When Sammy speaks with his superiors, his diction gets a lot worse. He doesn't do this on purpose—it just happens, as if some part of him has decided it's better not to look too smart.

"Lucky I'm not allergic," the boss says.

"Yeah," Sammy says, "I shoulda ask."

"Let me see 'im," the boss says.

Sammy opens the cat carrier and coaxes Tony out. He lifts the cat onto the coffee table.

"Nice lookin cat," the boss says, bending down to look at his nametag. "Anthony," he reads out loud.

The cat stares at the boss, locking eyes with him.

Tony knows what Sammy wants to discuss with his boss. He decides to move things along. He sends Sammy a message.

"So we got a deal?" Sammy says.

"Deal?" the boss says, still caught in Tony's gaze.

"I gotsum fammey obagashuns," Sammy says. "Like I says, I need ya ta cut me loose."

"What kinda obligations?" the boss says.

"My cuzn-law, Ray Palermo, drop dead coupla muntz sago."

"Yeah, sorry, I heard," the boss says.

"Right after dat, my cuzn Roselee, Ray's wife, lost bote her mudder and fadder."

"I sent flowers," the boss says.

"Buteful roses, I member," Sammy says.

"From Bianchi's, the best."

"Now, Roselee need me ta hep wid der restate biznus."

"What you gonna do?" the boss asks.

"She need me ta take Ray's place."

"You're sayin you're gonna sell real estate?" the boss asks.

"First I gotta getta licunze."

"So," the boss says, "you're tellin me you're gonna go from shakin down real estate guys to sellin real estate?"

"Lotta people make, ya know, career changes at my age," Sammy says. He's heard all about this on daytime television, which he's spent a lot of time watching while waiting around for his Outfit orders.

"Yeah, but lots of people ain't in your line of work, Sammy."

Sammy indicates the receipt.

"Can we jus'say we's square?" Sammy says.

The cat releases Sammy's boss from his deep look. The boss glances up at Sammy.

"Okay, Sammy," the boss says. "We're square."

❧

On the drive home, Sammy is euphoric. He's free. Free! His life is his own. Maybe he can do big in this real estate thing. With his psychic abilities, Sammy won't even need to hire building inspectors.

Sammy knows his boss would never have released him from bondage without Tony's powers of persuasion. The boss had even offered—offered!—not to ask for a street tax from Palermo Real Estate.

Sammy is free, free, free! The future stretches in front of him like an endless day on the beach in Cancun.

As he drives home in the hazy December evening, Sammy is unaware that the Lorenzos are in the back seat with Tony. But the cat can see the ghosts. He yowls—but Sammy thinks the cat was bothered by a pothole they'd just popped in and out of.

"We'll be home in a minute, Tony," Sammy coos to the cat.

Tony knows his screeching will do nothing to alert Sammy. His caregiver is psychic and a good receiver—but doesn't have the power to see spirits.

Tony figures he'll just keep an eye on the two ghosts. After a few moments, he realizes that the duo is related to Sammy and means him no harm. The cat curls up in his carrier and dozes off.

The ghosts relax. Cats always present problems—they can give you away, scare you off, and call on other spirits to make you sorry you ever showed up.

But now all is well. Just a peaceful ride past the forest preserves on the way to Sammy's house.

"It's nice Sammy gonna help out Rosalie," Aldo says.

"Yeah," Anne-Marie tells him, "Sammy always been a good boy."

"He got him a new pet, too," Aldo says, pointing at the cat. Tony opens one eye and gives the ghost a warning look.

"Yeah," says Anne-Marie, "they says cats is good for your blood pressure."

"They relaxing when you pet 'em on your lap," Aldo adds.

"So, what do you think, Aldo? Can we go on now?"

"You mean, Sammy got drugs from Virgin Mary statue Polish cleaning lady steal from us and give to boss and that got Sammy off hook so now he help out Rosalie in real estate?"

"Yeah."

"I guess," Aldo says.

The ghostly twosome gets out near the traffic light at North Avenue and Thatcher Road, where the Des Plaines River runs through the forest preserves. They walk toward the dark thick trees, then waft down to the water, step onto the frozen river, and glide upstream.

Sammy makes the sign of the cross. But he does that at just about every stoplight.

Tony falls into a deep sleep. He knows that, besides Sammy, he's now the only one in the car.

27
HEY, JOE

A FEW WEEKS LATER, Annette finishes painting the saint Joseph statues. There they are—all thirty-one of them, like chess pieces on the black and white tile floor.

Jerry puts his arm around Annette's shoulder. They beam at the statues like proud parents.

"I guess we can, like, thank Saint Joseph for bringing us together again," Annette says.

Jerry squeezes her shoulder.

"So, with your bad back," Annette says, "how you gonna lift the statues to put 'em around the neighborhood?"

"I got somebody's gonna help me," Jerry tells her.

"When?"

"Soon, couple days."

"So, when am I gonna turn you in?" she asks.

"Let's wait till after the holidays."

"So, what, like January second?"

"Somewhere around there. Don't tell me when. I gotta be convincing, like it's surprise when they come to get me."

Annette puts her arms around her ex-husband and hugs him.

"I love you, Jerry," she says.

Jerry tries not to cry, but in a few seconds Annette feels hot tears rolling against the side of her face.

She looks up at Jerry, wiping the tears from his face.

"You're doin the right thing, honey," she says.

Jerry looks at the Saint Joseph statues—thirty-one heavenly witnesses. If only, Jerry thinks, they could stand up for me in court.

In just six months, Virginia has made millions of dollars. This can go on and on. The business keeps growing and growing—each month, she doubles her receipts.

She'd heard that some people are going into serious debt to pay for her services. She'd heard the police had arrested several for robbery—money they'd stolen to spend at her establishment. Others had been caught embezzling—money they'd plunked down at Redemption Dry Cleaners.

Virginia takes a "don't ask/don't tell" attitude about where people are getting the money to pay for her services. Does the state of Illinois ask where people get the money to buy lottery tickets? Do the riverboats ask where people get the money they spend in the slot machines and at the gaming tables? Does the Catholic Church ask where each dime comes from that goes into the collection plate?

❀

Jerry rings Marek's back doorbell and waits. It's about a week before Christmas, a Sunday morning at ten o'clock. Jerry knows the Polish kid is home. He'd looked through the garage window and had seen his Nova.

As Jerry stands on the back steps, a light, airy snow falls around him. It's been snowing on and off for days and there's a thick covering on everything except the streets and sidewalks.

Again, Jerry rings the bell. He figures Marek's Grandma is away at church, where most old Polish ladies are on Sunday mornings. After awhile, he hears somebody shuffling toward the door.

Marek pulls back the curtain on the door window and squints out at Jerry. He wonders what the cop wants this time. Marek thought that Jerry was out of his life. He takes his time unlocking the door.

Marek stands in the cold wearing only jockey shorts. Still, it doesn't seem to bother him.

These Polskis, Jerry thinks, they're made of iron.

"What you are wanting?" Marek says, rubbing his eye. He was out very late and planned to sleep most of the day. He'd gone to Mass the previous evening.

"Let's talk about it," Jerry says, stepping through the door.

Marek shuts the door and follows Jerry into the kitchen. Jerry stands next to the chair that holds the plastic goose.

"You really should give this back," Jerry says, nodding to the goose.

"You coming at breaking day to telling this?" Marek says, grabbing onto the back of a chair.

"I need you to do a little job for me," Jerry says.

"O Bóg!" Marek says, slumping into a chair.

Jerry figures Marek had said, "O God!"

Well, Jerry thinks, prayers are always good.

Weak people are everywhere, Virginia tells herself—people prone to addiction, people who don't know where to draw the line, people who don't know how to regulate their own behavior. Is that my fault?

Some people can go into a restaurant and enjoy a cocktail or two and have a nice evening. Others will get drunk and cause a brawl. Should the restaurant close its doors because some patrons don't know how to behave?

This is true with any business—there are always people who will go to excess. An individual is responsible for his or her actions. Some people can find temptation anywhere. If every business that proves an "occasion of sin" shuts its doors, the country will be nothing but boarded-up shops.

Marek zips up his pants and tucks in his shirt. He hates wearing clothes—they're so confining. Then again, life is confining. There's always somebody who wants you to do something that you don't want to do.

As he brushes his hair, Marek smiles—remembering all the money he has in the bank. Money both earned and stolen in the robberies—money that will take him back home, to a new life and a new business. The cash is his insurance policy that he'll never have to be anybody's slave again.

✄

When they enter Jerry's house, Marek gets the feeling he's in a dream—an army of Saint Josephs stands on the basement floor. Jerry nods for Marek to get to work.

Marek feels uneasy carting the Saint Joseph statues from Jerry's basement to the cop's van. It seems that the Saint can see right into his soul—and Marek resents this intrusion.

More than anything, Marek wants a private space where no one will tell him what to do, where no one will talk when he doesn't want to listen, and where he doesn't have to wear clothes!

When he gets back to Poland, he'll have his own apartment—a place above the nightclub. There, he'll spend the entire day in bed—nude. When he gets up—late in the day—he'll walk around naked. Then, in the evening, he'll put on stylish, comfortable clothes and greet his club patrons. On his nights as a performer he will, of course, don the most fashionable hip-hop attire.

Marek engages in this time-passing fantasy as he totes the Saint Joseph statues. Soon enough, he's forgotten all about the Saint and his penetrating eyes.

✄

Virginia is peeved when the police show up to impound stolen money that thieving people had spent at Redemption Dry Cleaners.

"If they'd spent the money at a grocery store, would you go back and try to retrieve it?" she asks the officers.

"Not if the robber already ate the food."

"Well, these robbers have already partaken of my services—I have removed the sins from their clothes."

The police imply that her business might constitute fraud. They threaten to investigate Redemption Dry Cleaners—and perhaps close its doors—if Virginia doesn't return the money.

Virginia complies—anyway, in the big scheme of things, the money is little more than lint. The bulk of her customers don't steal—they just go into personal debt to pay for her services. They're stealing from no one but themselves.

�֍

After Marek places a load of the St. Josephs into the van, Jerry gives him towels and blankets to put between the statues—so they won't knock into each other and crack.

Jerry hops in the driver's seat, and Marek sits beside him. They take off to find Virgin Mary statues in the front yards of houses in the neighborhood. They'll place Saint Joseph next to her.

Marek is a hard worker. He knows just what to do. When Jerry double-parks in front of a house, Marek jumps out, goes to the back of the van, plucks up a statue, then runs to the front yard and rests it beside the Virgin Mary.

As Jerry had instructed, Marek rings the doorbells. When the owners answer, Marek informs them that, for their good works, they were selected by "The Society of Saint Joseph" to receive a statue for their front yards. All are honored and proud that their good works have been recognized.

28
THE ROAD TO HELL

AFTER SAMMY MANGANO PROMISES TO BUY THERESA A NEW FUR COAT, his wife agrees to having a cat in the house—well, the basement. But Sammy has a nice, finished basement.

Sammy's life is his own now. He has an interesting new career—and his cousin Rosalie has offered to bring him in as a full partner in Palermo Real Estate.

Sammy goes to Confession and admits all his sins. The priest gives him ten rosaries as penance. After Sammy's fingers drop from the last bead of the last rosary, he knows his sins are forgiven. Since Sammy won't have to commit more crimes, he can live the rest of his life free of mortal sin.

As the end of the year approaches, Sammy feels he's leaving his past behind. The new year will mark his transition, his new life.

This is Sammy's state of mind as he enters the Department of Motor Vehicles to get his license renewed. It's December twenty-third, three days before his birthday.

As Sammy stands in line, he reads the newspaper. He's in such a good mood that he doesn't even mind the long wait. But when Sammy looks into the next line, he sees a face that makes him forget his fervent resolutions to sin no more.

It's the now-ancient face of Franco LaRussa—the vicious landlord who'd murdered Sammy's beloved cat, Prince.

On Christmas Eve, Grazyna is invited to a party at Dorota's house. She asks Marek to come along, but her grandson says he has other things to do. She tries to find out what these things are, but, as usual, Marek pretends deafness when Busha pressures him for a response.

Marek hasn't told Busha that he intends to go back to Poland. In a few weeks, he'll take an afternoon flight while she's out of the house. But he'll at least leave her a note—which, after the way she's treated him, is probably more than she deserves.

He knows if he shares his plans, she'll try to talk him out of it. But Marek's determined to leave—to go home and forget his stay in America, as if it were just one long bout of acid indigestion.

✄

Sammy feels as if someone just kicked him in the gut. For years, he's been searching for LaRussa, without any luck. Sammy figured he was long dead or in Florida.

LaRussa glances over at Sammy. Recognition lights up his eyes—Sammy is easy to spot, because his face has changed little since childhood. LaRussa starts to smile at the tenant from the past, then in a rush remembers the details of their last meeting.

The old man sidesteps, trying to ease out of line and escape into the crowd without attracting too much attention. Sammy pretends to read his paper, but can see LaRussa in his peripheral vision—a skill he'd perfected during his years in the Outfit.

Sammy sees the old man drift like a brittle leaf toward the exit. LaRussa keeps looking over his shoulder to find out if Sammy's following him. But Sammy appears to have his eyes on the newspaper.

Sammy tries to figure out if the old man has anybody with him. LaRussa has to be at least ninety years old. It's hard to believe he'd driven himself—in heavy snow—to the Melrose Park facility.

But it looks like LaRussa is alone. Sammy watches the old man stumble through the door, then throws his newspaper on a chair and bolts for the exit.

�֍

When Marek wakes up on Christmas Eve, he feels a weight on his chest. He knows he's too young for a heart attack—but it's happened to people even younger than he is. Along with the weight on his chest, Marek feels dizzy and queasy. The flu? Still, he's hungry. He wouldn't be hungry if he has the flu.

Marek touches his forehead, which feels flaming hot. His heart and his head are pounding.

"Busha!" Marek cries out. "Busha!"

Then Marek remembers about the party at Dorota's house, where Busha is eating and drinking and dancing and singing. How could she! When I'm sick, dying here all alone!

Marek crawls to the bathroom, reaching it just before he retches in agony. The pains and spasms in his stomach are like daggers ripping him apart. He retches until there's nothing left inside, and still it keeps on with dry heaves that tear up his body.

He collapses on the bathroom floor—feeling as if he's just a shell with nothing left inside. He's too weak to move. He's bare-naked on the cold tile floor. The tile is a sickening Pepto-Bismol pink that makes Marek feel as if he's going to be sick again.

He puts one hand on his forehead and another on his stomach, trying to fight back the pains.

The pink tiles bombard his brain—they seems to speak. *You were supposed to rip us out and put in new ones—a nice, soothing light beige shade. But, no, you have not kept your word. You have neglected your duties.*

Marek writhes on the cold tile. Ah, ah, ah, he cries out. He looks up and sees the plastic goose staring at him from the bathtub. Her eyes seem to burn into Marek. It's as if she's projecting thoughts into his mind.

"Your soul is sick," the goose seems to say.

"No, I having wirus!" Marek moans.

"The virus of sin!" Gertrude responds. "Thief! Robber!"

"I only taking money from people affording losing it!" Marek says, covering his eyes against the goose's penetrating look.

"It is a sin!" the goose says.

"No, sin is what hurting someone else. I am not to hurting no one."

"Sin is what harms yourself," Gertrude says.

All at once Marek feels at peace, as if soothing rays are covering his naked body. He removes his hands from his eyes and turns toward the goose. Gertrude's black eyes bore into him. Marek hears her words inside his head.

She says: "Sin is what makes your soul sick."

Then an idea pops into Marek's mind. It's the last thing he wants to do. But he knows he has to do it right away.

Outside the Department of Motor Vehicles, Sammy sees Franco LaRussa stumbling toward his car, his black wool scarf draped around his mouth.

LaRussa can't weigh much more than a hundred pounds. He's trudging against the wind, his coat flapping like a sail behind him. The old man has to grab onto the sides of cars and drag himself along as he inches across the lot.

For a few moments, Sammy just watches his former landlord. He takes in how old and frail he is, how helpless he seems.

Sensing something, the old man turns around. He peers at Sammy through the slice of eyes that isn't covered by his stocking cap and scarf. Sammy catches the gaze all the way across the parking lot. The same eyes—the same mean, black, pitiless eyes that had glared down at little Sammy as the child had wept about his dead cat.

Before he knows it, Sammy is sliding in slick-soled shoes across the parking lot, the rock salt crunching like tiny bones under his feet. LaRussa sees Sammy barreling toward him. He glances around—and knows he has nowhere to run, no place to hide.

LaRussa backs up against a car, holding onto the front and rear door handles for support. The snowflakes fall onto his eyelashes—he blinks, then sees Sammy looming over him. It's their last encounter in reverse. Now, LaRussa is small and helpless—and Sammy is a big strong man glaring down at him with mean, black, pitiless eyes.

Marek places crisp bills into separate envelopes, then drives from one end of the city to the other—the criminal returning to the scene of his crimes.

Marek doesn't want to admit the robberies. Returning the money should be enough—why should he also go to jail?

Giving back the money without getting caught is easy. Marek just enters each place, sets the envelope on the counter, then walks out—pretending he's forgotten something.

By four o'clock, it's already starting to get dark outside. A fairyland lights up the landscape: Santas, reindeer, Nativity scenes, stars, angels, candy canes, toy soldiers. Some yards mix secular Santa with sacred baby Jesus—as if these figures are all equal.

Marek thinks it all very beautiful. It gives him a safe, cozy feeling—as if he'll get away with everything.

"Franco," Sammy says, "where you been?"

It's always better to be cordial at the start of these kinds of encounters.

"Here, there, you know," LaRussa says in a whispery voice.

"Wha'cha doin here?"

"I come up for Christmas from Boca."

"I mean here," Sammy says, pointing to the ground.

"Renew my license, you know," LaRussa says. He's trembling.

"You're still drivin, then?" Sammy says.

"Yeah, why not?"

"How old are you, Franco?"

"Two days, I be ninety."

Two days, Sammy thinks. That means they share the same birthday. But Sammy shrugs off this thought—lots of people are born on the same day—anyway, he doesn't believe in astrology.

"Happy birthday," Sammy says as he grabs LaRussa's scarf and begins to tie it.

"Sammy, don't bother," LaRussa whispers, acting as if he thinks Sammy's trying to help him out.

"I been waitin years for this," Sammy replies, as he grabs the two ends of the scarf and begins to move the knot up to the hanging flesh of LaRussa's throat.

The old man scans the parking lot—his eyes darting from one end to the other. People are coming and going, but they don't pay attention to him and Sammy. If they did, they'd just think it was a son helping a father bundle up against the cold.

LaRussa wants to cry out. But, at his age, can't raise his voice above a whisper. He watches as the knot moves toward his throat, then looks up at Sammy, who's staring right into his eyes. The old man knows this is a deliberate act on Sammy's part. Sammy knows damn sure what he's doing, and won't look away and pretend he doesn't.

By five o'clock, Marek has returned all the money—with one exception. He'll visit Redemption Dry Cleaners the following day and return the two hundred dollars he'd stolen. For some reason, Marek feels he needs to be there on Christmas morning.

✂

LaRussa tries to think of something to say that will convince Sammy not to strangle him. Even though his body is old and frail, his mind is still sharp. Thank God for that.

He closes his eyes, and can feel Sammy's hot breath on his face—it feels like steam coming from a radiator. But as much as the old man searches his mind, nothing comes.

LaRussa has never apologized to anybody in his life. He takes great pride in this. Sure, he's sorry about some of the things he's done. But he'd been under a lot of pressure, and people should understand that. People should know he's sorry. He shouldn't have to say it.

But right now LaRussa sees no other choice. He'll have to break his lifetime vow.

Sammy gets ready to pull on the two ends of the scarf with every ounce of his enormous frame.

✂

After she returns from Dorota's place on Christmas Eve, Grazyna calls for Marek, but he doesn't answer. The house feels empty and lonely.

Grazyna retrieves Gertrude from the bathtub—where the goose likes to sit, Grazyna feels, because it's like a small pond. She wraps a towel around the goose and takes her into the kitchen, placing her on the table.

Grazyna dresses the goose in a cute little Santa outfit, then makes a pot of tea. She sets a tiny cup in front of Gertrude, opens a drawer, and pulls out a small wrapped package.

"A present for you, Gertrude," Grazyna says in Polish.

Grazyna opens the package. Inside, is a shiny golden egg. She holds it up for Gertrude to appreciate.

"Like in the fairy story," Grazyna explains to the goose.

She hopes the goose will take pleasure in this wondrous gift. But Gertrude's eyes look like burned-out light bulbs.

※

"I'm sorry, Sammy," LaRussa says in his low, raspy voice.

Sammy looks down into the old man's eyes. He can't tell whether or not LaRussa means it—or if he's just afraid. Sammy yanks on the scarf.

"I prayed for you, Sammy," LaRussa says.

"You should pray for yourself!" Sammy tells him, still tying the knot.

"I prayed the Blessed Virgin and Saint Joseph would send you another cat you loved as much as Prince," LaRussa whispers into the icy air. The words seem to hang frozen over Sammy's head.

Prince! The miserable old bastard even remembers the cat's name!

"I been prayin for it all these years," LaRussa says, while making the sign of the cross.

Sammy's dead cat's name brings back the whole incident in vivid detail. Sammy can see it, feel it. He's six years old, poor and powerless—and at the mercy of a vicious, sadistic landlord.

Once again, Sammy experiences the fear, the hatred, the pain, the sorrow. The emotions race up and down his body, as if running over wires. The sensations are so strong, so powerful that Sammy feels as if he's going to blow a circuit breaker. Pains shoot around his heart.

Still, he doesn't fear his own death. At last, he'll get revenge on his life's enemy. If they die together, so be it.

But then something occurs to Sammy: *If I die, who'll take care of Tony?* He knows Theresa will get rid of the cat before

Sammy is even in the ground. She'll send Tony to the pound or dump him in the forest preserves. The cat will die for sure, one way or the other.

While Sammy feels these feelings and thinks these thoughts, his hands are locked in position, ready to give the knot one last tug over LaRussa's scrawny throat.

✼

"The goose that laid the golden egg," Grazyna says, giving Gertrude a hint.

Gertrude's eyes seem to grow darker in their sockets.

"It doesn't matter," Grazyna says, sipping her tea.

Still, Grazyna wishes the goose had shown some enthusiasm for the gift. It had taken Grazyna the better part of a morning to paint the old L'eggs container, trying to get it free of streaks, drying it on one side, before painting the other. She'd even bought—yes bought!—the spray paint at the hardware store.

Grazyna tells herself that all the work and all the money were a waste. Even worse, Grazyna feels hurt and embarrassed that she'd poured out her love in this uncharacteristic way—only to have her gift rejected.

Grazyna tries to pretend it doesn't matter—but she vows to get back to her normal pattern: A hard shell that no one can penetrate.

✼

"Just tell me one thing," LaRussa says, his voice cracking like an adolescent boy's.

Sammy still holds the scarf, ready to tie the final knot. He has to decide. Does he kill LaRussa and get revenge? Or does he let the miserable bastard go, and drive home to his adorable Tony?

When Sammy doesn't answer, LaRussa says: "Sammy, did the Virgin and Saint Joseph send you another cat?"

Again, Sammy thinks of Tony. He loves Tony. He has to admit that he loves Tony as much as he'd loved Prince.

"Yeah, so what?" Sammy shoots back.

"So, I prayed for it to happen," LaRussa says.

"So, what, I'm suppos'ta thank you?"

"No. Don't thank me. Just forgive me! Forgive me!"

The old man bows his head and begins to shake with tears.

"Asshole!" Sammy says, grabbing the old man by the shoulders and shaking him like a dust mop.

"I'm sorry, Sammy," the old man wails.

"What you did sent me on a life of crime!" Sammy says.

"You gotta take responsibility for your own actions!"

Like Sammy, the old man watches daytime talk shows and is familiar with the basics of popular psychology.

In the sky, a slit of sun breaks through the gray clouds. At the same time, an idea surfaces through Sammy's rage.

"You still own property?" Sammy asks.

"It's in the family," LaRussa says, wondering about this new turn in the conversation.

"Okay, I make you a deal," Sammy says.

"You want my property?"

"If you or anybody in your family sells any property, I want the listing. Hear me?" Sammy says.

He takes a business card out of his pocket and stuffs it in the old man's glove.

"So, if I do it, we got a deal?" LaRussa asks, sliding down the car. Sammy yanks up the old man by his shoulders and props him against the vehicle.

Sammy knows what the deal is: his forgiveness in exchange for the old man's listings. He knows it's only conditional forgiveness. This makes Sammy feel a whole lot better about letting LaRussa off the hook.

✄

Grazyna wonders which Mass she should attend the next day—though she doesn't feel like going at all. It's a Holy Day of Obligation, and she must fulfill her duty. But she wants to take in the services at Redemption Dry Cleaners, too.

Grazyna decides she'll attend nine o'clock Mass, then head to the eleven o'clock service at Redemption Dry Cleaners. She has a feeling that something exciting might happen over there.

29
SO THIS IS CHRISTMAS

AT THE MOST DRAMATIC MOMENT IN THE MASS— when Father Spinelli raises the communion wafer in consecration—a loud explosion booms through the church. Spinelli always gets caught up in this part of the ritual and thinks he's imagining a celestial sound effect.

But the congregation reacts not with awe, but with sheer fear. Nobody has the inclination to stay and pray—and trust that God will save them. People scramble for the exits, babies wail, and an old man in a walker almost gets mowed down in the chaos. The same thought occurs to most adult parishioners: *It must be another case of exploding gas lines! The City still has not managed to fix them all!*

But, after a few moments, the frantic activity stops as fast as it had started. The church has not exploded. The blast happened someplace else, somewhere nearby.

Two ushers open the massive church doors—revealing the smoldering scene across the parish grounds. The rectory is now a mere tangle of flames and rubble.

At the altar, Father Spinelli still holds the communion wafer over his head. He knows what caused the explosion: the forgotten bomb in his study, the same place where his musical compositions were tucked away—and he'd neglected to make copies of the sheet music.

The priest has one comforting thought: Lucky for me that I recorded those songs—at least those survived the blast.

With the furor at Saint Francis, Grazyna doesn't get to Redemption Dry Cleaners until a few minutes after eleven o'clock. She slips into the building as the proceedings are getting started. Grazyna has to wedge her way into a standing-room spot in the back—you'd think the Pope was going to appear for how many people have shown up.

As always, Virginia Martyniak starts the services by playing the organ. While Virginia plays, Grazyna glances around the room. Christmas trees decorate every corner, pine wreaths hang from the ceiling, and the entire place is festooned with red ribbons, hanging ornaments, and Italian lights. The place looks better than a downtown department store.

The music ends with a strong major chord that seems to hang in the air. Virginia pushes her now-hefty body from the bench and waddles to the center of the platform, a microphone in front of her. Grazyna notices the big belly bulging from the woman's pink choir robe. Really, Grazyna thinks, she should have that checked out.

"Happy Yuletide, customers," Virginia says.

The crowd murmurs a chirpy response.

"As you know, on this day we celebrate the birth of the Christ Child."

The crowd nods—taking great comfort in affirming the obvious.

"But here, at Redemption Dry Cleaners, we also celebrate dear Gertrude's birthday."

Virginia's face glows with mother love as she indicates the large painting of Gertrude suspended on the wall behind her.

"For on this day, five years ago, my dear husband gave me Gertrude as a Christmas gift."

The audience members crane their necks for a glimpse of Virginia's husband, who's smiling in the front row.

For months, Herb has been known as "Virginia's husband." One customer even calls him Mr. Virginia. Still, Herb doesn't let it bother him. As always, he turns to Saint Joseph as his model for behavior. How can one compete with a superior presence such as Mary or Virginia? You can't, Herb realizes. Best to just hop aboard, and feel lucky you're along for the ride.

"So, here, in this place established in Gertrude's honor," Virginia says, "we also celebrate her precious birthday. Hallelujah!" She raises her hands in the air.

"Hallelujah!" the crowd responds, glad for something to do.

"This is indeed a special occasion. For the spirit has informed me that today one lucky individual has the chance to hit the jackpot—absolute absolution for a lifetime."

"Oooohhhh," says the crowd.

"This individual must be willing to pay the price the spirit names, no questions asked."

Grazyna looks around—wondering who'd spend money in such a wanton way.

Virginia goes on: "The spirit has named a sum and told me to announce it. The spirit says this amount will ring a bell in the mind of someone here today. This person will have one chance and one chance only to pay the price and receive unconditional eternal redemption."

The crowd says, "Ahhh."

"That's right, customers, the person who pays the price can be assured that hell or purgatory does not await them in the afterlife. This individual will go straight to heaven after death!"

Again, the crowd expresses its audible awe and wonder.

Grazyna is intrigued. Who could it be? How much would the person have to pay?

"The individual is to walk forward, hand me their winter coat, and the transaction will be sealed."

Everyone in the crowd inhales at the same time—in anticipation of the sum that Virginia is about to announce.

"The figure the spirit gave me is $112,123.04."

The crowd lets out a collective gasp.

Grazyna understands right away. It's the exact amount she's netted from Spotless Souls Housekleening Service during the past few months. It's the money she intends to use as a down payment on a six-flat apartment building.

"I ask the individual to come forward now, or the opportunity will be lost forever."

The people turn in their chairs, bob their heads up and down, looking this way and that. Does anyone in their midst have that kind of money?

Grazyna doesn't want to lose her chance. But she doesn't want to lose her money, either. She thinks: *What if I go up now, give her my coat, and then later say I've changed my mind? This way, if I want to change my mind I can. But I won't lose my opportunity.*

"The spirit has told me to give the individual sixty seconds to make up their mind," Virginia says. "Customers, bow your heads for a minute of silence."

To Grazyna, the minute is a painful eternity. Her mind sprints back and forth between two extremes. Yes, no. I will, I won't. It's true, it's false. It's right, it's wrong.

As Virginia stares at her wristwatch ticking off the final seconds, something catches her attention.

She sees a young man proceeding in lockstep up the center aisle. In his outstretched hands is a box containing Gertrude and her clothes. The goose is wearing her wedding dress and veil—the outfit she'd had on during the robbery over six months before.

When she turns and sees her grandson, Grazyna is furious. How dare Marek return Gertrude to the dry cleaning woman! The goose belongs to Grazyna. She'd given Marek a week's room and board in exchange for the bird and the outfits.

Grazyna doesn't know Marek anymore. He's become so sullen and difficult to deal with. To Grazyna, it seems that

Marek has developed an overzealous conscience. First, he wants me to stop charging for cleaning away sins. Now, he returns the goose. And why—when the woman is doing so well without her?

Virginia recognizes Gertrude right away. She's different from all the other plastic geese in the neighborhood. She has a special aura, a presence—the result, in part, of all the love Virginia had showered her with during their time together, as if she'd given the goose part of her soul.

Virginia almost looses her balance as she navigates the platform steps. Somehow, she manages to scramble down to the aisle, where she lumbers toward Gertrude with extended hands and wet cheeks.

"Customers," Virginia says. "This is what the spirit promised! If the individual did not pay the $112,123.04, then Gertrude would be returned to me."

Virginia scoops Gertrude from the box in Marek's hands. She embraces the goose, then holds Gertrude high above her head for the audience to see.

There isn't a dry eye in the dry cleaners.

Herb elbows through the crowd, and at last reaches Virginia's side. He puts his hand on Virginia's back and guides her up to the platform. He's afraid that all the excitement—happy as it is—will send Virginia into a swoon or, worse, early labor.

Herb leads Virginia to the organ bench. She sits on the end of the bench, with Gertrude in what's left of her lap.

Herb trots down the steps and retrieves Gertrude's box of clothing from Marek, who stands stiff as a wooden soldier at the foot of the platform.

"Where did you find Gertrude, my son?" Virginia asks.

It doesn't occur to Virginia that Marek is the one who'd taken Gertrude—even though he's wearing the very same clothes, minus the black ski mask.

Marek wants to give back the goose, but he doesn't want to go to jail. Still, at this delicate moment, he can't lie and commit a sin.

"I finding goose in neighborhood, with this," Marek says, as he extends an envelope to Virginia.

"Bring it up here, my son," Virginia says.

Grazyna just knows what's inside the envelope. Her idiot grandson is also returning the money he'd stolen during the robbery. What's the point? The woman now has wads of money—she doesn't need another trifling two hundred dollars!

With his head bowed, Marek sidles up the platform steps and extends the envelope toward the waiting woman. Virginia nods to Herb, who lifts Gertrude from Virginia's lap and places her on the sermon lectern.

Virginia takes the envelope from Marek, rips it open, and removes two smooth, new hundred-dollar bills. She holds them up for the audience to see.

"This is the amount of money that was taken when Gertrude was stolen. And now it has been returned," Virginia says.

"Ahhhh!" responds the crowd.

During the moments when the crowd is savoring this dramatic turn, Marek peeks over his shoulder. He spots the stained glass windows where he's depicted stealing Gertrude. He feels ashamed and uncovered—his dark, sinful self memorialized for all time and for all to see.

Even though he's returned the goose and the money, Marek still feels guilty. He'd hoped to gain some relief, a lightened burden. But he still feels the same—worse, really. The stained glass windows have made him feel the full weight of his sins.

"Where did you find these things, my son?" Virginia asks, when the crowd noise quiets down.

Marek turns and spots Busha in the back of the room. Across even that great distance, Marek can see the black look in Busha's eyes. She thinks he's a fool. She's angry, believing he'll give himself away—and with himself, her as well.

What will people think if they find out she has a thief for a grandson? No matter that she's an inveterate thief herself. At least she's a smart one. She never gets caught and she never repents and she never has second thoughts and she never gives anything back.

Marek turns and looks at Virginia. Again, he admires her beautiful golden hair.

"Where did you find these things, my boy?" Virginia coaxes.

"It is me," Marek says.

"You?" Virginia asks.

Marek grabs a ski mask out of his pocket and pulls it over his face.

"Ohhh!" the crowd gasps, then, as one, looks to the stained glass windows where Marek's crime is commemorated.

Grazyna grinds her false teeth. *Idjota! Cielak!* At this moment, she thinks Marek the stupidest individual who's ever lived—even dumber than his fire-eating grandfather!

Virginia stands up and puts her hand on Marek's shoulder. Marek sees squares of light reflected in Virginia's hair. He looks into her bright blue eyes and begins to weep.

"I was robber," he sobs.

Women scream. Others faint. Men begin to storm the platform.

Virginia holds up her hand to calm the crowd. She knows the mass of people can become a mob with the slightest nudge.

"You have come here to repent?" Virginia asks the sobbing Marek.

Marek nods. He can't speak.

"Kneel down, my son."

Marek obeys. Virginia places her hand on his head and closes her eyes.

"Heavenly spirit, use your most powerful cleaning solutions to wipe the sins from this man's soul."

Right away, Marek feels as if his body has been plugged into a powerful current. He's sure that sparks are flying from his head. Then he feels as if the inside of his body is getting worked on by tiny vacuum cleaners, scrub brushes, and floor polishers.

When he opens his eyes, Virginia is smiling down at him.

"You are forgiven," Virginia says. "Go and sin no more."

She pulls the black ski mask from his head and flings it into the laundry basket in front of Gertrude's picture.

Marek stands up, dazed. He wobbles on his feet as he steps from the platform and staggers up the center aisle.

The audience breaks into applause. Marek offers the people a wistful smile. What he's just done begins to sink in. He feels embarrassed, exposed. He can't wait to go home and bury himself in bed.

30
NEW YEAR'S RESOLUTIONS

IN THE EARLY WEEKS OF JANUARY, Jerry Valentino is arrested, Marek Jablonski flies back to Poland, Sammy Mangano starts real estate classes, and Emmett Dobbs begins an extended leave from the post office to prepare for his first gallery showing.

Tony, Sammy's cat, settles into the Mangano household. Soon, he's no longer relegated to the basement—and lounges at will on Theresa's fancy furniture. Sammy is jealous about Theresa's growing relationship with Tony—he'd hoped to keep the cat for himself. But he knows better than let his possessiveness get in the way of a larger good—domestic peace. He'll have to share.

Virginia Martyniak continues to hold Sunday services at Redemption Dry Cleaners as her pregnancy progresses. There are murmurs in the congregation about the woman's growing belly, but Virginia never says a word about it—so the people figure she's just gaining weight.

After the debacle with the bomb, Father Spinelli has to take up residence at a rectory in a nearby parish. He buys back one of his CDs from a parishioner—who charged him double the purchase price. Some people will always try to capitalize on another person's disaster, thinks Spinelli. He spends many weeks transcribing the music. The priest waits for new compositions, but none arrive.

Antonio Vivaldi, the dead composer, will have nothing more to do with Spinelli. What a careless imbecile, Vivaldi thinks. I hand him masterworks and he allows them to get blown to bits!

Vivaldi pleads with Virginia to give him another chance. But, with the woman's booming business and her burgeoning belly, she has no time.

The dead priest decides to leave Chicago for the West Coast. He plans to try his luck with a famous Latino guitarist, who'd been channeling for other dead musicians—including John Coltrane and Jimi Hendrix. Vivaldi hopes that Carlos can squeeze in some time for him.

Annette Valentino puts Jerry's house up for sale to pay his legal bills. Because of the nature of his alleged crime, Jerry is denied bond. Annette withdraws her annulment proceedings and visits Jerry as often as allowed.

With the money she's netted in her housecleaning service, Grazyna Jablonski plans to buy an apartment building. Never one to turn down an opportunity to make even one extra cent, Grazyna puts a sign in her window—announcing she has a room for rent. With Marek gone, why should she waste the space?

31

NO PLACE LIKE HOME

FOR OVER A YEAR, EMMETT AND DENNIS HAD WORKED OPPOSITE SHIFTS. They'd spent most of their time together during the weekends.

But now that Emmett is on leave, the house seems as tiny as a shoebox. Dennis is always poking his head into the attic while Emmett is trying to paint—sometimes complaining that Emmett has the window open with the heat on. All these petty arguments and interruptions screw up Emmett's concentration, taking him hours to get back into the groove.

Emmett has serious thoughts about breaking up with Dennis. But it'd be too big of a change right now. And right now Emmett needs to concentrate on finishing his paintings for the show.

On this day, just as Emmett's ideas are starting to spark, he hears Dennis's footsteps on the attic stairs.

"You want rice or pasta with the chicken?" Dennis asks.

Emmett turns. Dennis has a cat slung under each arm. The cats look like huge hairy slugs.

Emmett doesn't answer. He doesn't want to lose his temper. He has to focus on his artwork. He figures maybe Dennis will get the message and leave.

"How about couscous then?"

Still, Emmett tries to maintain his focus.

"I could make mashed potatoes," Dennis continues.

A low rumbling starts in the back of Emmett's throat. He's growling. The cats recoil.

Emmett sets down his brush. He stands up, bending over because he can't rise to his full height in the tiny attic.

"How many times I gotta tell you!" Emmett says.

"It's just a picture!"

"It's my life's work!"

"Well, what about our relationship? Am I less important than your pictures?"

Emmett doesn't say anything. It'll do no good to argue. Yes, Dennis is less important to him than the paintings. Everything is.

✀

Grazyna sees Emmett staring at her through the windows up high in the door. She hasn't seen the mailman on his route in a few months—a new man had taken over.

When Grazyna opens the door, she asks: "Mailman, you having letter for me?"

Emmett explains that he's taking a leave of absence without pay. To Grazyna, this is a foreign concept. Who would take time off from work without pay?

"I'm working on my paintings and my sculptures," Emmett explains. He points to Dennis's front yard, which sports a carved wooden statue of Saint Francis of Assisi.

"I made that," he says.

"Italian saint," Grazyna says to herself.

Emmett inquires about her room for rent. He tells her he needs a quiet place where he can do his painting.

"You getting paint on floor!" she says.

"I'll be very careful," Emmett says. "How much you chargin for the room?"

When she tells him, he offers to pay double. Grazyna grasps his hands and looks up at Emmett with misty eyes. Then she invites him inside to discuss the particular arrangements.

As they eat pierogi and Polish sausage, Emmett tells Grazyna how Dennis is driving him nuts.

"I can't get no peace and quiet," Emmett says.

Grazyna shakes her head and looks up at Emmett with big brown sorrowful eyes. She pats his large hand. It doesn't occur to Grazyna that she'd never shown a drop of compassion for her own grandson—but here she is ladling it out to someone who's little more than a passing acquaintance.

Yes, Grazyna feels very sorry for Emmett. The poor man at last has the money to realize his lifelong dream, and he can't get a moment's peace. It's sad, so sad. She wipes a tear from her eye with her apron.

Just then, Emmett sees Grazyna in a new way. She looks like the sorrowful Madonna, the essence of all compassionate motherhood. He has an overpowering urge to paint her.

"Will you sit for me?" Emmett asks.

"I sitting," she says, wondering what the man is talking about.

When Emmett explains, Grazyna is flattered—but she doesn't let Emmett know it. She decides if she does this favor for him, he'll have to do something for her.

"What's that?" Emmett asks.

"You making statue Saint Stanislaus Krakow."

Grazyna needs the statue soon—if she wants to find just the right apartment building at a bargain price. For years she's promised the saint a statue. Now here, at last, is her chance.

"You got a picture of him?" Emmett asks.

Grazyna jumps up and grabs a framed icon from the kitchen counter.

"Here," she says.

"No problem," Emmett tells her. "I'll get going on it as soon as I get a block of wood."

"I having wood," Grazyna says. She'd scavenged it from a demolished building—Marek had hauled it home and put it in the garage. See, Grazyna thinks, you never know when something will come in handy.

"First, let me do some work on your picture," Emmett says. "Okay?"

"Tak," Grazyna says. "But saint statue you starting tomorrow!"

Emmett races back home to get his paints and canvases. He feels inspired and has to begin that portrait of Grazyna right away.

⁂

"Why you wanna throw good money away renting a room when you got all the space you need right here?" Dennis asks Emmett as he packs his things.

Emmett decides that—no matter what—he will not get into an argument with Dennis. He says nothing.

"You got somethin goin on with that old lady's grandson?" Dennis asks.

"Jesus, Dennis," Emmett says. "He back in Poland."

"The old lady, then?" Dennis says. He wants to start an argument in any way that he can.

"The old lady is like my grandma, for Christ sake!"

"You never even visit your own grandma, and here you're spending time with somebody else," Dennis says. He knows it's a weak sally, but at this point he'll try anything.

"My grandma live in Detroit."

"You don't love me any more," Dennis says, bringing up what he'd wanted to bring up.

"I love you, Dennis. I just need some space, okay?" Emmett says.

"No, it's not okay! It is not okay!" Dennis says. "First, I lose Punkin—and now I lose you!"

Emmett has an idea—a way to get Dennis off his case. It's dangerous, but Emmett is desperate.

"You not goin'ta believe this," he says. "But I found out what happen to Punkin."

After Emmett tells him, Dennis says: "So that's why you were talking to that guy after Mass that day?"

"Yeah," Emmett says. "I seen him with Punkin and I wanted to get the cat back. I didn't tell you so's you didn't get your hopes up for no reason."

�֎

Emmett's ploy had been the perfect antidote for Dennis's jealous snit. Right away, Dennis shifts his attention from Emmett and starts plotting how to get Punkin back. He rushes down from the attic and leaves Emmett alone.

As he packs his paints and canvases, Emmett prays Dennis won't do anything foolish or crazy. He knows how much Sammy Mangano loves the cat—and hopes Dennis doesn't get himself killed trying to retrieve his cherished pet.

✖

As he paints Grazyna, Emmett feels as if things inside of him are healing. All the hurts, all the slights, all the offenses inflicted by his mother are just washing away.

He'd posed Grazyna in her faded babushka and an old skirt and sweater. She sits in Marek's former bedroom—now Emmett's studio—on a rickety kitchen chair. Her hands are folded in her lap. Her brown eyes are filled with a range of emotions: sadness, compassion, suffering, love.

With each stroke of the paintbrush, Emmett gets the sense that he's painting in a new life for himself. After a lifetime of conflict, Emmett can make peace with the mother who lives inside him.

✖

In the morning, Dennis waits in his car down the block from Sammy Mangano's house. He'd used his investigating skills—the ones usually reserved for checking up on a boyfriend—to find out Sammy's last name and where he lived.

When Sammy leaves the house around 7:30, Dennis sees Punkin jump in the front window. The cat's eyes follow

Sammy as he gets in his car. Sammy blows Punkin a kiss and waves goodbye as he drives away.

At ten o'clock, Dennis sees Theresa Mangano walk out the front door. Again, Punkin jumps in the front window and watches her. She, too, blows the cat a kiss and waves goodbye as she takes off.

Dennis parks in the alley behind Sammy's house. He lets himself in the yard and walks up to the back door. He takes out a credit card and springs the lock.

Dennis walks through the kitchen and dining room—lots of mirrors and bad pictures in gold frames—and enters the living room.

Punkin is stretched out on the embroidered sofa washing his stomach. He jolts upright when he spots Dennis.

"Punkin!" Dennis says, racing toward his former pet.

He sits next to the cat and begins to stroke his back. Punkin tolerates the embrace, but doesn't purr or nuzzle Dennis's hand.

Dennis feels like crying. His favorite cat—one he'd lavished affection on—and this is the reception he gets! He picks up the now-plump Punkin, sticks the cat under his arm, and heads toward the back door.

Punkin starts to scream and yowl, clawing into the sleeve of Dennis's leather coat.

Dennis figures that once he gets the cat home, everything will be just as it used to be: Punkin following him around the house, Punkin flopping on the floor and rolling around, Punkin dozing in his lap, Punkin curled up next to him in bed at night.

The cat bites into Dennis's leather glove. Still, Dennis refuses to get the message. It's his cat and, by God, he's going to take him back!

�֎

The drive home is horrendous. Punkin runs around the car with his fur standing up, and spends most of the ride hanging upside down—his claws in the upholstered ceiling.

When they reach Dennis's house, Dennis grabs the cat and holds him down as he removes the purple collar and the "Anthony" nametag. On the way inside, Dennis throws the collar in the trashcan—while Punkin squirms and screeches in his arms.

✂

Dennis has many cats. He feeds at least a dozen strays, and relegates them to the backyard in summer and the indoor porch in winter. But he allows four cats—besides Punkin—in the house.

When Punkin jumps from Dennis's arms, the other four cats stroll into the kitchen to see what is going on. They surround Punkin and try to sniff him.

Punkin runs into the living room and hides under the sofa. He's been dethroned! He was a king at the Manganos's house—and now here he is just one cat among a throng. He feels as if his heart is crumbling into litter-sized pieces. He can't help it. He starts to moan and cry out in pain. Sammy! Sammy! I want Sammy, he thinks.

But then Punkin stops crying. He remembers who he is. He's a special cat, a medium. He'll send Sammy a message.

32
ASKING PRICE

AT THREE O'CLOCK, Sammy is scheduled to show a six-flat to Grazyna Jablonski. He's been showing her buildings for a few weeks. But he believes this one is a winner.

He'll make his first sale as a real estate agent! And it's his own listing—one of the LaRussa family properties—so he'll make a ton of money, plus get some payback from his old landlord.

Grazyna meets up with Sammy at the Palermo Real Estate office on Belmont Avenue, near the forest preserves. As they drive to the property, Sammy hears a loud message in his head. It's Tony. He's in trouble. Dennis Vitale kidnapped him. Right now, he's under Dennis's couch, waiting for Sammy to rescue him.

Sammy makes a U-turn and heads in the direction of Dennis's house.

"Where we are going?" Grazyna asks.

"I gotta make a little stop first," Sammy says.

"We having appointment," Grazyna tells him, tapping on her Cinderella wristwatch, a prized cemetery find.

Sammy turns and gives the woman his look of death. Grazyna decides to go along for the ride.

✤

When the doorbell rings, Dennis is in the shower. He has to get ready to leave for work at four o'clock.

When nobody answers, Sammy looks to Grazyna in the car, holds up his finger, then jimmies the lock.

He walks into the living room, bends down, peeks under the sofa, and says: "I'm here, Tony."

260

Tony leaps into Sammy's arms.

When Dennis steps out of the bathroom—stark nude—he sees Sammy hugging and kissing the cat.

"Get your hands off Punkin!" Dennis says, rushing toward Sammy. Tony crawls up Sammy's coat and perches on his shoulder.

"The effin cat is mine and his effin name is Tony!" Sammy says.

Dennis tries to grab the cat, but slips and slides on the wood floor with his wet feet. It's all he can do to keep his balance.

As Sammy heads toward the door, he turns and says, "Don't you ever, ever try this again—or I'll…"

Sammy stops himself. He was about to say, "kill you." But he's vowed to sin no more. Some habits are so hard to break, he thinks.

"…Or you'll what?" Dennis taunts, kicking toward Sammy's shin, but missing.

"Or I'll make you sorry, asshole!" Sammy says. He wants to kick Dennis back, but afraid the sudden movement might cause Tony to fall off his shoulder.

"It's wrong to steal somebody else's pet!" Dennis tells him.

Sammy knows it's wrong. But he didn't steal Tony. He'd rescued him from neglect at Jerry Valentino's house. The cop is the guilty party who'd nabbed the cat.

"The cat wants to live with me! End of story," Sammy says, slamming the door on his way out.

As they drive to the six-flat, Tony sits next to Grazyna in the back seat. The cat is relieved to get away from Dennis's house. How horrifying! Just thinking about himself as one cat in a big brood makes Tony tremble. After a few minutes, he falls into an exhausted sleep.

Grazyna strokes the cat as they drive along, and the worn-out cat puts up no resistance.

"What you are calling cat?" she asks Sammy.

"Tony."

"Like for cereal commercial?"

Sammy hopes Jerry didn't name Tony after the tiger in the cereal commercial. Sammy doesn't like commercials—and there were a ton of them in the shows he used to watch during the daytime.

But Sammy no longer sits around watching television. He's a businessman who works a regular, respectable, daytime job.

"No," Sammy says, answering Grazyna's question. "He's named after Saint Anthony of Padua."

Italian saints! Grazyna is so sick of them.

❦

The building is a beauty—a sparkling-clean, gorgeous six-flat in pristine condition. Grazyna gasps when she sees it. The building is the perfect embodiment of her long-held vision. And it's on a beautiful, tree-lined block in a nice neighborhood.

"How much asking price is?" Grazyna says as they tour one of the apartments. Lovely, lovely, lovely, she thinks—a lots of light, pristine walls, perfect floors, shining windows.

"Six fifty," Sammy says.

Grazyna holds her lips tight. She has to think! She really, really wants this building. But she doesn't want to pay this kind of money.

"How long building is for sale?" she asks.

"It just came on the market today. Everybody thinks it's gonna go in a few days," Sammy says. "If you want it, you better make a bid right away."

❦

Grazyna avoids paying full price for anything. At rummage sales, thrift stores, and flea markets, she usually starts out by offering half the asking price.

But this is different. Grazyna knows she'll lose the building if she places a low bid. Somebody is going to get that building right away—and Grazyna wants that somebody to be her.

Once, on a television show, Grazyna had listened as some kind of expert had said: "If you really want something, pay the asking price." This had stuck in Grazyna's mind—because, at the time, she'd found it so absurd.

But, here it is coming back to her. She knows it's the right thing to do. Still, she's a skinflint down to the spirals of her DNA—and her genes shriek at the possibility of wasting good money.

But, she reasons, no one will offer what the seller is asking. People will place their initial bids somewhat less, a bit less, or a great deal less than the asking price. Where, thought Grazyna, should I come in?

When they get back to Sammy's real estate office, Grazyna slumps into a chair, holds her head in her hands, and thinks hard. She picks up a pencil, writes a figure on a piece of paper, and hands the paper to Sammy.

When Sammy looks at the figure, he has to hold onto the desk so he doesn't keel onto the floor.

❃

All day, Grazyna frets. She busies herself around the house, getting partway through this task or that before moving on to another. Every half-hour, she calls Sammy.

"You getting more offer for building?" she asks.

"Yeah," Sammy says, "I'll keep you posted."

Still, Grazyna keeps calling back. After a while, he just refuses to take her calls.

To calm her nerves, Grazyna embarks on six different activities at once—she bangs pots and pans around, sweeps floors, polishes furniture, washes windows, vacuums, and cleans the bathroom. The house is a din of aimless noise.

Emmett hears the ruckus all the way out in the garage, where he's working on the carving of Saint Stanislaus of Krakow. He decides he'd better find out what's going on.

"You havin a party in here, Busha?" he asks when he tromps into the kitchen.

Grazyna collapses into a chair and starts to sob. She holds her apron to her eyes and weeps.

Emmett opens his mouth to speak, but doesn't want to disturb Busha—he's afraid he just might say the wrong thing.

He tries to figure out what's the matter. Did someone die? Is somebody sick?

At last, Grazyna speaks: "I bidding on new building."

"What you offer for it?" Emmett says.

Grazyna just shakes her head, raises her apron to her eyes, and sheds hot tears.

✄

Grazyna feels like the old rag doll that her German Shepherd used to play with—open seams with sawdust spilling out.

The six-flat is the first thing Grazyna has really, really wanted that she had a real chance to attain. And it's the first time in her life she's been willing to pay the price.

Yes! She'd not only offered the asking price—she'd offered more! She can't lose that building! But opening her purse after all these years has destroyed Grazyna. She feels as if her entire being is dwindling to nothing.

Yes, she thinks, maybe I will get the building, but I will no longer be myself. It will just be some broken shell of my former self who owns that building. Do I want it so much that I will risk losing myself—the self that has kept me going for all these long years of a difficult life?

Grazyna considers calling Sammy and withdrawing her offer. But something holds her back. She will wait and see what happens. After all, she can always say she'd changed her mind—that when she'd placed her offer, she'd had a lapse of sanity.

�

As Grazyna, inconsolable, weeps at the kitchen table, Emmett busies himself making dinner. Before taking up residence in Grazyna's spare room, Emmett had never cooked. But after moving in, he started to watch the old lady as she worked in the kitchen. Before long, he asked her to teach him how to cook.

Right now, Grazyna is so distraught that she doesn't even chime in with her usual orders and instructions. She just lets Emmett have the run of her kitchen.

Grazyna gazes at the chair where Gertrude used to sit. She holds her apron to her eyes and sobs even harder. The word "Gertrude" escapes her lips.

Emmett heard about what happened to the goose—Grazyna told him how Marek returned the bird to the woman at Redemption Dry Cleaners. Right now, Emmett wants to cheer up his landlady. He has an idea how to do it.

✷

Things have changed at Redemption Dry Cleaners. For one, Virginia no longer waits on the customers. People drop off their clothes with Giovanni, who now works as Virginia's second-in-command.

After collecting items of clothing from a dozen or so people, Giovanni tells them to wait in the lobby. Then he rolls a large hamper with the tagged items into an inner sanctum, where Virginia sits relaxing on a chaise longue—with Gertrude next to her on a golden pedestal.

Giovanni shows Virginia each item, and she tells him which sins to check off on the dry cleaning receipt. After each batch is completed, Giovanni rolls the hamper back to the lobby, where he tells the customers their fees and collects the money.

This new arrangement has created competition among the customers. No longer do they receive personal service from Virginia—and private discussion of their fees and sins. Now, an entire waiting room of people can listen as names are called out and fees are discussed.

"Antonelli—$16.99."

"Majewski—$16.98."

"Hudson—$56.25."

"Ignacio—$98.42."

"Kosinski—$27.55."

"Phillips—$102.76."

Customers with lower fees—and fewer sins—strut up to the counter, proud at the superior state of their souls. Customers with higher fees slink to the counter, shoulders sagging, faces red, as they cough up the cash or credit to pay for their sins.

But soon the inevitable happens. While Giovanni is in the inner chamber with Virginia, customers start laying odds about who'll have the lowest and highest fees. In no time, Redemption Dry Cleaners is the biggest gambling parlor on the Northwest Side of Chicago.

33
OUT OF CONTROL

WHEN EMMETT STEPS UP TO THE COUNTER WITH HIS POST OFFICE SHIRT, he demands to speak with Virginia.

Giovanni shakes his head and says, "Virginia, she no longer wait on customer."

"I need to see her. Now," Emmett says.

"No, is impossible, sorry, please excuse," Giovanni says, looking hangdog. Virginia had instructed him to always show empathy for the customers, most of all when denying a request.

Emmett pounds his fist on the counter.

"I demand service!" he says.

"Yes," Giovanni says, tagging the shirt. "Right back."

Giovanni speeds to Virginia's chamber and shows her the item of clothing. In no time, he's back at the counter.

"Is $212,414 for shirt."

Emmett stares at the little man. It's the exact sum he'd gained from selling his share of the cocaine to Sammy Mangano.

He grabs his shirt from Giovanni, shoves past the Italian shrimp, and barges into Virginia's special private room, where she indulges in her special private thoughts.

❇

Like many spiritual leaders, Virginia finds the responsibility daunting, demanding, and draining. Like others in her line of work, Virginia more and more retreats into the background— leaving the day-to-day drudgery to underlings.

And why not? After all, the spirit chose her as a special messenger. She shouldn't have to bother herself with drone work. Besides, she must have done something—or shown herself worthy of this blessing in some way. She deserves a life of luxury and ease.

For another thing, she's pregnant with a divine child—and the birth is imminent. She needs to rest and prepare herself for the forthcoming event. She wavers between wild happiness and deep depression—ecstatic that her long-held dream is about to come true, and deflated that her long-held dream is about to come true.

As Virginia stares at Gertrude, she wonders: What can I wish for now?

Virginia plays with a range of fantasies to lift her spirits—hoping that one will lighten her black mood.

When Emmett invades her private room, Virginia is imagining herself as the most famous spiritual leader on earth. She travels the globe, conducting services in huge arenas. Her picture is on the cover of *Time* and *Newsweek* the very same week. She's on television. She meets on a regular basis with the president of the United States, offering counsel and advice.

These thoughts paint a blissful smile on Virginia's lips.

Emmett takes one look at the woman and figures she's high on some kind of drug. But Virginia is high on fame, high on success. She's high, feeling she deserves all her good fortune—that she's a notch above the average Joe or Jane in this world. She doesn't have to plod or struggle—she just knows, she just does, she just lives and breathes and it all comes with such ease for her.

"This bird belongs to a friend 'a mine," Virginia hears Emmett say—snapping her back to the present.

Emmett tosses his post office shirt over Gertrude and looks for a back exit.

"What's going on?" Virginia says, trying to rise to her feet. But she's as round as a rising moon, and can't manage to sit upright, let alone stand.

"You!" Virginia says, pointing her finger at Emmett. "You have the shirt with $212,414 worth of sins on it!"

"Yeah," says Emmett, "and I ain't leavin it with you!"

"Giovanni!" Virginia yells.

Small, but brave, Giovanni leaps into the room brandishing a wire hanger he'd just pulled apart. The wire dangles in the air before him. He whips it in Emmett's direction, but his adversary has found the back exit, and has whisked the goose—and her box of outfits—out of Redemption Dry Cleaners.

Outside, Giovanni runs after Emmett, lashing the black wire in the air. The wire flies backwards and hits Giovanni straight in the face, just missing his eye. Giovanni put his hand to his stinging cheek. When he looks up, Emmett is gone.

✖

As he drives off with the goose in the back seat, Emmett is overcome with the giggles. Yes, that was fun. Really fun! He showed Virginia! He stole her precious goose—and got away with it! Ha ha!

After his laughter subsides, Emmett sighs. He'd set out on a mission, and had achieved his goal. But he's happiest just thinking about how glad Busha will be when she sees Gertrude again.

✖

When Emmett returns to Grazyna's house, he calls for the old lady, but gets no answer. He finds her in bed with the covers pulled over her head.

"Busha, I got a surprise for you," Emmett says.

Grazyna peeks out from under the covers. She raises an eyebrow. This is all she has the energy to do.

Emmett removes his post office shirt from Gertrude as if he's a magician making something appear.

"Ta da," he says.

Grazyna's eyes open wide. Tears well up. Emmett smiles wide, pleased as hell that Grazyna is so moved by his gift.

"No!" Grazyna tells him. "Giving goose back! Is bad luck!"

"But," Emmett says, "you told me the goose belonged to you."

"No! No! If keeping goose, somebody dying!" Grazyna says, remembering what had happened when she'd stolen the Virgin Mary from the Lorenzos's yard.

Grazyna has never told Emmett this particular story. She's too ashamed. And, right now, she doesn't have the strength to relay it.

"Giving back goose!" Grazyna sobs, then ducks her head under the covers.

"If I try to give it back, I might get in trouble," Emmett says.

The phone rings. Grazyna knows it's Sammy Mangano calling about the building. After phoning the realtor all day, now that he's calling she doesn't want to talk to him.

Grazyna crawls deeper under the covers. What should she do? What if she was the successful bidder? What if she was not the successful bidder? One option seems as bad as the other. For the first time in her life, Grazyna understands why people jump off bridges.

When Grazyna hears Emmett walk toward the phone, she screams out in a quilt-muffled voice: "Leaving for answering machine."

❈

Sammy slams down the phone. He's tried to reach Grazyna at least five times. What the hell is going on?

His face softens when he looks over at Tony, who's asleep in a wicker basket in the corner.

After rescuing the cat earlier in the day, Sammy realized he'll have to keep Tony at his side 24/7. It's the only way to make sure Dennis won't abscond with him again.

During the afternoon, Sammy had stopped at a pet store and picked up a litter box, litter, bowls, and cat food, plus some cat toys and the wicker bed. He'd also replaced Tony's missing collar and tag.

Tony would prefer to spend his days at the Mangano residence—with its plush chairs, cushy sofa, and thick carpeting. Still, the Palermo Real Estate office is better than Dennis Vitale's cat menagerie. Tony intends to accept the current setup without mouthing even one "meow" in complaint.

While Sammy's cousin Rosalie would prefer a cat-free office, she doesn't feel it's worth getting into an argument about. Losing her husband and both parents during the past year has put things into perspective. Next to death, everything else is a minor annoyance—better ignored.

As Sammy gets ready to leave, he realizes he forgot to buy a cat carrier for the office. He'll have to carry Tony with him when he stops at the Jablonski house on his way home.

Sammy can't wait to see the old broad's face when he tells her she has the winning bid.

✄

When Emmett opens the door, Tony squirms free from Sammy's arms and bolts into the house.

Like most cats, Tony can disappear for hours—even days if he wants to. Sammy doesn't like the idea of sticking around the place that long. The whole house reeks of cabbage and Lysol. Holy hell, get me out of here, he thinks.

Sammy scoots around, looking for Tony under the sofa and chairs, in the closets, in cabinets, and behind doors.

After a while, he hears Emmett say: "Awww," in an "ain't that sweet" voice.

He finds Emmett standing in a bedroom doorway. Sammy peeks around Emmett's shoulder and sees Tony in bed with the old broad. The cat is cuddled up next to her, and she has both arms wrapped around him.

"Kotek, kotek," she says.

Sammy thinks she's saying, "Kotex." He figures that maybe she has cramps or something. But the old broad is too old to be having a period. Still, she keeps talking about Kotex.

Sammy looks at Emmett and raises his eyebrows.

"Better get her some," Sammy whispers.

"Some what?" Emmett says.

"Whichacallit, sanitary napkins."

Emmett laughs as if this is the funniest thing he's ever heard.

Sammy watches as Tony curls closer to Grazyna and rubs his face on hers. Sammy looks away, jealous and hurt. He likes to believe that Tony loves only him—and everybody else is just in the background.

To make it worse, Emmett is still laughing.

"What the hell's so funny?" Sammy asks.

"She says 'kotek' not 'kotex.' Kotek is the Polish word for kitty."

"You speak Polish?" Sammy says.

"Busha's teachin me."

What a crazy household, Sammy thinks. But he doesn't give a damn. He just wants his cat. He wants the old broad to sign the papers. He wants to get the hell out of this stinking dump and go home!

Sammy elbows past Emmett and walks over to Grazyna's bedside. He reaches down to pick up Tony, but Grazyna clutches the cat, crying: "Nie! Nie!"

Sammy tries to pry Tony free from Grazyna's embrace, but she holds the cat in a viselike grip. While Sammy and Grazyna tug on him, Tony remains passive—not wanting to claw or bite either of them.

"This is my fricking cat!" Sammy yells.

"Nie! Nie!" Grazyna wails, hanging onto the cat.

In a second, Emmett is boxing Sammy's ears and yanking him away from the cat.

"She says no!" he tells Sammy.

Again, Grazyna embraces the animal. The cat's purring is so loud that Sammy can hear him across the room.

That's gratitude, Sammy thinks. You rat! I turn my back for a second and you're in bed with somebody else.

Of course, at this moment, Sammy neglects to remember that Tony had once been the beloved pet of Jerry Valentino. That Tony had switched affections and had lavished all his love on Sammy—leaving Jerry lonely and bereft. And before that, Tony had left Dennis for Jerry.

Sammy should have realized that Tony was capable of doing the same thing again. And now he is—snuggled up with a perfect stranger, and rubbing Sammy's face right in it.

Still, Sammy doesn't care that Tony has betrayed him. He just wants him back. He just wants things to be the way they were before.

"Get the hell out our house!" Emmett orders.

"I go, I take the effin cat with me," Sammy says.

"Watch your language!" Emmett says. He's now sitting next to Grazyna, stroking the old woman's hair.

Even though he feels betrayed, a part of Sammy is detached. He looks at the scene, as if from far, far away.

He sees the old Polish woman stroking the cat. He sees the black guy patting the old lady's head. All of a sudden, Sammy imagines the whole thing multiplied out. Somebody is patting Emmett, another person is patting that person, and on and on. People trying to comfort each other to infinity.

He can't help it. He laughs. He laughs because he realizes something. For the first time, he sees the folly of trying to control things over which you have no power. Shit, he thinks, who in the hell can tell a cat what to do?

Sammy sits at Grazyna's kitchen table with Emmett. They'd left Grazyna and Tony alone.

While Emmett eats boiled cabbage, potatoes, and carrots, with slabs of baked ham on the side—Sammy sips a Screwdriver that Emmett had prepared with cheap vodka and generic orange juice.

"So, she gonna sign the papers or what?" Sammy asks.

"She won't say," Emmett says. "And I ain't askin her."

Sammy sighs. The remaining offers are from other real estate offices—and all the bids are lower than Grazyna's. It's Sammy's listing—and if he can sell the building himself, he'll get a huge commission, something like thirty thousand or so.

He wants to make this sale! It's a matter of personal pride. It's also revenge of sorts on Franco LaRussa, whose son owns the building—papa had forced sonny to put the building on the market and give Sammy the listing.

They hear sounds coming from Grazyna's end of the house. In a few moments, she's shuffling into the kitchen. She drags her feet to the table and plops into a chair. Grazyna looks up at Sammy with weary eyes.

"Anton telling me signing paper," she says.

"Who's Anton?" Sammy asks.

"Kitty in bedroom."

Anton! Now his name is Anton, Sammy thinks. The effin cat does have nine lives!

"The cat belongs to me, and the cat's name is Tony," Sammy says, pleased that he 'd omitted any curse words from his statement. It's at least one more venial sin he's avoided—maybe two, because he'd wanted to curse twice.

Anyway, no need to start an argument. Just state the facts. Besides, good old Tony has done his job. He'd talked the old broad into buying the building.

"Needing kitty here," Grazyna says. She puts her hands over her eyes and starts to cry.

Emmett watches his benefactress's every move. He doesn't want anything—or anybody—to disturb her. She needs that cat—period.

He turns and glares at Sammy. The former mobster tries to sum up the situation. Maybe, he thinks, I'll act like I'm going along—just leave Tony here for a day or so until the deal is done.

When he leaves, Sammy ducks his head into Grazyna's bedroom. Tony has his head on Grazyna's pillow, with the covers pulled up to his chin. He doesn't even look up when Sammy says goodbye.

✼

Tony—or Anton, as he's now called—has a therapeutic effect on Grazyna. Soon, she's just like before—bustling around, giving orders, stealing flowers from the cemeteries, and taking buckets and boards from construction sites.

The building sale is moving ahead. Grazyna has made a small fortune from Spotless Souls Housekleening Service— plus Emmett is throwing in a hundred thousand dollars from his lottery winnings. Grazyna offers to put a fifty-percent down payment on the building. With her successful housecleaning business as a reference, Grazyna has no trouble getting a mortgage.

Emmett will use one of the apartments as an art studio, and get a prorated share of the rents each month from Grazyna. They'll be partners. Grazyna will continue to live in her tiny house—with Anton as her charming companion.

Tony likes his new name—he thinks it sounds exotic, as if he's a big cat in the jungle. Grazyna also pampers Tony in strange new ways that thrills him and sends his tail shooting straight up in the air.

Until this time in his life, Tony has only experienced male caregivers—Dennis, Jerry, and Sammy. He's had some passing experience with Theresa Mangano—still, she hadn't been his primary caregiver.

Tony's relationship with Grazyna is so new—so different. For one thing, she has a wonderful soft cushiony lap. Men don't have such laps—their legs feel hard and unyielding. But Grazyna has such a lovely, pillowy lap. Tony sinks right into it.

For another thing—and this is the best part—she has those wonderful soft breasts. Tony loves to jump in her lap, rest his head on one breast, and listen to Grazyna's heart beating.

Tony brings out all the repressed maternal tenderness in Grazyna—feelings she's tried to lock away since abandoning her sons so many decades ago. The cat is about the same size and weight as a human baby—and Grazyna loves to hug Tony, to cuddle him, to scratch and pet and nuzzle him. Whenever the cat is nearby, Grazyna feels her heart open wide. She realizes this is the way the poor woman at the dry cleaners felt about her goose, Gertrude.

After the sweet cat enters Grazyna's life, she has no time for the goose—the neglected fowl has been wearing in the same outfit for days. Grazyna decides to return Gertrude to her rightful home.

After losing Gertrude for the second time, Virginia becomes sullen and remote. She will no longer analyze the customer's clothing for sins.

Giovanni waits on the customers, piles the clothing into the hamper, and rolls it into the back—pretending that he's conferring with Virginia.

But he assumes the duty himself. At first, he tries, really tries. He closes his eyes tight, feels the clothing, then attempts to figure out which sins to check off on the dry cleaning receipt.

But, after a while, he has no choice—he just checks things off at random. The customers don't seem to notice the difference. Giovanni is careful never to check off sins like murder or other horrible crimes. People would know for sure if they've committed these heinous acts. But, for the most part, people have no idea how often they'd lied, cheated, or lusted.

A part of Giovanni feels bad about the deception, but another part is more practical. The business needs to keep going. Since Virginia can no longer run things, he'll just have to fill in.

Giovanni is in the back of the store when Grazyna arrives with Gertrude in a large knapsack. Right away, the sharp woman notices all the gambling action going on in the waiting room. Grazyna is drawn to gambling, but never takes part in it. She doesn't believe in throwing money away.

"Where Wirginia?" she asks a customer, who fills in Grazyna about Virginia's desire to lead a quieter life.

"Who wait on customer?" she asks.

As if on cue, Giovanni bustles in with the results of his latest sin-detection services.

"Putka—$98.43."

"Lemka—$89.34."

"Bender—$34.89."

"Manelli—$43.98."

He continues until he's shouted out all the names and sin removal fees. In the background, people exchange money—paying off their bets.

"Where Wirginia?" Grazyna calls out over the heads of the customers at the counter.

"Virginia, she commune with spirit," Giovanni says.

"Giving her this," Grazyna says, handing over the knapsack.

Giovanni takes the package and nods to Grazyna. He'll get to it later. Something more important has just come up. While in the back room, Giovanni was roughed up by a couple of thugs. They want Giovanni to make sure they win their bets. They held a gun to his head to get the message across.

Giovanni knows it's pointless to put up any resistance. The fix is in.

By closing time, Giovanni is exhausted. The thugs had set up a series of complicated hand signals. Giovanni was supposed to make a person's clothing the highest or lowest fee —depending on the signal.

There is so much to think about, so much to worry about, and now this, too! And, after all, this is supposed to be a holy place. The gambling is bad enough. But fixed gambling! What kind of sin is that—how much will it cost to remove it?

Giovanni gets all his clothes cleaned for free—so he doesn't have to worry about his own soul. Each day, he throws his clothing into the dry cleaning bin, then unwraps cleaned items that he keeps in the back room.

Giovanni is about to tell Virginia he's leaving for the day when he remembers the knapsack the old woman left. He picks it up and carries it back to Virginia. But Virginia isn't there.

34
BENEDICTION

AFTER GERTRUDE'S SECOND KIDNAPPING, Virginia loses all interest in Redemption Dry Cleaners. It's as if the soul of the business has been ripped out.

Virginia comes to work less often, stays for shorter periods, and, when she is around, seems as if she's in a trance.

Virginia thinks she might be suffering from prepartum depression—which she's never heard of, but figures must exist, seeing as how there's such a thing as postpartum depression.

Thinking it over, Virginia realizes that she feels about the divine child the way she'd felt about channeling Vivaldi's musical works. It's a daunting responsibility. And is she up to it? Good Lord, she's now a sixty-year-old woman with arthritis.

Only months before, Virginia's life had been ordinary—even dull. The same routine—slave away six days a week from seven a.m. until seven p.m. Go home, fix dinner, go to bed, get up, and do it all again. On Sundays, go to church, do laundry, grocery shop, clean the house. Then Monday, start all over.

After founding Redemption Dry Cleaners, Virginia's life has been nonstop excitement. She has a successful business, and is doing important work. She is renowned and respected. Her life has borne out the promise of her golden hair.

Yes, her life is golden! People adore her—even worship her as a saint. She has millions in the bank, the latest model Lexus, and a magnificent new home in River Forest. She has a loving, doting husband. She has new friends, new clothes, and new household appliances. She gets frequent manicures and pedicures. She dines at the finest restaurants.

Then why is she so unhappy? Yes, she's sad about losing Gertrude. But after Gertrude's first kidnapping, Virginia had gone on to start a successful business and assume an important role as a spiritual leader.

But now Virginia lacks the energy to even walk across a room. She wants nothing anymore than to spend her days in bed with the shades drawn.

Virginia searches her soul for one thing she wants, one reason to go on living. She looks at the holy image of the Black Madonna on her bedside table. She sits up in bed. She thinks of something: She wants her mother.

�֍

When Grazyna gets home from Redemption Dry Cleaners, she heads straight for Tony, who is asleep on her pillow.

"Anton, my little Anton," Grazyna chirps as she pets the cat.

Emmett comes into the room.

"Everything work out okay?" he asks.

Grazyna doesn't say anything. She's mad that Emmett refused to return Gertrude himself.

"Want somethin to eat? I made meatballs and gravy," Emmett says.

Grazyna shakes her head, and waves Emmett out of the room. She rests her head on the pillow next to Tony and falls asleep.

✖

In the middle of the night, Grazyna wakes up to the most horrific sound she's ever heard. Tony is screeching and flinging himself against the front door. What could be wrong?

Soon, Emmett is in the living room, trying to figure out what's going on.

"Anton maybe sick. Needing eating grass," Grazyna says.

Tony looks deranged. His fur is standing straight up all over his body, his eyes are bulging out, and his mouth is held in a perpetual snarl.

"Getting Princess leash kitchen drawer," Grazyna commands. She's referring to the leash that had belonged to her now-departed German Shepherd.

When Emmett returns with the leash, he tries to calm down the cat.

"Anton, buddy, whatsa matter?" Emmett asks.

Again, the cat flings himself against the front door.

Grazyna attaches the leash to Tony's collar, while Emmett holds the frantic cat in place.

Grazyna opens the front door, and the cat bolts down the stairs—almost causing Grazyna to tumble headfirst into the darkness.

Tony races down the block into the night. Then he turns and sees Emmett on the porch. He runs back to the house—dragging Grazyna behind—gallops up the steps, and screeches at Emmett.

Emmett stares at the cat's yellow eyes, glowing in the dark. Then the cat turns and races back down the block.

Worried, Emmett walks down the stairs and follows Grazyna and the cat. When they're half a block away from the house, they hear rumbling, as if a volcano is about to erupt. They turn around just in time to see Grazyna's house explode —and blow to bits from its foundation to its roof. They duck behind a tree to avoid the blast of bricks and lumber.

Tony positions himself between two parked cars, sits down, and begins to wash his face. Then he flops down and dozes off.

But Grazyna and Emmett are paralyzed. The house is now in flames. And their first thought isn't relief that they were not in it—or that Tony has saved their lives.

Their first thought is their money—Grazyna had all her cash hidden under the floorboards in her attic. Emmett had his nest egg in his art box—and all of his paintings had been in the house. The only thing remaining is the statue of Saint Stanislaus of Krakow, which somehow has survived the blast and is still standing upright in what used to be the backyard.

Emmett and Grazyna cling to each other and sink to the curb. Soon, Emmett's head is in Grazyna's lap. He's sobbing for everything that he's lost. But then he's outside himself. He sees himself and Grazyna as if from above. They look like a sculpture—Michelangelo's Pietà.

"Mama," Emmett cries over and over. "Mama."

❉

The fire department calls it the latest "incident" caused by the City's unpredictable natural gas lines. It's a miracle no one was killed. A photographer from the *Chicago Tribune* arrives and takes pictures of Tony, credited with saving two lives— plus his own.

It's not yet sunrise, but the block is thronged with people— gapers and helpers and neighbors and passersby. Emmett and Grazyna sit on the curb with their arms around each other. They weep, refuse to speak—and seem on the verge of complete collapse.

Tony wanders through the crowd, enjoying his newfound celebrity. He's patted, petted, stroked, fed, and cuddled by person after person. As he mingles among his admirers, Tony looks up and sees a familiar face coming toward him. It's Sammy—and Tony is surprised at how happy he is to see his former caregiver.

❉

Sammy grabs Tony from a little girl who's cuddling the cat like a baby. The little girl tries to keep her arms around the cat, but Sammy pries Tony free.

Sammy slings Tony over his shoulder and marches to the next block, where his car is parked.

Sammy feels conflicted. He's proud that Tony averted disaster. But he's afraid that now a lot of people might try to take the heroic cat away from him. One thing for sure—he's never, ever going to let Tony out of his sight again.

✦

Soon, Grazyna is ensconced in Dennis's two-bedroom house, along with the prevailing cat occupants.

Dennis, with his soft heart for strays, doesn't hesitate to take her in. Besides, now he can keep close watch on Emmett. Emmett welcomes Dennis's fawning and attention. It's just too much—all his money and paintings had blown up in the explosion and burned away in the fire. He needs somebody to take care of him for a while. Dennis is glad to oblige.

By the next morning, Grazyna has snapped back. She's been through much worse things. Besides, all that money had done something to her—made her feel like a spendthrift, somebody she didn't know and didn't even like.

Grazyna makes a big breakfast for everybody, then heads out to take part in the activities that made her really, really happy.

✦

Virginia seldom manages to get out of bed—thanks to her bloated body and bleak mood. Again, she thinks of her mother —a kind, simple woman who'd lived like a martyr most of her life.

Virginia weeps thinking about her mother—a young widow, a slave on the assembly line at a clock factory who'd spent her life painting glow-in-the-dark clock faces on the second shift at a miserable dirty plant in Franklin Park.

If only she were here now, Virginia whimpers. I'd give her all the things she never had. Then Virginia remembers the one thing her mother had wanted most of all—a grandchild. But Virginia—an only child—had failed to make this wish come true. Now her mother is dead, and Virginia is old enough to be her own child's grandmother.

At the cemetery, Grazyna is excited. It's spring and there are so many nice silk flowers in the ground. She has her pick of new stems, in all colors.

Later, she'll visit construction sites and try to find some rope and lumber.

Grazyna ambles through the cemetery, then stops and hides behind a large headstone. From her spot, Grazyna watches a gravesite about twenty feet away.

She sees Virginia Martyniak, her golden hair shining in the sun and her body round like a beer barrel. She makes the sign of the cross, holds onto the gravestone, and kneels down. Grazyna watches Virginia pray for a while, then try to push herself up. But she's so large she can't get to her feet. Instead, she tumbles over and rolls on her back. Then she starts to groan in pain.

When she sees Grazyna hovering over her, Virginia is relieved. She was afraid she'd have to stay here all day before somebody found her. She didn't mention to Herb or Giovanni where she was going. She'd left the house early and hadn't gone to work at Redemption Dry Cleaners.

This morning, something told her to visit her mother's grave—to do it right away, before going into labor with the divine child.

But here she is in labor—she's sure of it. Even though Virginia has just celebrated her sixtieth birthday and has never given birth to a child, this is something she just knows.

The sky is overcast, and it has turned cold—the way it does during April in Chicago. Virginia is only wearing a light flowered dress. She's shivering on the ground.

Grazyna removes her black woolen sweater—one she'd knitted—and drapes it across Virginia's chest. She bends down and holds Virginia's hand.

"Ohhh," moans Virginia.

Virginia didn't expect this. She figured a divine child would be borne without pain. Oh, how wrong she'd been. She wants to die. It's too, too much pain to bear. She feels as if her entire body is getting pulled and pushed by sharp magnets in the earth.

"Owwww," she screams.

Grazyna holds her hand tight.

As she writhes on the cold ground, Virginia has the sensation that she's falling into the earth—into her mother's grave. Yes, she and the child will die right there—and three members of her family can share the same burial plot.

Virginia rolls on her side. Her ear touches the hard earth. Virginia thinks she hears something. Someone is whispering in her ear. It seems to come from the ground, from her mother's grave—as if Mother Earth herself is speaking.

"We give birth to our self," the voice whispers.

But Virginia hears: "We give birds to our shelf."

Virginia sees an image of Gertrude standing on her lectern—this is the only bird on a shelf she can recall.

The pains come again, stronger and faster. Really, it's too much to stand. Virginia wants—really wants—to die. It's impossible to endure such pain and still live.

Her body stiffens and jerks—fighting the stabbing she feels in her middle. She's breathing hard, the jolts and jabs stopping for a moment before starting again—with more force and fury.

Virginia turns on her other side, her ear to the ground.

Again, she hears a voice. It says: "You are the pain." But Virginia hears: "You are the rain."

"Stop talking nonsense!" Virginia cries out.

Grazyna takes off her pink babushka and mops Virginia's forehead. Virginia is out of her mind, saying crazy things. Grazyna tries to think of something that will take Virginia's mind off her misery.

She starts to sing a Polish lullaby.

Virginia stops thrashing and ranting and stays still, letting the pain wash over her. She's forgotten most of her Polish, but still understands enough to grasp the meaning of the song.

Hushaby, don't you cry, you are in my arms, safe and warm.

Grazyna's voice is sweet and strong. The lovely melody enfolds Virginia like a well-worn quilt. The music seems to seep right into her body, mixing with the pain.

Virginia reaches out and grabs Grazyna's hand and squeezes it until Grazyna feels as if her bones are melting.

❦

Virginia curses herself. Oh, she had been so sure, so smug—thinking she was singled out, deserving of some special privilege. This is what she got—pain, pain, and more pain.

And what is all this about telling other people their sins? Who am I to tell anybody anything, Virginia thinks. Who am I to judge? I am no better than anybody else. I am only here through the grace of God.

With that thought, Virginia feels something move inside her— a heavy weight pushing down. Grazyna, a mother herself—and a midwife many times in her life—knows what is coming.

She puts her hands below Virginia, and holds them there, waiting. Then a child is in Grazyna's hands. The child is smiling, with wide-open eyes. It is a girl.

Grazyna hands the child to Virginia, who wraps her in the black wool sweater.

The child breathes out and her breath fogs the frosty air. Then the mist rises upward, floating toward the cloudy sky.

The clouds open and drink in the child's breath. Then snow starts to fall—large, light, dancing flakes.

The snow falls on the trees heavy laden with the blooms of spring. The snow falls on the grass, the flowers. The snow falls on people and houses and the whole city in benediction.

It's an April snow. It's a blessing and a gift. It's a special grace.

Virginia gazes down at her divine offspring. The child does not resemble Virginia—does not have her golden hair or blue eyes or white skin.

The little girl has a crown of soft black hair, large shining black eyes, smooth dark skin, like the Black Madonna.

The white snowflakes fall on the girl's dark skin and melt. All at once, Virginia knows what to name the child.

She calls her Grace.

ABOUT THE AUTHOR

MELANIE VILLINES is a novelist, playwright, screenwriter, television writer, biographer, and editor. Her published work includes the novel *Tales of the Sacred Heart* (Bogfire Press), the family memoir *Reason to Fight* (co-written with Hiram Johnson), a celebrity biography *Beyond Hollywood* (co-written with J. Herbert Klein), *Anna & Otto*, a novel for children (Inklings Press), and a variety of ghostwritten books and screenplays. A founding member of Chicago Dramatists, she is the author of twenty plays. Her original screenplays include *Calling Oz*, finalist in the Austin Film Festival and many other screenwriting competitions, and *Just Say the Word*, top-10 finalist in Illinois-Chicago screenwriting competition. She co-wrote the critically acclaimed 90-minute drama *Crime of Innocence*, based on the life of Emmett Till, for the NBC affiliate in Chicago. Her play *Bernice* (co-written with Hiram Johnson and Jessica Everleth) had a workshop production in Dallas (2013) and Los Angeles (2015), and her story "Windy City Sinners," an excerpt from her novel of the same name, appeared in *Chicago Quarterly Review* Vol. 17/2014. Since moving from Chicago to Los Angeles in 2007, she's worked as a scriptwriter as well as a producer and researcher for true crime TV shows.

vivaldi
psychic Mafia guy
redemption dry
          cleaners
60 yr old wo— wants
        a baby)

printers

love of cat

Crazy no sells dope
Dead - ghost
            110
        haunt
      grazyna

soothes souls
Mafia guy guilt
cop- mafa guy & mailman
        deal coke

48484783R00159

Made in the USA
Charleston, SC
04 November 2015